HOPE UNDER FIRE

Caroline Dunford

ACCENT

First published in 2024 by Headline Accent
An imprint of HEADLINE PUBLISHING GROUP

1

Cataloguing in Publication Data is available from the British Library

ISBN 978 1 4722 9541 5

Typeset in 10.5/13pt Bembo Std by Jouve (UK), Milton Keynes

Printed and bound in Great Britain by Clays Ltd, Elcograf S.p.A.

MIX
Paper | Supporting responsible forestry
FSC® C104740

Headline's policy is to use papers that are natural, renewable and recyclable products and made from wood grown in well-managed forests and other controlled sources. The logging and manufacturing processes are expected to conform to the environmental regulations of the country of origin.

HEADLINE PUBLISHING GROUP
An Hachette UK Company
Carmelite House
50 Victoria Embankment
London EC4Y 0DZ

www.headline.co.uk
www.hachette.co.uk

Having previously worked as a journalist and the[illegible],
Caroline Dunford enjoyed many years helping other people shape their personal life stories before taking the plunge and writing her own novels. She has now published almost thirty books in genres ranging from historical crime to thrillers and romance. Caroline also teaches creative writing courses part-time at the University of Edinburgh.

For further information about Caroline Dunford's Hope Stapleford adventures, and to find out all about Caroline's Euphemia Martins mysteries, set during World War One, visit: caroline-dunford.squarespace.com.

Praise for Caroline Dunford's novels:

'A sparkling and witty crime debut with a female protagonist to challenge Miss Marple'
Lin Anderson

'Impeccable historical detail with a light touch'
Lesley Cookman

'Euphemia Martins is feisty, funny and completely adorable'
Colette McCormick

'A rattlingly good dose of Edwardian country house intrigue with plenty of twists and turns and clues to puzzle through'
Booklore.co.uk

By Caroline Dunford

Hope Stapleford Series:

Hope for the Innocent
Hope to Survive
Hope for Tomorrow
Hope Under Fire

Euphemia Martins Mysteries:

A Death in the Family
A Death in the Highlands
A Death in the Asylum
A Death in the Wedding Party
The Mistletoe Mystery (a short story)
A Death in the Pavilion
A Death in the Loch
A Death for King and Country
A Death for a Cause
A Death by Arson
A Death Overseas
A Death at Crystal Palace
A Death at a Gentleman's Club
A Death at the Church
A Death at the Races
A Death in the Hospital
A Death on Stage
A Death of a Dead Man

Others:

Highland Inheritance
Playing for Love
Burke's Last Witness

This novel was written during the 80th anniversary of D-Day, so it seems only fitting to dedicate it to the brave men and women who made D-Day a success, even at the cost of their own lives. D-Day is a sombre reminder of how lucky we are to live free, how much we owe those who ensured that we could, and how we must defend and protect those freedoms.

Prologue

From the window, up on the ninth floor, I could see the East End. Almost all of it was ablaze. In the reflection I also saw the man behind me, and the gun he levelled at my back.

I was caught as off guard as any poor person living down by the docks. The Nazis had taken their raids to a new level. As the flames licked up against the night sky, the ghastly mixture of orange and black created a hellscape on earth. I wondered if Harvey had got his father out in time. If he had got out in time. Who would the fire take this time, and who would be blamed.

'You're very calm,' said the figure behind me. 'In fact, you don't seem surprised at all.'

I took a deep breath. 'You were one of several suspects.'

The man gave a low laugh. 'Yes, that sounds like you. Hedging your bets until the last minute. But this time you've left it too late.'

'I didn't want it to be you. But you can't have been doing this alone? Who are you working for?' It was too far to jump out of the window, even if I could have smashed the pane. My only chance was to keep him talking until an opportunity presented itself. If an opportunity . . .

'Oh, I was to tell you, from Prometheus himself, that this isn't personal.'

'That's your head cheese's code name? I am honoured.' This time I couldn't keep the sarcasm out of my voice.

'But it is. Personal. I'm taking all this very personally.'

'I'm sorry about that,' I said. 'I liked you.'

There was a sudden intake of breath at that. I struggled not to tense my shoulder blades. Would he pull the trigger now?

'So tell me, little Sunflower. How would you like to die?'

Chapter One

Earlier

I realised things weren't going to plan when Leo swore at the guard. His face suffused with red. His normally bright blue eyes were cloudy. His lower teeth bit into his neat moustache as if he was physically trying to hold back the words that boiled inside him. He was angrier than I remembered seeing him, but then my stepfather can have that effect on people.

We had left my new stepfather and my mother behind to make their final preparations for travelling out to Cairo. My stepfather, Fitzroy, is in military intelligence. So is my mother. Their sudden marriage after the death of my father, had caught me utterly by surprise. They had been agents and partners during the Great War, and had worked on and off together throughout my childhood. How much espionage they had been involved with, and at what level, I was only now beginning to discover.

They had thought, like others, that the Great War was the war to end all wars. (Now, we knew it was only a tragic overture.) But having created a great many enemies through their work, they had trained me from when I could first say a few words and toddle about, to observe and evade. Despite raising me in the Fens, both of them had always feared someone would come for me. For revenge. For something they had done.

So when we went to war with Germany I was, if not a fully trained agent, well on my way to becoming one. My stepfather, who was then still only my godfather, had missed the whole show down in Ireland in the twenties, and managed to stay in intelligence right up until the present day. He was connected in more ways than I understood, and a master at pulling strings and generally getting his own way. I realised Leo's anger was almost certainly directed at Fitzroy and not the poor man in front of us.

'I'm so sorry,' I told the elderly man who had checked our rail passes, 'we didn't realise this train was going to London.'

'Well, you can't get off. We're not stopping now. We're as full as we can hold.'

'No, of course, not,' I said.

Leo was by now making a nuisance of himself and pulling his bag down from the overhead rack. There were two other men in the compartment with us, both officers, a captain and major, and both frowning heavily.

'Right you are then,' said the guard. He moved out of the way as Leo swung the bag down. 'I'll leave you to it.' He paused before he opened the door. 'I hope neither of you pair is leading any of our chaps anywhere.' Then he slipped out before Leo could rail at his small joke.

'Hold these,' said Leo, piling clothing into my lap.

'You can't,' I hissed at him.

'I bloody well can,' said Leo. 'He's done the dirty on me. Bloody man. Bloody, bloody man.'

'I say,' said the captain, who had an extremely full moustache, 'that's no way to speak in front of a lady.'

'She's not a lady,' snapped Leo, 'she's a lieutenant in the army.'

'A lieutenant by gad,' said the captain, reaching over and holding out his hand. 'Charles Willard, Captain, Royal Engineers.'

'Hope Stapleford,' I said, shaking his hand. 'Army administration.' Leo made a scornful huff at this, but as his face was still half-buried in his bag, Willard either didn't hear him or chose not to.

'Off to straighten out London, are we? Getting lots of files shipshape?'

'Something like that,' I said.

'You're not in uniform,' said the major suddenly. He had the kind of voice that you associate with men disappointed in life, and ready to take it out on anyone who crosses their path. A scratchy sort of voice with a slight nasal whine.

'We had to leave very suddenly,' I said.

'Filing having an emergency, was it?' said Willard, but he laughed in a friendly manner. 'What about you, sir? Rummaging in the luggage? You an army man too?'

'Yes,' said Leo unhelpfully. He pulled out the heavy envelope. 'Put that stuff back in, Hope,' he said. 'And keep it neat.'

Fortunately, Leo rolled his clothing, so this was easy enough to do.

'Orders you about a bit, doesn't he?' said Willard, who I was beginning to think might have had a bit of a send-off before pouring himself into the carriage. Either that or he was looking for a fight.

I looked up and smiled. 'He's a major,' I said.

'Oh right,' said Willard. 'Sorry, sir. No uniform.'

Leo ignored everyone. He went to the far end of the compartment, pulled the blind down so there was no reflection, and tore open the envelope. He spent a couple of minutes reading and rereading the papers it contained, then he began to swear under his breath. He thrust the papers at me, and turned to face the blind, his fists balled in his lap.

I'd realised when the guard had said we were headed to London that my stepfather's chauffeur had not delivered us to the train we expected to be on. However, it was unlike any of Fitzroy's people to make a mistake, so I had assumed that we would simply be changing trains in the capital. Leo, who hadn't enjoyed his enforced stay with Fitzroy and my mother at their castle – it was going to take a lot of getting used to that my mother was now a duchess – had clearly suspected a plot before I had.

I read the orders he had passed me. It stated clearly at the top these were not to be read before we exited the train, but that seemed moot now. Besides, I had been raised to always consider any order carefully before complying.

The instructions were brief. Instead of going to Scotland to support the first batch of SOE recruits Leo and I had helped pick, we were going to the Ministry of Information. Leo had been fretting for some time over the fate of the amateurs he had picked for the SOE project. These brave souls were to be given seven weeks' training and then dropped into occupied France to aid the Resistance. The selection process had been rigorous, and we had only been one part of it, but the nearer we got to the first deployment the more responsible Leo had begun to feel. He had changed from the charismatic undercover officer I had first met, to a man who kept whisky in his office and brooded. I suspected this might be why Fitzroy had sent us elsewhere. I knew he didn't approve of the SOE, but he wasn't directly involved. I had been seconded to them, and now it appeared Leo had been seconded back in return. I reflected that it was probably better for Leo's mental state that he hadn't gone to Scotland, and it might even have been a kindness. However, now was not the time to point this out. I decided it was time to distract the other members of the compartment, and broke out the sandwiches the cook had given us for the journey. As Fitzroy was now a duke, with a castle and extensive kitchen gardens and farms, I was able to refocus the attention of the two officers. In fact, by the end of the journey we were on rather good terms. Leo had stayed sulking in the corner with his face to the drawn blind. I wondered just how much trouble I was going to have with him.

We had almost kissed once, and I had been holding out some hope that we might, if not become lovers, at least be friends. I did not have a surfeit of these, or even a sufficiency.

We arrived in London late in the afternoon. At several points the train had stopped on the tracks and waited for other trains to pass. Clearly there was a great deal of troop movement going on. Climbing down on to the platform was like dropping into another world. London is always a shock after the countryside, but the sheer mass of people moving along the platforms, the huge tea stands, to which we almost immediately lost Willard and his friend, the shunting of stock and the bustle of the guards was astonishing. The noise of the engines and the shouted commands, the whispered goodbyes, the loud camaraderie of those heading off to war buffeted us like a body blow of sound. My instinct was to get clear as soon as possible, and I headed directly for the exit.

I emerged into the cold sunshine and buzz of the city. I felt a little electric shock surge through me. London might be busy, and the press of people put me on edge, but it was always exciting. I had no idea what the Ministry of Information was. It did sound as if it might be some kind of deep-cover intelligence work. I turned to see how Leo was faring. His face told me everything I didn't want to know.

I hailed a cab. Our orders had implied we were to go straight to the ministry, but as our train had been so delayed I doubted anyone knew when we were due to arrive. I gave the cabbie the address of my London flat. Maybe some decent coffee could get Leo into a better mood. Clearly, turning up in the state he was in would not start us off on the right foot. Why, I wondered silently, do people always think women are the emotional ones? In my experience it is men who wear their hearts on their sleeves, certainly their sulks.

Leo didn't say anything on the journey, but followed me up to the flat like some kind of automaton. I made him some coffee, and sorted quickly through my mail. Nothing of great interest, although a letter addressed to my late flatmate, Bernie, gave me a strange cold feeling in my chest. I placed it on the side. I hadn't liked her husband, but I supposed I should pass it on to him.

I came back through. Leo was staring into the distance, but he'd drunk his coffee. 'Do you think I will get to stay here?' I said. I was more thinking aloud than expecting a response, but Leo surprised me, by answering.

'I don't have a billet,' he said. 'I was meant to be staying in Scotland, permanently assigned to the training team.'

I sat down opposite him. 'You mean, you'd been moved off recruiting?' I asked. 'You didn't mention this.'

He frowned. 'It was need-to-know and you didn't. You were assigned to my department, not to me.'

'Of course,' I said. 'I shouldn't have presumed we would . . .'

'I'm well aware your stepfather wants to coerce me into being some kind of guard dog for you . . .'

'Now wait a minute—'

Leo held up his hand. 'You don't need one. I know. But for whatever reason, your stepfather isn't prepared to let you out unattended.'

'That's ridiculous.'

'It is when there's a war on, and you could be a lot more useful in the field than in a propaganda unit. As could I.'

'Is that what the Ministry of Information is?'

Leo gave me a hard look. 'What else could it possibly be?'

'Cookbooks. Oh God. That would be worse.' Leo frowned even harder. 'I'm not mad,' I said. 'Fitzroy had my flatmate working on trying out recipes for the home front. You know, cheap and easy meals that taste good with whatever you can dig up for victory.' I smiled slightly. 'He chose her because she was the world's least competent cook. Or as close as.'

'I am not spending the war writing cookbooks!'

'No,' I said. 'But Fitzroy is flying out to Cairo. If they haven't left already. My mother thought they would be gone at least a couple of months. Surely he can't keep pulling my – our – strings from over there?'

'I should never have tried to kiss you,' said Leo gloomily. 'That was my big mistake.'

I felt myself blushing. 'Well, you didn't, so we can put all that behind us.'

Leo snorted in a way I didn't find particularly complimentary. We had both been a bit overwrought at the time. The realisation that we had helped choose a number of perfectly nice people, who would in all likelihood die in unpleasant ways abroad, had just hit home for both of us. That my then stepfather had chosen that moment to burst into my flat had prevented us kissing – which would almost certainly have been a mistake, not least because Leo was of a higher rank – and the whole potential kissing scenario had been avoided.

But then the last person I had kissed had gone to a fiery death in an aeroplane crash, and I was still dealing with that. That, and the death of my father, the remarriage of my mother, and the intolerable interference of my god/stepfather, who had been the person I had been second closest to my whole life. And then, Bernie, my best friend, was suddenly dead.

Some of what I was thinking must have shown on my face, because Leo suddenly became a lot more animated. 'Buck up, Hope,' he said, standing and carrying his coffee cup to the sink. 'You're right. In a couple of days I can put out feelers and contact my old commander. I'm pretty sure he'd be eager to have me back. He can't have been keen on seconding me out. With Fitzroy out of the way I'm sure I can get us up to Scotland. I take it you'd rather be doing that?'

I shrugged. 'I'd rather do anything other than typing,' I said.

'I don't suppose I could bunk in here, could I?' Leo asked. 'It would be simpler if I didn't have to go through the process of getting another billet. Make us easier to move too.'

I blinked. 'I never cleared out Bernie's room,' I said.

'Would it be that hard?' said Leo.

I got up wordlessly and led the way through to the second bedroom. Bernie had been the messiest person I had ever known. In her mind a drawer was only in proper use if it was open, full, and dripping stuff all over the floor. Either that or she'd open out the drawers and stack books, shoes and make-up in staggering piles on top of them. Obviously, there were frequent avalanches and collapses. I opened the door. 'Have a look,' I said.

Leo peered in. 'I suppose I could get something from stores if you don't have any linen,' he said.

I slipped in front of him to see what he was talking about. The room was completely empty of Bernie's possessions. A stripped bed, a chest of drawers and a wardrobe were all that remained. Even the carpet was pristine.

'I don't understand,' I said. 'I didn't do this.'

'Her husband?' said Leo.

'He doesn't have a key – or I don't think he does. Anyway, he wouldn't . . .' I took a deep breath. 'Fitzroy,' I said.

'He had a key, didn't he?' said Leo. He blushed slightly, clearly remembering the awkward moment once more.

'Fitzroy no doubt has keys to the gates of heaven,' I said through gritted teeth.

'That I sincerely doubt,' said Leo.

Chapter Two

The Ministry of Information was in one of those amorphous white office blocks that litter the centre of London. Built in the 1800s for the then more aristocratic civil servants of the day, they had white, sharp-edge brick fronts, with impressive stairways inside and out. The imposing nature of the building was slightly diminished by the sandbags piled up outside and the criss-crosses of black tape across the windowpanes.

'They are taking the possibility of bombing seriously,' said Leo.

I shrugged. It had been far too long since I'd had eyes on any intelligence reports. I had little idea of how the war was going. 'Better to be prepared,' I said.

We went up an imposing set of steps together. We'd both changed into our uniforms and brushed up as well as we could. We reported to the front desk. Or rather Leo, being of senior rank, did.

'You're late,' said the corporal behind the desk. 'She won't like that. And when they say the bark is worse than the bite, they don't mean her.' He handed us both an identification badge. 'I'd hop to it if I were you. Third floor, and as good an excuse as you can conjure up on the way up.'

Leo and I exchanged looks, but had the good sense not to comment on whoever this dragon might be within earshot. We eschewed the lift and trotted smartly up the wide marble stairs. Arriving out of breath when you are late always looks better than stepping leisurely out of a lift.

Our last mission had been in the Highlands, and both of us were fitter for our encounter with the Scottish countryside. However, since then Leo had sat at a desk and slunk around London and its nightclubs recruiting for the SOE, while I had been training as an auxiliary – the last line of defence should we be invaded. By the time we marched into the assigned room, entering on the echo of our knock, Leo was panting and I hadn't broken a sweat.

It was a large space filled with a number of desks, filing cabinets and large tables. Both men and women in army uniform criss-crossed the room. All walking purposefully, often carrying manila folders and only stopping when they met to talk in low voices. The place had a hum and a feeling of energy about it. I briefly took in that some of the larger tables had photographs on them and overhead magnifiers, but what got my attention was the clack-clack of typewriters.

Fitzroy had previously placed me undercover as a typist – although he had not told me at the time, nor even yet confirmed it – and I had learned to hate the machines and the boring, endless tasks inflicted on their operators.

'Oh no, not again,' I said under my breath.

Leo gave me an odd look, but before I could explain, a woman with iron-grey hair and features that must have once been pretty before life had soured her, and the pips had been put on her shoulder, walked so quickly up to us, that I took a step back, fearing collision.

She eyed us from the soles of our shoes to the tops of our caps. She took barely any time to do this, but I still felt as if someone had run a torch up and down my skin. 'This won't do at all,' she said. Her voice was deeper than I expected, and with a crispness that told us she demanded everything was done her way.

'You're a major,' she said accusingly to Leo.

'Yes, ma'am,' he responded, even though he doubtless outranked her. Later, he told me that he hadn't felt so guilty about anything since his mother caught him stealing his younger brother's biscuits when he was four.

I saw Leo straighten as if on parade. The female officer's top lip curled slightly. She was not impressed. 'Well, we can't have you here. Besides, you're far too good-looking. No brains, I expect. Fleming should take you in his unit only he's got a full complement. Go up to the fifth. They'll find something for you.'

'The fifth?' said Leo.

'Fifth floor.' She didn't add the words 'you idiot', but both of us heard them. Leo nodded. 'Well get! I don't have time to waste on you!'

Leo turned and left. The expression on his face was a mix of indignation and disbelief. If I hadn't been so worried about what was going to happen to me I would have laughed.

'So you're Sunflower? I'm Masterton. You can call me ma'am. There's not much of you to look at is there? Mind you, you're carrying a bit of weight around the middle. Privileged no doubt. You'll need to watch that while you're out of the field. Now, can you type?'

It is never worth lying to anyone in intelligence – well, not on your own side. Within minutes I was stuck at a desk with enough typing to take me the rest of the week. People passing my desk would slap a file down on the top of my pile. 'This takes priority,' they would say. Then someone else would come over and rearrange the pile. Other than Masterton, I had no idea who was running this show, and could only look on in bewilderment as this weird game of pass the parcel played out on the corner of my desk.

A lot of what I was typing made no sense. I did wonder if any of it was in code, but gradually I realised that I was typing such different reports that they had little or no common context. Everybody wanted everything *now*, so the words fairly blurred under my fingers. One minute I was typing about how many portions a housewife was making out of a tin of Spam, the next I was typing up conversations that were so artificially stilted I couldn't believe they were real.

When someone finally tapped me on the shoulder and told me

I could get lunch in the canteen in the basement, and that I had twenty minutes to get it, I looked at them in confusion. Surely it must be dinner time by now? I checked my watch on the way down, and realised I had been typing for less than two hours. I didn't think I would enjoy working in this department whatever it was. I also utterly failed to see what contribution I was making to the war effort. Had Fitzroy sidelined me again? Or had I been placed here to weed out a traitor?

If I was asked under oath to swear I was working for my stepfather I couldn't have done it. But if not, why on earth was Leo here? There had been no reason to derail him from the SOE operations he had been going to support. Fitzroy might be many things, but if he was angry with another man, he was more than likely to punch them in the face. He might be sneaky, sly, contriving and downright frustrating, but he would never take an asset like Leo out of the field for no reason. So I had to be here for a reason. Unless he was truly worried about Leo's mental health. But then wouldn't it have made more sense to send him somewhere to recuperate rather than dropping him back into vital intelligence work?

The canteen smelled of meatloaf and cabbage. I repressed a gag. Being at the castle had spoiled me. Fitzroy's estate had been growing their own produce long before the war began and, of course, he'd only encouraged them to do it more. I tried to imagine my stepfather in a place like this and failed. Could it be there was some secret counter-intelligence canteen where they kept the good food? I sighed as someone pushed roughly past me on the stairs. It seemed more likely Fitzroy dined with Churchill. I wouldn't put it past him to get to any table if there was a good meal on offer. In some ways the pair of us were alike. Except Fitzroy's form never showed how much he ate.

'Are you going down there or what, love?' said a voice behind me.

I turned, and he caught sight of my pips. An army corporal in khaki with a face like a pickled walnut and balding tonsure of greying hair. He must have been at the top end of the enlisting age. 'Er, I mean ma'am. Sorry.'

I indicated for him to go past me, and followed him down into the steamy room, filled with long tables and benches. It was about three quarters full and with a quick selective scan, I reckoned there were about seventy people. A lot of them were smoking, so the actual counter where the cabbage was presumably being served, was obscured in a foggy mixture of steam and smoke. Lovely. I doubted it could make the food taste worse. (In this I would shortly be proved wrong.)

I obediently filed into the snaking queue for food. I didn't see anyone of rank higher than lieutenant, so maybe there was another canteen. The queue inched forward. I had yet to visually confirm actual edible items were being served. It began to seem unlikely that I would get back in the twenty minutes. Around me people were talking about films, cigarettes, weather and nothing of the least important. Clearly they cracked down on loose lips here. My mind was wandering, mulling over the last conversation I had had with Fitzroy, when I saw someone get up from a table across the room. Army uniform, tall with a distinct limp. He walked across to stack his tray, and then exited through the door. My mind and my tongue did not communicate in time. I gave myself a mental shake. There was no way that could be Harvey. When I'd left him in Scotland he had been on his way to train as a pilot. He'd also proved himself to be a surprisingly adept aero engineer. If he hadn't got on in the pilot training, they would surely have kept him on as an engineer.

I reached the counter and took a tray. 'What do you want, love?' asked the hair-netted troll behind the counter. Her bright pink lipstick and the cigarette attached to her lower lip momentarily distracted me. 'Come on, duck. Lots of people need to eat.'

I seriously could not tell what the slush in front of me was, so I pointed at a couple of the trays. 'Chicken à la King and potato gratin. Girl with taste,' she said as she ladled brown and yellow mush on to my plate. 'Puddings further down. Jam roly-poly today.'

I ducked out before the sweet section, but I did remember to give my name and number to the cashier. Behind me the queue surged forward. I found a stand with cutlery, water jugs and mugs. It also had a tea urn, but there was no way I was touching that.

Feeling somewhat down I took my tray to the nearest table and sat in a vacant space. My plate looked as inviting as I feared. Normally, I love desserts, but if they could do this to potato gratin what hell would have been inflicted on a jam roly-poly? I nudged the edge of what I hoped was a potato slice with my fork. It sank down into the striped beige and white sauce.

'You can be assured that will taste as bad as it looks,' said a well-spoken man on my right. I turned to see an older man in a sharp civilian suit. I say older, but he could have only been the same age as Fitzroy, but no one ever thinks of my stepfather as old.

'I feared that.'

'But,' said the man, holding up an imperative finger, a thin, aristocratic and well-manicured finger, 'when you've not been home in three days, and only managed to grab a couple of hours sleep at your desk, it will seem like manna from heaven.'

I felt myself blushing slightly. 'Yes, I see that.'

'Probably the best thing that can be said for the food is that it is hot,' he continued. 'As winter bears down on us, I believe that will make the substances that come out of the kitchen much valued. Even the plates lightly sprinkled with ash.'

I smiled at that and held out my hand. 'Lieutenant Hope Stapleford,' I said. 'Working on some floor, doing something.'

'Ahh, very hush-hush?'

I shook my head. 'I'm new here and haven't a clue what I'm doing yet.'

'Don't expect it to get any better,' said my new friend. 'Daniel Dashwood, actor and raconteur, at your service.'

My surprise must have shown.

'I'm in the war films.' I must have still looked blank because after a short pause he continued, 'You know, the "how important it is to get to an air-raid shelter" and the like. They often run them before films in the cinema. Increased my big-screen time no end. Used to be more of a stage man.' He gave a charming smile.

'Oh, propaganda,' I said.

'The director doesn't like us calling it that. It's more helpful hints for the hard of thinking.'

Despite the cruelness of the remark I gave a small laugh. It was very much how Fitzroy would have described it.

I was rewarded with another even more charming smile. 'Now, that's more like it,' he said. 'We clever people have to stick together in these difficult times.'

Chapter Three

The smell of shepherd's pie greeted me as I opened the flat door. Leo popped his head around the side of the kitchen. 'I got off early, so I thought I'd start dinner. Afraid my skill is pretty basic, but I've got some wine open. Come and have a glass.'

It did strike me that drinking with Leo after a long, tiring day, considering last time we'd shared a glass I had more or less ended up in his lap, might not be a good idea. 'Oh, what the hell,' I said and went over to accept a glass. 'Chin-chin!'

I took a sip. 'This is one of Fitzroy's,' I said. 'You've decanted it well.'

'Oh heck,' said Leo. 'Another thing he'll be on to me for.'

'No, I meant he gave it to me. All the best wines I have are from him. It's not the expense so much as he knows a lot more about wine than I do. Besides, I think he used to "borrow" them from his father's cellar. Give me a moment to get out of my uniform.' I slipped to my room to change, and mysteriously by the time I came back I was carrying an empty glass. Leo was waiting for me in the living room. He refilled it.

'I have to say, seeing your castle was a bit of a shock.'

I slumped down on the settee. 'Likewise,' I said.

'I assumed you'd been visiting since childhood.'

'No, he only inherited it recently, and that was a matter of attrition. He was never meant to be a duke.'

'Duke.' Leo said the word slowly with consideration. 'He does seem to be a man who falls on his feet. What's next? Supreme Commander of the British army?'

I took another sip. I felt a touch light-headed, so I rested against Leo's shoulder. 'I doubt it,' I said. 'He likes playing fast and loose in – in all sorts of ways. But he'll be in Cairo or on the way at least by now. So, he'll be out of our hair for a while.'

Leo gently disengaged himself. 'I wish I could believe that. That man's influence seems all pervasive to me. I'm waiting on the telephone to ring and him shouting at me to get the hell out of your flat.' He stood up. 'I need to get the food out of the oven.'

At that moment the telephone rang, and we both jumped. I answered it and a posh female voice asked for Leo. I handed the telephone over and went to rescue our supper.

In the oven I found a surprisingly decent-looking and large shepherd's pie. It smelt amazing. I set it carefully on the side and searched for some plates. I served us both portions, and collecting the cutlery I headed back through.

'There's plenty more,' I said. 'I thought on two glasses it would be foolish to attempt to carry the whole dish through.' I didn't ask who was on the telephone. I knew if he could Leo would tell me. He took a plate from me and sat down. His handsome face was marred with a heavy frown. We ate off our laps like savages. When our glasses were empty Leo refilled them without a word, finishing the bottle. He was clearly lost in his thoughts. While I was happily lost in what was proving to be a remarkably flavoursome dinner.

'Hope,' he said finally, and so suddenly I started enough that food fell off my fork – but fortunately not on to the floor. 'I'm going to be getting calls like that one, and having to come and go at all kinds of times. It might be better if I found a billet elsewhere.'

'I wasn't expecting you to cook me dinner every night,' I said lightly.

'It's not that,' said Leo. 'I can't tell you what I'm doing, and the damn thing is, I suspect you would be ideal for the project.'

'Oh,' I said.

'I hope they've got you on something decent on the third floor.'

'Typing.'

Leo's eyes opened wide. 'I have the strong inclination to open another bottle of wine, but I won't.' He sighed. 'I can only think the reason you're not on this with me is Fitzroy's interference.'

'It does usually work out that I am in the right place,' I said. 'Even if it often doesn't feel like it at the time.'

'Humph!' said Leo. 'But I bet that's when Fitzroy is still in the country to tow you out of trouble.'

'I was attacked once,' I said. 'In this flat. I'd be happier not being alone in it. Besides, the telephone line is as secure as you're going to find outside an official office.'

'So, I am your guard dog?'

'Perhaps,' I said. 'But at least you get decent wine and coffee. I get the odd food parcel from the estates too.'

'Estates?'

'Mine or Fitzroy's.'

Leo's eyes narrowed. 'I forgot you're an heiress in your own right.'

'That,' I said, standing up, 'is hardly my fault. I'm going to bed. You can move out if you want, but I would prefer you to stay here.'

After I'd washed and changed, I lay in bed with my thoughts wandering. I wondered if Leo would do the washing-up or if everything would be all crusty and hard in the morning. I wondered if he might try my door. I'd left it unlocked in case he did. I thought about what a bad idea it would be to get involved with him. I wondered if Fitzroy had got the cellar reinforced as a shelter and thought I should have already checked. I fell asleep wondering if I would ever lie in the arms of a man I loved before the war blew me to bits.

I awoke in the morning feeling slightly less self-obsessed. I opened my curtains to brilliant sunshine and felt my mood immediately lighten. It improved further when I discovered that although

Leo had already gone, he had done the washing-up. I peeked into his room and accidentally saw his civilian clothing was still in his wardrobe. He hadn't left yet. After a brief breakfast, I hurried out and made my way to my new working environment.

I was half an hour early for going on shift, but the room was as buzzing as before. People still walked at a carefully considered pace. No running allowed here, but it was brisk, coordinated and with purpose. Masterton gave me a slitted-eye look when I arrived and checked her watch. In return I gave her a respectful nod and big cheerful smile. She didn't smile back. I settled at my desk, and within moments I had enough files to type that if they didn't exactly tower over me, they were in serious danger of toppling on the floor.

The files proved about as interesting as the day before until I came to what could only be a film script. It wasn't long before I found myself sniggering. I tried to keep this as hidden as possible, but phrases like, 'My goodness, my dear, do you think Hitler would bomb little old Ivy Lane?' and 'Now then, my darling, I want to know you and the boys are safe while I'm overseas doing my jolly old bit', were the least egregious of the sketch. It seemed to be a short film that was attempting to ensure people either went to air-raid shelters or built ones in their back gardens. When I saw the line, spoken by 'a cute, curly haired tot with a lisp of common stock, but not too rough, as it surveys the new shelter', 'Now that nasty man Hitler won't be able to harm me or teddy, will he, Mama?', I gave a sudden bark of laughter. No tot, and I had met plenty of the local children back at White Orchards, my childhood home on the Fens, had ever been so literate or thoughtful.

'And what would you have written?' asked a voice at my elbow.

'Now my sweeties are safe from Hitler?' I said. 'But only if it was an older child, wearing glasses to show their intelligence. A tot, as is described here, isn't likely to go beyond "Mama!"' I looked up into the handsome face of Daniel Dashwood.

'I must say that is better than what is written here,' said Dashwood. 'Although I think it still needs tweaking. We have some awful young woman, who is related to one of the commanders, and thinks she is going to be a famous author one day dashing out these scripts. They are dire.'

'I shouldn't have laughed,' I said, handing him the completed copies. 'It was very rude of me.'

'Not at all,' said Dashwood, 'you're only reacting as I suspect our audience will.' He frowned for a moment. 'I say, is this what you're doing all the time. Typing stuff?'

I gave a wry smile.

'If you're not allowed to say I will quite understand.'

'No, your assumption is correct. But it is only my second day.' I looked around the room. 'Although there is a lot of typing to be done, and I do seem to be one of the faster ones. Drat it!'

Daniel smiled. He flicked through the file. 'And no mistakes. I see how they might value you right where you are.'

I made a non-committal sort of noise as I had spied Masterton out of the corner of my eye. It seemed that Daniel had spotted her too. He stepped sharply away from my desk, saying quickly, 'Never mind, fair maiden. Perhaps a dashing knight will rescue you yet.'

I didn't spot Harvey at lunchtime, and I knew he would never miss a meal. If Fitzroy had been around I would have been able to ask him where Harvey was currently stationed. My godfather never minded me asking questions about previous assets, especially if he had been involved himself. He thought keeping track of such people was wise. Or in his words, 'Once you've got someone on your team you keep your hand on them. You never know when they will be useful again.' It was something of a mantra for him and explained his remarkably wide circle of influence. However, any request of this nature to any other officer would be met, I had no doubt, with short shrift.

'Stapleford, summarise the document you have just typed!'

I looked up into the familiarly unfriendly face of Masterton. 'I'm sorry,' I said. 'I wasn't paying attention to what I was typing.'

She fairly snatched the papers out of my machine. 'Excellent! No mistakes and no understanding. You are an ideal typist,

Stapleford. Glad they sent you here.' Something strange was happening to her face. I managed to prevent myself from squinting, and realised that the lines around her lips had changed. Her eyes too seemed less interrogating. This must be as close as she got to a smile. I smiled back although my heart was rapidly sinking. 'I had hoped, ma'am, that I might be able to do other work here,' I ventured.

Masterton shook her head. 'Empty minds like yours are exactly what we need in the typist section.'

I felt like banging my head on the desk. I had finally made an impression, and it was exactly the opposite of what I wanted it to be.

That night I told the episode to Leo, framing it as an amusing anecdote, but secretly hoping he would be what Dashwood had termed 'my dashing knight'. Leo didn't find it funny. He even stopped scoffing his way through the pot pie I had made to comment, 'It's a damn shame, Hope.'

'Yes,' I said, 'it looks like the only thing that's going to get me off this assignment is a bomb landing on the building.'

'Not funny,' said Leo. Then he went to bed leaving me with the washing-up.

I left my door unlocked again, but nothing and no one disturbed my rest.

Chapter Four

'It's good we haven't had any air raids recently,' I said to Leo over a breakfast of French toast (my recipe). 'Maybe the danger has been exaggerated.'

Leo shook his head. 'I think we've been lucky. I expect that will change.' He took an extra slice from the plate in the middle. It was his fourth. I'd only had two, but I still had hopes for Leo, either in the bedroom, or as a rescuer, so I didn't complain despite the unfairness of it pinching me inside. 'By the way,' continued Leo, 'I had a look downstairs. Seems like it's been made bombproof, or as bombproof as you can make a shelter without digging a mile underground.'

'Are there shelters that deep?' I asked, intrigued.

'Forget I said that,' said Leo, and rather than it being a conversational remark, I heard the tone in his voice that meant this was an order. 'Still, we won't have far to go if the siren goes at night.'

'No,' I said. 'Have you decided if you're staying here?'

Leo nodded. 'For now. Leave the plates in water and I'll walk in with you.'

It was another unseasonably hot day, and I wished very much that I wasn't in uniform. It was thick and scratchy, and I could feel the sweat breaking out on my brow before we'd reached the end of the street. Leo had been setting a cracking pace, but he suddenly seemed to remember I was with him and slowed down. Around us people were milling about waiting at bus stops, bustling along to their offices with their umbrellas clasped to their sides, and women with baskets were queuing hopefully outside butchers and bakers. The men heading into the offices in their uniforms of black jackets and pinstripes were fewer in number and older in age than before the war and, of course, the number of men and women in service uniform was high, but despite this, London was wearing a very ordinary look this morning. The sky had the required number of fluffy clouds and was a cheerful blue. It could have been any day at any time. Leo glanced up, and said, 'I read that during the last war one of the things that amazed the men in the trenches the most was that the birds sang every morning.'

'It does feel too ordinary today,' I said.

'I expect that's influenced by your work,' said Leo. Then he stopped. We were standing under an elm tree in a small pocket from the crowds around us. 'I'm sorry, Hope. I did try to get you out of there. But it seems Masterton has taken a shine to you, and frankly no one is prepared to deal with the hassle of upsetting her. I've told them how good a field officer you are, but it doesn't seem to have made any difference. I wanted you to know that I had tried.'

I swallowed the lump I could feel building up in my throat. 'It was good of you to try,' I said. 'Thank you.'

'I don't know if you'll think of this as good news or bad, but I'm going to stay billeted with you for the foreseeable future.'

We both started walking again. There didn't seem a lot more to say. I expressed pleasure at having Leo around, but tried to downplay it. I rummaged around in my thoughts trying to find something playful or interesting to signal my continued interest in him, and failed. During the lull in the conversation I noticed him glancing over to the other side of the street a few times. I followed his eyeline and saw he was looking at a thin blonde girl in a Navy uniform. She was very pretty in a perky, slightly horsey way that the upper classes can have. 'Excuse me,' said Leo. 'I think I see someone I know.'

He ran across the street, dodging a bus, and I saw the girl react with obvious pleasure at their encounter. At that point I stopped looking. Could the day get any worse? Then, as I crossed a side road I came face to face with a familiar man in civilian dress, Cole, who raised his hat to me and sidestepped around me. I was so surprised I tripped over my own feet, and did one of those silly hopping trot things you do to avoid falling on your face. By the time I'd recovered he had gone. Or at least I could not see where he was, which wasn't quite the same thing when it came to Cole. My eardrums thudded, and my heart raced. My breath was coming so fast I had to stop and lean against a garden wall. I told myself my mind was playing tricks, but I knew, down into the core of me, that it had been Cole. No matter how ridiculous it sounded, we had run into each other in the city. Only with Cole there was no such thing as a coincidence. It was some time before I could pull myself together and walk on.

For once I was relieved to get inside my office building and sit at my boring little desk. The files came thick and fast during the day, and lunch turned into a hurried fifteen minutes. If I had been asked afterwards what I'd eaten, I wouldn't have been able to say. It had no particular flavour and I couldn't even remember what I had asked for. Many of today's files were filled with numbers, and in all likelihood encoded. I had to concentrate particularly hard to transcribe these correctly, and by the end of the day I felt as weary as if I had been wrestling alligators all day.

Once more I was home before Leo, so I made a quick supper out of toasted cheese on bread and some beans, leaving his in the oven to keep warm, and went and lay down on my bed. I'd hoped I would get a second wind. I certainly had plenty to think about, but within minutes I was fast asleep.

Leo bursting through my bedroom door woke me. He was wearing striped pyjamas and his hair was sticking up at crazy angles. 'Come on, Hope,' he shouted. 'Move!'

'What?'

'The siren? Didn't you hear it?'

He came over and tugged my arm. I got up quickly, but my

brain was reeling. At least I still seemed to be dressed. I followed him out the door and downstairs with very little coherent thought. In truth, I was fairly sure I was still dreaming. But Leo was in his pyjamas and that might lead to an interesting dream.

At the bottom of the stairs, he threw open a door I had paid no attention to, making this even more likely to be a dream, and led me down a set of wooden steps. At the bottom was a short passageway, and then a metal door. It led to an underground room with a couple of cots. Leo threw himself down on one. 'I'll say one thing about your stepfather, when he does a thing, he does it properly. I doubt anyone else round here has as good a shelter. Must be nice to have someone take care of you like that.'

I sat on the edge of the other cot and waited for the pieces of my brain to fall into place. 'I think I was deeply asleep,' I said.

'No kidding,' said Leo. 'That siren was louder than – whatever, you must have been practically unconscious. Been knocking back your stepfather's wine in secret?' He paused. 'The wailing of that thing. I would have thought it would wake the dead.'

'It's an unearthly sound,' I agreed with a shudder. 'I suppose they wanted a noise that no one would confuse with anything else.'

Leo rolled back on to his cot. 'Well, it's that,' he said. 'I'm going to try and get some shut-eye. I have a long day tomorrow. You should do the same.' He plumped the pillow behind his head and stretched out his legs. 'Good old Fitzroy. It's not even cold in here. Check under your pillow. I bet he's even left you a nightdress!'

Leo was joking, but I looked and there was one. I changed into it. It wasn't the kind of thing I would normally have worn. The material was thicker than I liked, but it was a glorious royal blue. I hoped wearing it would make me feel like sleeping. It didn't.

I continued to sit on the edge of the cot straining my ears. Despite sleeping like the dead I generally have good hearing. This time I registered something at the very edge of my hearing, in that way when you're not entirely sure if the sound is real or your mind is tricking you. It was a low humming sort of sound. I'd worked last at an airbase in Scotland, so I knew the sound of an incoming plane. But this was a deeper noise, a low thrum that seemed to echo up from the centre of the earth itself. I knew if I was on the street I would feel it vibrating in my bones.

I stood up and began to pace. The sound of my slippered feet on the wooden floor was slight, but enough to push the other horrible noise away. Leo gave a sudden snort, and began to snore.

We had a small emergency bulkhead light. One of those ones that is shaped like a lozenge and is bandaged in bars, so if it explodes the glass doesn't go everywhere. It was set high in the wall, casting light down into the space, and making it feel less like the pit it actually was. Everything about the design of this little retreat was clever and well thought out. If you'd told me Fitzroy had borrowed Churchill's builders to create it I wouldn't have been surprised. I assumed he had done the same under his apartment, and the one I had recently found out he had bought my mother during their time working together. He hadn't bought me mine. I was renting it from a Mr Goldbloom, who I only knew as a signature on the bottom of my lease, so how he'd got permission to build the shelter, I didn't know. Though it was possible he'd gone ahead without asking. He was a great one for acting now and only seeking permission afterwards if he absolutely had to. He generally assumed everyone would understand he'd done the right thing.

I turned and began to pace in the opposite direction, now going widthways instead of lengthways. I was especially concerned about waking Leo. I wouldn't do it deliberately, but I did think it was callous of him to fall straight asleep and leave me to worry.

The humming was getting closer. Would they bomb Kensington? What would be the point? To demoralise us and cause property damage? Wouldn't it make more sense to bomb the docks? London needed the East End docks working to function.

Immediately, I berated myself for wishing the bombs on anyone.

My preference was for them to go back to where they came from or blow up mid-air.

But that wouldn't happen. And no matter how well designed Fitzroy had made this shelter, he had had neither the time nor the ability to build as far underground as I suspected the war chambers of the government would be.

I should be grateful. Lord knows it was better than those hideous brick structures on the London streets. Did anyone really think they would be safer in those outside shelters than under their own stairs in a tenement building? Again, I understood the point of them was to give reassurance, to show the government was considering the people's safety. How well would that work when the morning brought the sight of them cracked open like eggs with the dead and dying spilling out of them?

I considered slapping myself, and stifled a sound that might have been the start of an hysterical giggle. I switched to pacing lengthways again. I must be beginning to wear out the floorboards.

Leo gave a tremendous snort and began to snore. A moment later I was violently shoved on to my cot. Face down. Traces of earth pattered down around me. I heard Leo say, 'Hey what?' in a startled sleepy voice. I hung on to the far end of the cot and buried my face in the pillow. Beneath us and around us the world moved in sudden jerks and spasms.

Silence.

I turned over slowly and pulled myself to a sitting position on the cot. Clots of soil fell from my hair. I brushed at it automatically, and as thought returned, felt over my scalp for injury. Leo's cot was empty, and it took me a moment to understand he had rolled on to the floor.

'Bloody hell,' he said. 'Why would anyone bomb Kensington?'

'Morale,' I tried to say, but my voice came out broken and wheezy. Leo pulled himself up off the floor and came to sit beside me. Both of us were looking up.

'You okay?' he asked.

'Ah ah,' I said. 'Only loose earth. I don't think it's coming down.'

'No,' said Leo. 'Bit of a surprise all this.'

'My legs hurt,' I said, reaching down. 'I bruised them on the side of the cot.'

'Just a bruise?' asked Leo in a worried voice.

Then, without knowing why, I began to sob uncontrollably.

Chapter Five

The next morning, after we left the cellar, we went outside first. There was rubble all along the street of Georgian terraced houses. The roofs of the porticos lay smashed on their sides, and most of the once-imposing pillars were no more than debris. A green tea wagon had been set up halfway along the street, and there was a stream of people queuing for tea out of those giant tin urns.

'That's not good,' said Leo. 'They only send those to the worst-hit places.'

I stood there trying to make sense of what I was seeing. The street had been perfect when I'd come home. My side of the street was entirely unscathed, but on the other side windows were blown out, the white stone was blackened, and fire engines were spraying water on to three separate terraced houses that were still burning. Across the road lay books, bits of furniture and paintings – I couldn't imagine how they had got there, and in such neat piles, until I realised this must have been people trying to rescue their possessions.

I caught a glimpse of blue through the window of one of the upper windows of the house opposite and realised I was seeing sky. The whole roof had caved in. The chaos was remarkably organised. I saw two men carrying a stretcher from out of one of the ruined houses. They passed close to me and I saw the tiredness on their grimy faces, but they walked upright and at a steady pace. I automatically looked at their patient, only to see their face was covered and the blanket over them soaked in shockingly brilliant red.

Leo had to pull me back as they walked past. 'Shall we go get ourselves a cuppa?' he suggested.

I moved backwards, responding to his touch, but my eyes were searching for the people who had lived in the houses. I hadn't really got to know my neighbours. No more than a morning nod or a bright, 'Lovely weather, isn't it, for the time of year?' Living with Bernie hadn't exactly endeared me to the locals. She liked to sit out on our little balcony smoking a cigarette and drinking a cocktail in the early evenings. She had made us look like the socialites we had been as debutantes last summer. Until . . .

Why hadn't I bothered to get to know these people? I might never have the chance. I saw one woman, holding a soiled bandage to her face, being helped along by a nurse. Ambulances had arrived at the other end of the street. At least she looked as if she had the competence of a nurse, though she was wearing some kind of overall.

'Did you come out from one of 'em houses?' asked a man in civilian clothes. He was wearing a tin hat and some kind of armband. 'Do you need help?'

'No, we're from the other side,' said Leo. 'We were in the cellar.'

'Bloody lucky,' said the man. 'Family over the way were down in theirs and the whole thing came down on top of 'em. Least it was quick. Incendiaries, that's what it mostly was. But once it burns through the roof, these old buildings just seem to give up the ghost. It's the beams in them. Not been strengthened in over a century I reckon. Most of the poor buggers didn't stand a chance.'

'Yes, we were lucky,' said Leo in a remarkably calm voice. 'We'll give the Germans hell for this. You see if we don't.'

'That's the spirit! Here, look, your girl doesn't look too good. You'd better get a cup of tea down her pronto.' He patted my arm. 'You'll be right as rain, miss, soon as you've had a brush-up and changed back into your clothes.'

It was only then I remembered I was still in my night clothes.

'Yes, thank you,' I managed to say. I took a couple of steps towards the house, and tottered like an octogenarian. Leo got me to sit down on something. I didn't register what, except it was hard.

'Stay there. I'll get you some tea.'

I tried to protest that we had tea in the flat. I didn't want to take supplies from the tea wagon, which were for the people who really needed it. But I didn't get further than 'but'. My mind and my mouth were not yet sufficiently connected.

Leo brought me back tea; milky, strong and sweet. He stood looking down at me, a worried expression on his face. He was running his fingers through his hair, which with the effects of sleep had changed his normal sleek style into curls. He looked absurdly young in his pyjamas. 'I need to get in,' he said. 'Do you think you'd be up to going back in when you've finished that?'

I nodded, and swallowed the rest in one gulp.

Leo returned the cup to a passing helper. 'Tell you something,' he said. 'I'm sleeping in my uniform from now on. It's mighty chilly out here dressed like this.'

'Is it?' I asked.

Leo hooked my arm through his and walked me back to the flat. Once inside he was something of a blur of motion. He splashed his face in the kitchen sink before heading into the bathroom with his shaving kit. I started making toast and coffee, but I'd barely cut the bread before Leo appeared in the kitchen, spruced up with his hair slicked back into place, and his uniform looking so sharp you'd have thought it could cut cheese.

'What have you been doing?' he asked, looking from the bread knife to me.

'Coffee. Breakfast before we . . . No time for eggs,' I said, and sat down suddenly and involuntarily on the kitchen stool.

'Were you hit on the head by anything?' asked Leo. He peered closely into my eyes. 'I can't see anything, but I'm no expert.' He placed his hand on my forehead as if that would somehow make everything better. 'I have to go, Hope. But I can't leave you like this. Can't you tell me what's wrong?'

I was saved from answering by the ring of the doorbell. It struck me as hugely funny that we still had doorbells, and I began to laugh softly.

Leo went to answer the door. I heard the words as if from a long distance, 'Old family friend.'

'There's something wrong,' Leo said. 'I don't know what. We were in the cellar. I'm afraid she must have fallen harder than I realised. I should take her to the hospital only—'

'Don't worry,' said the familiar voice. Then both voices dropped to a level I couldn't follow. This seemed rather rude, but I couldn't quite summon up the energy to comment. Some time later, whether it was seconds, minutes or a day I couldn't have said, I heard the door slam. Then came the sound of heavy footsteps walking towards me. I looked up into the grey-blue eyes of a man, dressed all in black, with slight greying flecks at his temples. He was tall and broad-shouldered enough that he loomed over me. He smelled faintly of petrol, and beyond him I saw a coat and motor goggles cast down on the couch. This was the man who had claimed to be an old friend of my mother's, before he had tricked me into killing one of our own agents. He was also the man who'd overcome my assailant when I had been attacked in this very flat. I had been in the bath at the time or I'm sure I could have dealt with him myself.

Cole stood in front of me without saying a word. I could feel tears welling up as I looked up miserably through my eyelashes. So it was quite a surprise when he slapped me. Slapped me hard enough it made me rock in my seat.

'You bastard!' I said, springing to my feet and adopting a defensive pose. Cole backed away, holding his hands up.

'I don't know why your little boyfriend couldn't have figured that out for himself.'

'He's not my boyfriend, you snake!'

Cole chuckled. 'Apologies, Hope. You were in shock. The adrenaline rush snapped you out of it – or more exactly your desire to punch me in the face.'

'Why on earth would I be in shock? I've killed men!'

A wide smile spread over Cole's face. He sat down on the couch furthest away from me. 'That's more like my girl.'

'I am not your girl!' I growled. 'You made me kill one of our own.'

Cole pulled a face of mock horror. 'Is that what you think of me? I certainly helped you take the shot, but he was a traitor.'

'Fitzroy would never have done such a thing to me!'

'Probably not,' said Cole. 'He's always been too soft on you. You're more like your mother than you realise.'

'Oh yes, I can just see my mother standing in the middle of a bombed street crying in her nightgown.'

'I'd pay money to see that,' said Cole. 'The nightgown not the crying.'

I looked down at my clothing, before I realised he was talking about my mother not me. 'Really, he was a traitor?'

'I'm surprised you thought anything else,' said Cole in a colder voice. 'And apart from giving you some of the training you desperately needed, saving your life more than once and letting you ride pillion on my bike, which I never let anyone do, what exactly gave you the idea *I* was a traitor to the crown?'

'I don't know,' I said. 'You seemed to keep showing up and I wasn't sure what you wanted, and then you told me stories about Fitzroy training as an assassin before he was a spy—'

'No,' said Cole. 'I said that he learned to be a sniper first, and he was sent on kill missions. That's part of being an agent of the crown, as you should know.'

'But they never mentioned you,' I said, sounding even to my own ears petulant.

Cole gave me a long look. 'I don't believe they ever wanted you in their world.'

'Who?' I began, but he interrupted me. 'You were in shock. Being bombed the first time, wherever you are, is something of a shock. You see the world literally torn up around you. Everything you considered safe is not. But then a lot of chaps in the last war saw their comrades being blown up beside them – literally vanishing into clouds of crimson.'

'I didn't see anything like that.'

'I know you didn't,' said Cole. 'You were stuck underground like a rabbit waiting for the farmer to send his dog down. It's not what you're meant for. You're not someone to wait on the sidelines, whatever your parents might have thought.'

'Fitzroy is not my father,' I said hotly.

'Of course he is,' said Cole, brushing my comment aside. 'That's not important. You might have been trained in evasion and observation, Hope, but you were always meant to be in the field. Waiting for those bombs to drop on you is anathema to your soul. Like it is to mine.'

'Where were you?'

'On my motorbike. On the streets.'

'Pulling people out of buildings,' I said with as much sarcasm as a girl in a nightdress facing a man she knows fancies her mother, can muster.

'Oh no,' said Cole. 'Something far more important. But it's what you need to do. Get out there. No hiding behind your puppy-eyed boyfriend.'

'He is not my boyfriend.'

'If you go and get dressed I'll get you to work in time. Masterton can't have changed that much. You'd have to be dead to be excused being late, and maybe not even then.' He chuckled again, clearly remembering something he had no intention of sharing. Before he could say anything else I grabbed my clothes from my room and headed into the bathroom.

I emerged not many minutes later. While I didn't look the polished young lieutenant, neither did I look scruffy and woebegone. Those few minutes had given me pause to reflect on what Cole had said. I had felt trapped and helpless in the cellar. Maybe he knew me better than I knew myself.

Chapter Six

I ran up the steps to the building, flashed my ID at the doorman and was behind my typewriter only moments before I heard Masterton's stentorian tones as she flung open the doors to the office. She didn't even look over at my desk. The morning progressed and a number of people I didn't know either dumped files in my in tray or rearranged them into their preferred order. I felt like I should object, but it was hard to bring myself to care. Besides, I had no idea of the importance of anything I was typing. Much like other typing positions I had ended up in, it took a while before the jargon, the code words and the general sense of these reports made any sense. Usually I was just beginning to understand things when I was moved on. That was something to hope for.

I was sipping my tea in between typing up papers on resilience – though resilience to what was unclear – when Daniel Dashwood appeared at my side. He gave a low bow and said, 'One shining white knight as ordered.'

'Stop it,' I hissed. 'You'll get me into trouble with Masterton.'

'Rubbish,' said Daniel. 'She's one of my biggest fans.'

And rather like some demons that were believed to have been summoned by the saying of their names, Captain Masterton appeared in front of my desk. She only needed a whiff of sulphur and a smattering of smoke to complete the image.

'Ah, fair lady,' said Daniel, possessing himself of one of her hands and kissing it. 'I tremble to see your ethereal beauty – a poise and elegance that even khaki cannot obscure. Hateful colour on everyone.'

I clenched my fists to prevent myself from putting my hands over my eyes and cringing. This wasn't as bad as being bombed but at that moment it felt close. Then the incredible happened, and Captain Masterton, the iron-clad mistress of all she surveyed, simpered. She even gave a little giggle. She batted at Daniel's hand and told him he was a 'bad boy'.

He told her he'd like to be 'a very bad boy' where she was concerned, and I seriously considered throwing up in my wastebasket.

Without warning, she turned to me and snapped, 'You'll be part of Daniel's crew every afternoon from lunch. In the mornings, you'll be working double hard up here to make up for missed time.' Then she turned on her heel and strode off.

'Magnificent woman,' said Daniel. 'I can't help feeling that should we parachute her into Berlin she'd have this whole thing cleared up by the weekend. Anyway, come along. You're in the film industry now. At least for afternoons.'

The film studio was in the basement. Or perhaps it was the lower basement. This was one of those buildings that went down and down, but access to the nether regions was granted only to a few. The studio was a series of enormous rooms attached to some smaller offices. The larger areas were filled with sets such as a domestic kitchen, or even a country garden. Nothing bore too close an exploration, but Daniel assured me that the wonders of lighting and the right film could make miracles happen.

He took me into a little office where my heart sank to see a typewriter. 'You want your scripts typed up,' I said.

'Well, yes,' said Daniel. 'But I've sort of convinced the major, who's running the show, that you are a wonder child when it comes to scripts. Awful woman we had stormed out. Said we didn't value her talent, and she would go where she was wanted. I can't imagine where that might be, but wherever it is they're welcome to her.'

'You told the major I would write the scripts?' I said. 'Are you crazy? I've never written anything in my life!'

'Yes, well, you can do a damn sight better than her. Besides, the major is greener than a gherkin. Barely knows his fades from his floods. And if I asked him for a Gobo he'd probably faint.'

'Gobo? Goblin?'

'No, it stands for Go Black Out – it's a . . . well, you don't need to know.'

'I don't understand!' I protested

'You're only doing the words.' He handed me a file. 'Look, here's what we were working with. See what you can do with that and then give us six copies. I've made sure you have carbons.'

'Just type it up?' I said, looking over the eleven pages, which were filled with things like 'EXT' and 'INT'.

'No, rewrite it. You need to use the same settings but change the dialogue.'

'Can't you rewrite it?'

'Darling girl, actors never write their own lines. All hell would break loose if they did. Quite against the natural order. Now chop. We need them in fifty.'

'Fifty?'

'Fifty minutes. I'll close the door behind me and tell the others to leave you alone.'

It took me under the hour to complete my first film, a short, very short piece on the importance of digging up your rose beds to grow potatoes. As I reread it, I didn't think I would win any prizes, but it was undoubtedly better than the dreadful stuff I'd been handed. It was only a first draft, but I didn't know that at the time.

'Gave you an extra five,' said Dashwood sticking his head around the door. 'New director needs the pages now. He might come and have a word. Should say I've talked you up a bit, but I'm sure you can carry it off.'

He held out his hand for the pages. I got up and passed him the bundle. It hadn't occurred to me that anyone would request changes, so I gave him the seven copies I had made. I saw by his raised eyebrows that I might have made a mistake. I gave him a hopeful smile, and he doffed an invisible cap to me.

Then I went back to my desk and stared at the wall. I hadn't been given anything else to do, and the desk was quite bare. I would be going up the stairs any minute if this director didn't like what I had done. And what did Dashwood mean he'd talked me up? That was a worrying thought.

Less than ten minutes later, the door opened and I heard Dashwood say, 'She's in here, Major. Bright little thing. Might not think it to look at her, but she's got the brain of an engine when it comes to creativity. Fires on all cylinders.'

I heard a loud 'Humph' in answer to this. I stood up to see around Dashwood and looked straight into Leo's face.

'You!' we both said in what must have seemed comical unison to Dashwood, because he sniggered. Leo turned on him with a snarl. 'Out!' he shouted in a voice quite unlike the Leo I knew. I'd seen him annoyed before, but never quite so authoritative. Dashwood left quick smart.

As soon as the door closed behind him, Leo went over and pulled down a blind over the glass top of the door. Then he stalked over to me. 'What the hell are you doing here?' he said. His tone was slightly less aggressive than it had been with Dashwood, but his cheeks were flushed red with anger.

'I don't know what you've been told,' I said carefully, 'but I suggested a couple of changes to the script to Dashwood, and he seems to have turned that into an opportunity.'

'So it was his idea, not yours?'

'I admit I told him I was bored in the glorified typing pool, but I had no idea he would put me forward or that you were the director.'

'And the man at the door today.'

'Cole,' I said. 'You remember him. He's been in the service as long as Fitzroy.'

Leo snorted. 'What is it about you that you have all these middle-aged men falling at your feet?'

'Do I? I wasn't aware I had anyone at my feet.'

'Humph,' said Leo. 'I don't suppose I can get rid of you now.'

'I'm only here for part of the day. And I'm pretty sure you can get rid of me. You're in charge.'

'Yes,' said Leo. 'But,' he slapped the papers in his hand, 'these are the best I've seen since I got here, and believe me I've read through thousands – well, hundreds – of dire pages.'

'Maybe we're fated to work together,' I said lightly.

'You mean Fitzroy intended this?'

'I didn't mean that at all. Why would he? And how?'

'The how doesn't come into it,' said Leo crossly. 'That man could fix the Derby to run on the moon.'

'Okay,' I said. 'But . . . why?'

'Never mind that,' said Leo. 'Come and watch this being shot. It's good, but once you see it on its legs, you'll understand more how dialogue works. Hearing your own words . . .'

I followed him out the door. 'Did you try writing one?' I asked.

'Yes,' he said, dropping his voice so low only I would hear, 'and it was pretty grim.'

Chapter Seven

It was a lot of fun watching the actors go through their lines. Especially as they were my lines. However, I quickly learned that how I thought they might sound didn't necessarily sound the same from the actors' mouths. What's more, Leo also had an idea of how they should be said and it was often neither how I nor the actor had imagined. Fortunately, our disparity in rank had kept me from saying anything the first time Leo corrected a line, and as I watched I realised that in this role no one dared correct him. He behaved very differently from how I had seen him at the SOE, or even back at the castle. He was belligerent and bombastic. There was no kindness about him, and he was ruthlessly direct if he didn't like something. I wondered if they were on a tight schedule, or if he was, in a slightly different manner to how Fitzroy's dog Jack might have done it, effectively marking his territory. If he really knew as little as Dashwood claimed, it made a kind of sense in that odd way the male brain can. But then if he knew nothing about this world, why was he here?

The hour passed swiftly, and by the end I knew even if Leo didn't know what a Gobo was, he still knew a lot more about putting a film together than I might have expected. I recalled at the castle he had had a few private chats with my stepfather. I had presumed this had been Fitzroy's way of entertaining himself. He didn't like Leo much as a person, but I thought that had as much to do with him catching me in Leo's arms as anything. There were very few people he cared about, but those he did, he defended with the ferocity of a lion. Although he did seem to respect Leo as an operative. Perhaps this was what Fitzroy had been instructing him in? But wouldn't he have mentioned this? After all, we had both been expecting to go to Scotland until the train went in the opposite direction. Or had we? I could see now just how good an actor Leo was.

Lots of people in SIS were good at acting. For field agents it was frequently part of our role to pretend to be someone we weren't. I didn't think this was one of my strengths. Could Leo have known all along what was going on?

The next day, these thoughts and other more morose ones occupied me while I typed away diligently back upstairs. In previous typing pools I had got to know the other girls, but here the typists were separated across the wide office. In between us people bent over tables looking at maps through large lenses or shifted through piles of papers jotting down barely legible notes I had to puzzle out later. People were constantly bustling about, and now I realised, also buzzing between different offices. Ours seemed to be one where information was finalised, but in between the various personnel often disappeared for up to an hour at a time, only to return with more wretched typing. Clearly this department was connected to lots of other offices, but I currently had no excuse to go and investigate these. My current position reminded me of something Fitzroy had once said to me about war on the battlefield. He had described it as long periods of boredom interspersed with short periods of terror.

When I was given permission for my fifteen-minute tea break, I trotted quickly downstairs to the canteen and sat in a corner sipping something that was almost, but not quite, like tea. However, the mug was hot and comforting to hold in my hands.

'Whatcha, Lieutenant,' said a cheery voice. I looked up to see the chap with the pickled-walnut face I had run into earlier. 'Thought I should introduce myself now you're down in the movies with us. I'm Perkins. Lights and props. Though lights itself is work enough.' He held out his hand. I took it and gave a small smile.

'Mind if I pull up a chair?' I felt I could hardly say no, so I nodded. 'Cor blimey, you're a young 'un, aren't you?' He pulled back and looked a little worried. 'If you don't mind me saying. Must be the same age as my daughter. She's just turned twenty. Still not given her the key of the door! Though seeing how she's off fighting for King and Country I suppose now I should.'

I was nearer thirty than twenty, but Perkins didn't give me a chance to speak. All I could think was that Leo was right. Do I have something about me that makes older men feel protective towards me?

'Anyhow, you were sitting there with your face as long as a wet Monday, so I thought I'd pop over and be cheery. Me wife says that's my main talent, being cheery. Bloody annoying she finds it.'

By this time I was smiling. I couldn't help myself. 'Yes, you are rather good at that Corporal Perkins.'

'If I might be so bold, can I ask what has got you so down? Aside from there being a war on and all that. Wasn't our major, was it? I've noticed as long as you do your job proper he doesn't rip into you. Can't stand people wasting time or not putting the effort in. Drives him bananas. Not really the right sort of cove to work with theatrical types.'

'Is that what you did before?'

'No, bless you, love. I operated the projector at the movies. Army clearly thought that good enough to put me into lighting. Though it's nothing close. I've had to learn on the job. Rather glad I started in the post a while before our new major came along, or you'd be picking over my bones now.'

'My street got bombed last night.' The words fell out of my mouth before I realised.

'Oh, you poor love. Did you lose anyone?'

I shook my head. 'I felt so helpless down in the shelter waiting.'

Perkins nodded. 'I know exactly what you mean. You're like me. Waiting around grinds your nerves down.'

'Exactly,' I said. 'I expected you to tell me to hold my nerve.'

'Nah,' said Perkins. 'I could tell looking at you you're a girl who likes to be doing things. Like my Laura. Have you thought about joining the ARP – air-raid protection? You get to wander around yelling at people to put their lights out. Even the posh folk.'

I laughed.

'Yeah, but we also do more serious stuff. We're often first on the scene, which you know, can be awful, but at least you feel like you're doing something. Or there's the tea wagon. They always need more helpers.'

'ARP,' I said firmly. 'How do I join?'

By the time Leo got back to the flat I had a hotpot in the oven and was resting on the sofa. 'That's smells good,' were his first words through the door. 'It's for me, isn't it?'

'Us,' I said. 'I feel a bit like a wife.' I then blushed furiously. When would I think before I spoke?

'I made food yesterday,' protested Leo.

'So you did,' I said, looking down at the book I had in my hands in the faint hope he wouldn't notice the colour I had gone. 'By the way, I'm going out shortly. I'm joining the ARP.'

Leo came over to sit next to me. 'Is that a good idea, Hope? It's dangerous.'

'There's a war on,' I said. 'Lots of things are dangerous. It's not like I'm heading to the front line.'

'Going outside when there are possible raids is not different.'

'You're meant to help people not get bombed,' I said.

'You also help get people into shelters, organise the fire-watchers and report on the on-going raid,' said Leo.

'I didn't know,' I said.

'Fitzroy would be furious if I let you do this.'

In much the same way as a cat might, I could feel my hackles rising. 'You might be my commanding officer on the film unit, but I wasn't aware you had any other jurisdiction over me. Unless you've known all along that we were coming here, and this is another of those assignments within assignments Fitzroy is so fond of?'

Leo didn't answer immediately.

'Tell me I'm not being kept in the dark again?' I asked.

'I'd better get that pie out of the oven,' said Leo.

'It's a hotpot. And you can eat it all yourself.'

I got up and picking up my coat slammed out of the door. My exit was made slightly less dignified when I had to reopen the door to retrieve my gas mask. I hated the wretched thing, but it was unlikely anyone would enrol me as a warden if I showed up without it.

'Hope, don't be foolish. Come and eat some dinner.'

'Will you tell me the truth?'

'You know truth is subjective in our world. Now come and eat!'

I left.

Chapter Eight

Walking along to where Perkins had told me they were recruiting, my stomach made it quite plain how foolish I had been to forgo food. It was growling loudly by the time I reached the church hall, so the sight of a tea urn and a plate of biscuits was very welcome. Lots of people were milling around waiting for the information session to start. It was one of those ubiquitous places that are attached to medium-sized churches. It had a little stage built along one end, which still had its curtains. I imagined it wouldn't be long before those heavy drapes were confiscated for blackout cloths. The few windows around the room had all been boarded over. Daylight wasn't getting back into this place while the war was on-going, but nor was any light getting out. The ambience here was black and cold and, for me, somewhat forbidding.

There were women wearing headscarves, more than one of whom had a smut on her face. These must be ammunition workers. I found it rather cheering that although they hadn't had a chance to wash, they had all put on bright red lipstick. There were five of them, all with muscular arms, and a set to their chins that suggested they had the sass to take on a working man's job. I liked the look of them, but I felt too shy and too different to say hello. In the past I would chat to anyone, but having a duchess as a mother had unnerved me. I spotted another woman, who dressed exactly as the newspapers depicted a wife, neat, tidy and nervous. She'd brought her handbag and her gloves with her, and was constantly shifting them from one hand to the other. I spotted a couple of retired services men, probably army judging by the puffing barks of laughter they exchanged between them, and that wafted out of their thick white moustaches like tiny sea tides above their lips. There was a young man, who I would have expected to have been recruited, and perhaps he worked in my building, but he stood a little apart from the rest, looking at his feet and unable to meet anyone's gaze. He hadn't even got himself a cup of tea. There were others too, many more than I had expected, but they didn't make a particular impression on me.

I snagged myself a cup of tea and three biscuits. I even ate the crumbs that landed on my chest.

'Only two biscuits each,' said a voice at my elbow, and I turned to see Perkins' grinning face. 'We'll let it slide this time.'

'I'll only have one next time,' I said.

'Who said there would be any next time? It's getting harder all the time to get supplies.'

'I'll make some.'

Perkins gave a chuckle. 'Well, that's you in, girl. Anyone who provides snacks is right for us. I saw you watching the "Rosies". Those girls have got muscle.' He tilted his head to look past my shoulder. 'Oh, heads-up, here comes the boss!'

The door behind us had opened, and a man in blue overalls, much like the ones I noted Perkins was wearing, came in. Of average height and with a slender frame, I would have placed him in his forties. He was probably just, possibly by months, too old to be called up. He strode into the centre of the room like a man used to commanding respect and attention. Before the war this could have meant he was anything from a cocky car salesman to a brigadier. Only I got the impression he wasn't services. The set of his shoulders was a bit off. Not the straight line one would expect of an army man. Of course Fitzroy also had something of a cock-of-the-walk stride, but then he wasn't a regular soldier, and rarely undertook any kind of group command. I couldn't quite put my finger on it, but I got the impression this man was used to ordering people around. Perhaps he had been a floor walker in one of the better department stores.

I was still trying to figure him out when he made encircling motions and the group drew quietly up around him. I followed Perkins, who without any warning gave me a quick nod, and trotted over to the stage, which he leapt up on to with ease and disappeared behind the curtains.

'Er-hm, if I could have your attention. All your attention.'

I swung round to meet the speaker's eyes. Immediately I adopted a meek non-confrontational pose as I would have done if I had been undercover. At least here, I couldn't be on one of Fitzroy's hidden missions. Joining the ARP had been quite my own idea.

'Good evening, ladies and gentlemen. I am Larkin Prentice and if at the end of this session you decide the ARP is for you, and we decide you are for us, then we will get to know each other rather well. But for now if you could all collect a chair from the stack at the back and line them up neatly in front of the stage, Mr Perkins will give us a basic introduction to the items you might be using.'

People bustled about trying to make up lines, which I presume was the point. The 'Roses' had themselves in a group at once, but others had started other lines in other places. The two older men placed their chairs right in the middle in front of the stage, closer to it than anyone else. I found a midway space between two groups that made it more into a line in a quiet, team-player sort of way.

Perkins then walked along the stage as if it was a catwalk, introducing us to his overall uniform. I laughed at the way he minced along, but listened to the reasons for the blue costume; not bright, but identifiable by the public; pockets, but no protruding flourishes to catch on anything; hardwearing and practical for climbing over rubble. 'When I started,' he said, 'you only got an armband. We've gone up in the world. Not only do you get this,' he indicated his overalls once more, 'but this!' And like a conjurer performing a trick he slapped a flat metal helmet on his head. 'Very handy for the preventing of shrapnel in your brain box, fending off falling debris, stopping your hair catching fire, and entrancing the opposite sex with your debonair style! Especially when worn with your deluxe gas mask!'

Most people were either smiling or laughing outright at Perkins. I thought he had missed his vocation and after the war should consider going on the stage. 'Now this here,' he said, reaching behind the curtains and bringing out a long metal pole with a wicked-looking hook at the top, 'is not an ancient oriental weapon, but a ceiling pike for poking the ceiling. Not if your neighbour is snoring or being too noisy, but to check if the ceiling in a bombed building is stable. Of course one does not poke at ceiling from directly underneath, but from a convenient doorway.' He did a little mime of prodding upwards and getting showered in debris, and then another where he poked the imaginary ceiling from an imaginary door frame. People were laughing less now.

He went on to show us the gas rattle, that one swung around one's head to warn of gas; the bucket stirrup water pump for putting out small fires; a first-aid kit, which included a triangular bandage that was cleverly covered in illustrations for its multiple uses; and finally the forms we had to fill in when we arrived on scene. 'We're part of a wider network,' said Perkins, 'and these forms get passed up the chain by foot messenger or by phone. Bomb disposal, nursing units, firemen, you name them, they count on our accurate reporting. Telling HQ what is on-site and who is here already and what we need is what we have to do to save lives. Jokes are over now. We're into the business of saving lives and keeping alive ourselves.'

Prentice put one hand on to the stage and bounced up. Perkins immediately retreated behind a curtain.

'Now, ladies and gentlemen, you understand we are the first line in Britain's civil defence. We are often first on the scene and accurate recording of what has occurred, which is communicated quickly up the chain, is what will save both lives and property.'

'That's what I said,' said Perkins in my ear. I suppressed a jump, but twitched slightly. It is unusual for people to be able to sneak up on me. 'Came down the side stairs,' said Perkins. 'Captain Prentice,' he said the 'Captain' with heavy emphasis, 'he likes to do the serious stuff. He'll be interviewing everyone next to see if they make the cut. Waste of time. We need everyone we can get. Anyone not up to it will wash out during training.'

I put up my hand. 'Excuse me, how long do we need to train for before we are allowed on the street?'

'Well, Miss . . .?' said Prentice.

'Lieutenant Stapleford. I am trained in emergency first aid.'

'I am sure you are also good at the clerical side too,' said the odious man on the stage, 'but being out there in a war situation always comes as a shock to a young lady, and we like to ensure you are properly prepared.'

'Bloody hell,' I muttered under my breath.

Prentice finished speaking, and everyone was told to get another cup of tea.

'Problem?' asked Perkins.

I sighed. 'I find it difficult being down in the shelter. I'd rather be outside even when there's a raid on.'

'Claustrophobic?'

I frowned. 'Perhaps. I don't like being helpless.'

'You and me both, doll,' said Perkins. 'But the captain,' he said it again with too much emphasis, 'he is right about what it's like coming across a . . . well, a scene.'

'I've been in some hairy situations,' I said. 'I've seen dead bodies before.' I didn't add that I caused more than one of these to be dead.

'I'll see what—' began Perkins and then the air-raid siren went off.

Chapter Nine

'Ruddy hell!' exclaimed Perkins. 'These German buggers can't give us a single night off, can they?'

'I'm afraid,' called Larkin Prentice, 'that this evening's session has been terminated by hostilities. You can shelter in the church's crypt. Perkins will show you the way. I must get to the station point.'

'Right, ladies and gents, this way, if you please,' said Perkins.

'The crypt? Are you serious?' I said.

Perkins gave me a warning glance. Then he opened the door to the short gap between here and the church. The siren wail grew in intensity, but there was no sound of aircraft yet. I saw him look out and check the sky, before pulling the door to, and saying, 'Church door is open. Nice and orderly now, but quick smart. Once inside you'll see the sign to the crypt.' He opened the door and the banshee howls rent the air once more.

If British people know anything it's how to form a queue in a serious situation – like when you're trying to get decent chops from the butcher. It took almost no time at all to get us all across, Perkins coming in last.

Inside, the church was dark and cavernous. A couple of candles stood either side of the stairway down, so the top of the steps were lit. The rest of the church disappeared into inky darkness. I could smell wood polish and candle wax, but these normally reassuring smells did nothing to calm my heart, which was beating extremely fast. Beads of moisture stood out on the top step leading down. I knew without going there that the crypt would smell of damp, the walls would drip, and the effigies of the long dead would be crumbling. Stone faces would no longer have noses, or would be no more than a rough plane. I had no fear of the bones that would have outlasted their coffins beneath the statues. The dead are dead, but the sight of those who have been forgotten, and the cold wetness of the place, frightened me in a way I didn't understand. I was frightened enough to tell Perkins a secret.

'I trained alongside the auxies,' I said. 'Have you heard of them? A British resistance group should we be invaded. I could help.'

It didn't occur to Perkins to question my outrageous claim. 'I don't know,' he said. 'It's going to be bad out there tonight. I can feel it.'

'Then all the more reason to have an extra pair of hands who knows how to help the wounded!'

'Oh blimey,' said Perkins. 'You're already shaking like a leaf.'

'That's about going down there,' I said, pointing into the darkness. 'What's out those doors doesn't frighten me one bit.'

'Then you're mad,' said Perkins. 'Stark staring . . .' The sirens wailed again, and in the distance we heard the booming thud of a bomb landing. It was far away enough that nothing shook, but there was a change in the air. I don't know if I can describe it. It wasn't a pressure wave as such, but a weird kind of feeling that rolled over you, and then came the warm smell of the explosion.

'If Syd hadn't come down with the runs, I wouldn't even consider this,' said Perkins. 'Here, take this,' and he thrust a bag from beside a pew into my hands. 'That's his kit. Stupid blighter, I told him not to eat that green meat, but he would have it.' He was moving swiftly now, and I followed. As soon as we were outside, he led me along the edge of the wall towards the noise.

We could hear the bombs now. They whistled as they fell. Then the impact became more of a long, low boom than a bang. Ahead we could see the skyline lighting up with fires, brilliant orange against the dark sky like some kind of dystopian Van Gogh painting. It was still far enough away we were in no immediate danger. Perkins stopped at the edge of the wall. He tugged my shoulder and put his lips to my ear. 'Out in the open, dangerous,' he said and pointed up. 'Those buggers will shoot anyone.'

In the heavens above, swarming towards us, were the shadows of countless aeroplanes. They were larger than any flying craft I had ever seen before, and their propellers caused the air above us to start to hum and vibrate. Suddenly, the darkness was peppered with flashes, and sharp snapping sounds chased one another at enormous speed. An outpost on the ground was firing. As if this was a signal, other guns began to fire. A huge beam of light broke out across the night. On top of a department store a giant lamp was being turned on the bombers.

They were closer now and I could see the bombs falling. They looked like grey outsized bullets. I saw one go down behind a row of houses. The next moment the world shook apart and a great roar rent the air. I was thrown to the ground like a rag doll. All the wind was knocked out of me, and I lay there for a moment stunned. My ears were buzzing, and dust was everywhere. I couldn't hear. I couldn't see. But I knew. I knew the devil had done his work, and people had died in that moment, between one breath and the next – that bomb had stolen their lives away.

All I could think was how, how could any living man or woman do such a terrible thing? How could they cast down such a bombardment of death. The world must be ending for one person to do that to another.

Perkins grabbed me under the arm and hauled me to my feet. He was off and moving before I understood what was happening, but my body responded and I ran with him. I still couldn't see properly. The dust and grit was all around us, and it was in my eyes. Tears streamed down my face, but even in that state I registered that my eyes were not burning; there was no gas. It felt like no time and it felt like all of time, but we reached the ARP shelter. It was all sandbags, and the air was heavy with the smell of sweat. At every new boom, men crouched holding their tin hats to their heads like that thin metal half-sphere could save them. We were in a hutch of a building that huddled up close to a larger edifice. There were doors into this. I could hear people coming and going. But this area was all too much like a sandcastle. The bags were piled high around us. Not only along the outer sides, but across the middle, dividing the area into two.

The bombing outside was only intensifying. It only occurred to me then that we might wait until the worst of the raid had passed before we went out again. But at that moment a telephone rang. It was such an ordinary sound, and I was still so disorientated my brain conjured up the vain hope that this was my early morning alarm.

I wiped my streaming eyes, and saw Perkins bending over a table that had a map on it. He was gesturing to another man, who was pointing out a section. A boy ran into the room. He couldn't have been more than twelve or thirteen. My hearing wasn't back yet, but I saw several of the men welcome him, as if he was expected. He was covered in grime, and his knee was scraped and bleeding. However, he was grinning from ear to ear. He had a cloth bag slung over his shoulder, and he pulled out a pile of papers and put them on a tray at the end of the table. Someone produced a cup of tea from somewhere – I assume the main house – and a heel of bread. The boy squatted in a corner to consume his feast, which he ate with the relish of a king at a state banquet.

Perkins came over to my side. I managed to make out most of what he said. 'You all right?' I nodded. 'We're heading out to the West. There's been a sighting of a lot of damage out that way. Still up for this?' I nodded again.

The all-clear sounded as we made our way towards the devastation.

Chapter Ten

It was an ordinary little street. Nothing as grand as where I had my flat, but a respectable lower middle-class kind of an area. There were little gardens in front of the terraced houses, all turned over to vegetables now. Not a flower in sight. Leo and his masters would be pleased. All the railings and gates were gone to the war effort. The tape on the windows held the jagged glass in place – mostly. Here and there I could see windows that were completely blown out. Doors hung off their hinges, but I flicked my eyes upwards, the roofs were intact. These houses had basement kitchens, and looking over one wall I saw a coal cellar. Lots of places to shelter, but there was no one on the street yet. Blast damage, but no impact. I thought I saw flames flickering in one window.

The air smelt burnt. Ash and dust had settled over everything, like an evil powdered snow. Enough hung in the atmosphere that both Perkins and I were coughing. My eyes were still tearing and blurring everything.

Perkins carried the stirrup pump. It was eerily quiet at first. Unseen fires crackled. I could now smell wood burning, and there was a terrible, sickly odour of burning meat. 'Oh God,' I muttered under my breath as I realised what this meant. Incendiaries? Small bombs meant to set off fires must have fallen near here.

Perkins caught me sharply by the arm, his fingers pressing into my flesh enough to bruise. 'Watch it, girl!'

I looked down and realised the road in front of me was split wide open. Another step and I would have been in the hole. Perkins crouched, and pulling his torch from his pocket, shone it into the crevasse. The light slid along the side of a sleek metal object. Nearest us were the fins and the cone end was buried in the dirt. What took me aback most was the size. Longer than a tall man, and wide enough I would have struggled to get my arms around it. For an absurd moment I had an image of myself and Perkins trying to grapple this thing out of the ground and ending up staggering, almost waltzing with the bomb.

Perkins gave a long, low whistle. 'It's a big 'un.'

'Why hasn't it gone off?'

'No idea, but we need to get this section cordoned off, and get those bomb chappies down here fast. Can you go back to HQ and file a report? We call it a UXB.'

I looked at him blankly.

'You haven't a clue where you are, have you?' said Perkins. 'This is why . . . lord, never mind that now. I'll leave you the pump, and you can have my ceiling pike. Put the pump over there, and then head down to the cellars on either side, there.' He pointed along the street some distance away from the bomb. 'If there's anyone in there, you can see if you can get them out. No closer to this evil bastard though. Who knows when it will blow.' Somewhere in the distance I heard the roar of a motorbike.

I looked down into the crater and felt a cold chill wash through my entire body. 'It's not ticking,' I said. 'That has to be good.'

'Who says it needs to tick,' said Perkins. 'Don't assume a thing out here.'

'Warden!' called a man. 'Over here, my wife needs help!'

His shout was only the first. Now, almost like animals coming out from hibernation, people started to emerge on to the street, their faces a mixture of ash and milk-bottle white. Perkins took charge. Within a few minutes, he had picked out some of the men and set them to stand warning others until a proper cordon could be formed.

'Warden!' called the man again, more urgently.

'Go see what you can do,' said Perkins. 'I've got to get back and report all this. Remember your training – blast it, use your common sense. Don't put yourself in danger, it only means the rest of us have more people to rescue. If you can't handle it, wait for help.'

And with that he set off at a loping run. I left the pump like he'd said and went over with my ceiling pike, and the small first-aid bag I had. Although he was covered with grime, I could see the man was barely into his twenties. He stood shaking at the top of the cellar steps. 'She's in there,' he said, pointing. 'I can't get her to move. It's all my fault. I didn't think they'd be back again tonight. I wanted to get the kitchen set up for her. She wouldn't go to the shelter without me. What if she's dead?' His voice rose hysterically.

'What's her name?'

'Doris. Doris Mayhue. We only got married last month. I've got my call-up papers. I'm off tomorrow.' He followed me down the stairs, his mouth running on and on. He told me how he'd met her and was embarking on a description of her wedding dress by the time we'd reached the bottom of the steps. I let his words flow over me. 'Stay here,' I said. They'd chosen to hide in the empty coal shed rather than the basement flat. I could only imagine they'd thought it would be safer under the road.

'What? No! I'm coming in to help.'

'No, you're not,' I said. 'I don't need an extra casualty. Stay here!' I channelled both my grandmother and Fitzroy into the order, and it seemed to work, at least for now. I shone my torch into the darkness. I could see all the plaster from the ceiling had come down. I prodded it with my pike and another shower fell.

'Here! You'll bring the ruddy thing down on top of her!'

'Shut up, Mr Mayhue,' I said in a cold voice. 'If you want your wife rescued stay out of my way.' I could see that a section of the ceiling had come down. Not entirely, I couldn't see the sky through it, but some of the old bricks had been shaken loose when the bomb landed in the street. The thought of what it would have done if it had actually exploded sickened me. I edged a little further in. It stayed dark and cold. Good, no fires then.

The floor was uneven under my feet. I was fairly sure Perkins would have told me to wait for help. It was more than possible Doris was already dead. Then I heard a faint moan, low like an animal in distress. I went further in, kicking a piece of coal out of my way, and my torch picked out a woman half-lying, half-sitting on the ground. She was leaning against the far wall.

There had only been a small amount of coal in the shed, but it had all come down on Doris's legs.

'Come in, Mr Mayhue,' I called. 'But be careful!' I shone my torch for him to make his way across. 'Right,' I said, 'first we need to move this coal. It'll go quicker with two, so you can help, but you mustn't try and move her.'

Doris, whose hair was escaping in long curls from her head scarf, turned her head from one side to the other and moaned again. 'Hello, Doris,' I said, as I began moving the coals to one side, one by one. 'We're going to get you out. You're going to be fine.'

'Should I get the shovel?'

'We need to be more careful than that,' was the politest reply I could manage. The man was an idiot.

It took us maybe ten minutes, perhaps longer, to move the heap. It felt like for ever. I could hear other cries now, and people weeping. I was horribly aware of being the only person on-site to help, but I couldn't rush it. Once she was clear I checked her legs, and miraculously there were no breaks. I used one of my very few bandages to bind her bloodied head. She turned her gaze on me, but there was no focus.

'Right, we need to get her out. Go grab a man from above to help you carry her up. She's moving her head, so hopefully her spine is intact. She can't stay here anyway. Get her up top. Ambulances are on the way. You need to get her out of the cordoned area. I'll stay with her while you get someone.'

I had to repeat it all again, before he understood. Although to give him credit he returned quickly with a neighbour, and I left them to get Doris to the surface. There was nothing more for me to do there.

Up top, three people ran up to me at once, demanding my attention. Two young women, from different houses, had injured housemates, and one elderly woman stood behind them wringing her hands. It was her I went with first.

It turned out her husband and their grandson, an infant of no more than two, were trapped in their basement by a fallen ceiling. Their house was right next to the bomb. Of course it was. The two-year-old was terrified of the dark, so they hadn't taken him to the shelter. His mother was working overnight at the ammunition factory and his father was already on duty overseas. All this she told me, while crying. As the ceiling had come down her husband had thrown himself across the boy to protect him. She could hear the boy crying but couldn't reach him.

This family were lucky. The man, who had been only knocked unconscious, and the boy, had ended up in what rescuers often call 'the triangle of survival'. The ceiling and one beam had come down but caught on top of the kitchen table. The boy was trapped by his grandfather, and once I'd crawled in and brought him round, we were able to get both out.

This time when we emerged there were others on the scene. The national guard were out with stretchers, and they took all three of them away. I insisted the woman also lay down. Her face had become mottled and I was worried for her.

'Good job, love,' said the stretcher-bearer, a middle-aged man with a very fashionable moustache. 'Ambulances are standing by. How many more?'

'I don't know yet.'

'We've not got long to get them clear,' said the man meaningfully.

I followed the girls who had come to me one then the other. In the first case, there was nothing I could do. The young woman was clearly dead. I passed her friend on to a neighbour and told them to get her some tea. With the second woman, I thought we were going to be all right. Her friend, whose lower half was trapped under fallen debris, talked to me cheerfully as I used my pike to lever a beam away. I was beginning to shift it, when she suddenly stopped mid-sentence. I looked down, and saw – I've seen death before and the best way I can describe it is an absence – she was gone. Her friend pleaded with me to get her body out until I had to forcibly remove her from the building.

At this point Perkins found me. He was covered in grime, his left sleeve was in tatters, and there was blood on his chest. 'Not mine,' he said at once. 'Getting a bloke out from under a load of stuff. His chest was all caved in. Doubt he'll live. Anyway, the troops are here now.'

'Troops?'

'Ambulance, fire brigade – all the professionals. We can go back to bandaging and splinting, and whatnot. People with better equipment than us can go into the buildings. Besides, we're drawing back shortly. They need to deal with the bomb.'

'But if there're still people trapped?'

'Hope, love, we do what we can. We can't save everyone. Besides, if they're not shouting for help, at least they won't know anything about it. They'll come back and clear the area in daylight. Just in case anyone else has made it through.'

I nodded. I felt bile rise in my throat, but I understood.

'Where's my pump?' asked Perkins.

'I'll get it and meet you behind the cordon,' I said.

Perkins nodded. 'Make it quick, love. Equipment isn't in short enough supply yet that it's worth your life.'

Chapter Eleven

The stirrup pump wasn't where I had left it. I stood looking around, turning on the spot. People were running everywhere, but there was an order now, of a sort, and I could see a clear progression away from the bomb. I saw another child with a cloth bag run by, a determined look on his face. Through his torn shirt I could see that he had a long scrape on his arm, but he wasn't trailing blood, so I stepped aside to let him pass.

I couldn't see the pump anywhere but on the edge of my hearing I heard another low moan. I retraced my steps. It came from a house whose windows were all blown out, and one that was well within the detonation range of the UXB. The door was off its hinges and lying flat on the ground. I went cautiously, but quickly, down the steps. The coal cellar was empty, and I couldn't see anyone through the window of the basement. I was about to give up when I heard the sound again. It came from within the house. I was fairly certain that Perkins would tell me to get out of there. Another moan.

I couldn't. I couldn't leave someone I knew was alive. The hallway was a mess of rubble and ash. The noise came again. At least it seemed to be on this floor. I called out, but no one replied. The ceiling above me was creaking in an ominous way. I quickened my pace. Near the back a door stood firmly closed. This was odd. The others had all come down. I didn't think before I opened it. Flames burst out at me. I threw myself backwards and landed on my back. My face felt too hot. The fire couldn't have been going long, and I could just see through the flames a number of people sitting around a table. They weren't moving. The initial burst of fire had fallen back. I could reach the nearest one, I was certain. They must be overcome by the smoke.

Keeping my head bent low, I ran in. It was infernally hot, but I could see the fire ran largely around the edge of the room. I coughed and felt the heat burn my throat. I grabbed the shoulder of the nearest person. Instead of responding to my shake, they fell off the chair and on to the floor. It was then that I saw the blood down the front of their chest. It was a man. An average-looking man in civilian clothes of around thirty. A perfectly ordinary man, except his throat had been slit from ear to ear.

I stood stupefied. Then the moan came again. Except this time I heard it for what it was, a mew. I hunkered down to the ground, ready to crawl my way out, the flames were rising around me far more quickly than I had expected, and came face to face with a kitten. I scooped it up in one hand, although it made things more awkward, and made my way out of the house. I fairly flew up the steps. I expected the animal to jump from my arms, but it sank its claws into me and held on tight.

Beyond the cordon I found Perkins, to whom I apologised for the loss of his pump.

'Glad you're out, girl. People's been saying how some girl did a bloody good job before the rest of us turned up. Sounds like a right foolish lass to me.' He smiled. 'We'll have to get you properly trained.' He noticed the kitten and reached out to stroke it. 'Who is this then?'

'Ashes,' I said. 'I think he's mine now.'

'Well, you and Ashes better get further back. If the lads get this wrong it'll be the biggest boom either of you will have ever heard, and probably the last.'

I found Leo at the flat. We'd been lucky again and, apart from a broken window, it was fine. Leo was in the kitchen cooking his breakfast. He looked smart and well rested. 'I take it you had no trouble sleeping?' I said.

Leo moved the pan on to the heat. The oil hissed and immediately the smell of bacon filled the air. My stomach turned over and the little cat leapt out of my arms. I put the back of my hand up to my mouth and fought down the nausea. Leo jumped. 'What the hell was that?' he asked.

'A cat,' I said. 'He attached himself to me.'

Leo took his pan off the stove, and looked at me properly. 'God, you're a sight,' he said. 'Are you hurt? What happened?'

'I went to the training hall, but I ended up out in the field helping the ARP wardens.'

'Why doesn't that surprise me? I still expect you to be at your post on time.'

I looked at him in horror. 'But I've had no sleep.'

'That was your choice. I told you not to go. You're needed elsewhere.'

'Typing incomprehensible notes and creating your silly scripts?' Tiredness was catching up with me.

'If we were on duty I would take grave exception to that, Lieutenant.'

'Sorry, Major,' I said, sounding not in the least bit sorry. When your stepfather is a colonel who thinks rank is of far less importance than ability, you tend to regard those who rely on it as weak. Leo's face grew dark. He opened his mouth to speak, but before he could a crash made us both jump. While we were arguing the cat had seen his opportunity and stolen the bacon from the pan, and in so doing knocked it on to the floor. He stopped halfway across the kitchen floor, the rasher in his mouth, and his back half arched with tail curled under.

'That bloody animal has my bacon!'

Leo's voice was loud enough to frighten Ashes, who raced out of the kitchen as if he was rocket-propelled. I failed to stifle a giggle. Leo thrust his finger into my face. 'If that animal is here when I come back . . .'

I stopped laughing and raised an eyebrow. It was my flat. Leo must have realised this because he uttered an exclamation of disgust, snatched up his coat and slammed out the front door.

*

Two hours later I arrived at my desk. I managed to coax Ashes out from behind a wardrobe with a small amount of milk, and I'd even found time to have a bath. The hot water and the feeling of being clean once more, along with a strong cup of coffee, had got me to the office, but as I sat down at my desk, the adrenaline had long worn off. I felt like I had been slammed in the head with a cricket bat. I was so tired I could barely see straight. The files on the side of my desk were already six high. I took the top one, opened it, and the words literally swam before my eyes. This was no use. I managed to stay at my station until Masterton had seen me there. Then I explored the corridor outside and found a nice little cleaning cupboard. I curled up beside the mop and bucket and was asleep within moments.

It was the clatter of shoes on the marble floor that woke me. I glanced at my watch and realised I had slept through the entire morning. I stood up, straightening my uniform as best I could, and went straight down to the canteen. There would probably be hell to pay tomorrow, but with any luck the building would be bombed overnight and I wouldn't have to worry.

As I stood in the queue I assessed the offerings as slop one, slop two and slop three. The main differences were slight variations in the shade of brown and texture. I went for the darkest, thickest slop and was told I had picked lamb hotpot. I sat down at the long table where I had met the film crew, and it wasn't long before they came up from the depths to dine. There was no sign of Leo, which made me all the more certain there was some kind of officers' canteen somewhere that was being hidden from me.

'What did you get?' asked a well-spoken male voice.

I looked up to see Daniel had slid into the seat opposite me. 'Lamb hotpot,' I said, 'but this,' I lifted my fork and let some of the stuff drop off it, 'tastes more of leather than lamb.'

'I've got Welsh rarebit,' said Daniel, proudly displaying his plate. 'You can't beat a toasted cheese sandwich.'

'How?'

He tapped the side of his nose. 'If you'd been in the Saturday morning matinees then you'd get special treatment too.'

'You're that famous?'

Daniel winced. 'Beryl remembers me. I was her first crush.'

I smiled. 'Stranger things happen at sea or so I am told.' I stifled a yawn. 'Sorry. So tired.'

Daniel pointed at my face. 'What?' I said. He reached out gently, and stroked a finger lightly down my face. I flinched, but was quite proud of myself for quelling my instinct to punch him in the face, which was my initial reaction. Sometimes Fitzroy's influence really showed through. 'Pillow creases,' he said.

'Ah,' I said. 'Cleaning cupboard.'

He grinned, and I saw that when he had been a young actor he must have been very charming. 'Our secret,' he said. 'Why so tired? In love? Always a good time to fall in love, during a war.'

I shook my head. 'I went out with the ARP, and ended up helping some people out of bombed-out buildings.'

'I didn't think the ARP did that,' he said, frowning.

'We were waiting on the other services to get there.' I might have told him more, but the frown on his face stopped me.

'Getting yourself into trouble only adds to the work the rescue crews have to do. From when I first met you in that typing pool I could see you were spoiling for action, Hope, but really, being in the trenches is . . . is ghastly.'

'You were in the last war?'

'The Great War to end all wars. Yes, I was. And no, I don't want to talk about it.'

'Of course,' I said, and switched the topic to the new film. This time they were making one on Anderson shelters.

We walked down to the film set together, discussing whether it was possible to get shots from inside the shelter, and if we used a cutaway would it seem too unreal. We were about to go through the final set of doors, when I glimpsed Harvey off to my right.

My neck ricked, I turned my head so sharply, but he was already gone. I gave myself a mental shake. Dashwood didn't seem to have noticed, he was talking about how he had fewer lines than the woman playing the mother part, and how as patriarch he should have more. I locked the puzzle away in the back of my mind, and reassured him I would talk to the director.

If I thought Dashwood's scolding was harsh it was nothing to the reception Larkin Prentice, the local ARP coordinator, gave me.

Back at the church hall, in full view of the other candidates, he questioned me closely about what exactly I had done. I told him almost everything. When he was finished he turned to the group. 'Can anyone tell me what this young woman did wrong?'

The Rosies exchanged a few glances, their mouths set in grim lines, but they said nothing. I thought I caught the flicker of a wink from one of them. One of the old soldiers started on a rant about how I might have caused extra trouble for the rescue services by getting myself into trouble. 'Important thing in military life,' he said, huffing into his moustache, 'knowing one's place and obeying orders. In times of war, one needs the efficiency of doing exactly what one is told, and not getting out of place.'

A middle-aged woman piped up. 'She could hardly have ignored that young man's request for help, could she?'

'Yes, madam, she could,' said the moustache. 'She could have made him a nice cup of tea, and told him that the proper help was on the way.'

'Tea wagon hadn't arrived by then,' said one of the Rosies.

The moustache shot her an evil look.

Prentice raised his hand. 'The important point is not to endanger yourself unless you have no other option. Clearly if someone is on fire then you use the stirrup pump and not ask them politely to wait for the fire brigade. But your help must be proportionate to your role and to your abilities. Overconfidence is the sure way to disaster. I hope you can understand that, Miss Stapleford?'

'Lieutenant,' I said.

'What?'

'I'm a lieutenant in His Majesty's Army.' This occasioned muttering from the moustache and his friend.

We then broke for tea. One of the Rosies, the one who had

winked at me, came over. 'I'm Lulu, and this is Sam and this is Daisy.' Lulu was the most feminine, short and with a large bust. Sam had a wiry frame, and I wouldn't have minded her having my back in a fight. Daisy had an Amazonian-like figure, but a masculine jaw, and her eyes seemed a little duller than the other two, whose eyes sparkled with intelligence.

'Don't worry about them, pet,' said Sam, indicating the old soldiers. 'Their war was in a different time. It's all hands on deck now. Help wherever you can.'

'But we have to follow rules,' said Daisy, 'or people get hurt.'

Sam gave Daisy a pat on the arm and passed her a biscuit. 'She's a bit slow,' she whispered to me. 'Bit of an accident at birth, but heart of gold and strong as an ox. You just have to be careful how you explain things.'

'What's your story?' asked Lulu.

'I'm doing clerical stuff, mainly. Although I get to help with the information films sometimes.'

'Ooh!' squealed Lulu. 'Do you get to be in them? I'd love to be in the movies.'

'I edit scripts,' I said. 'I'm not an actress.'

'Do you think—?'

Before she could ask me for an introduction we were called back for a first-aid demonstration. Perkins was role-playing being an unconscious person with a head injury and we all had to show what we would do. It was going pretty well until Daisy's turn when she gave him a huge smacker of a kiss. Perkins shot up so fast he caught her on the nose. Blood went everywhere. By the time it had all been sorted out, and we learned that Daisy had misunderstood the concept of the kiss of life, the evening's training was over.

'Right,' said Prentice. 'Good effort, everyone. Please take care going home, and be aware of your nearest shelter. Germany hasn't graced us with her presence yet, but we can be pretty sure she's on her way. It's a bomber's moon.'

Chapter Twelve

I caught Perkins on the way out to ask him if I could accompany him tonight. 'You've got to be joking,' he said. 'Prentice will have my guts for garters. I should never have taken you out in the first place. Stick with the training, Hope. You're a brave girl. Too brave.' He patted my shoulder. 'Now, I have to scarper and get some dinner down me before the balloon goes up. See you tomorrow. Get yourself home safe.'

I walked slowly back to the flat only to find Leo sitting amid a pile of papers. The moment I came through the door he started to shuffle them up and, standing, reached for his briefcase to stuff them into.

'If they're that secret should you have brought them back?' I asked.

'They're not that kind of secret,' said Leo with his back to me. He finished stuffing them into his bag. 'They're secret to me.'

'What are you doing? Writing a novel?'

The back of Leo's neck went bright red.

'Leo! Really? Let me see?' I came forward and reached for the briefcase but Leo whipped it out of my reach.

'Stand down, Lieutenant!'

'I'm not on duty,' I said. I jumped up to try and reach it, but he was too tall.

'Stop it, Hope. It's just the beginning of an idea. I'm not showing anyone yet.'

I recognised the seriousness in his tone. 'So when did this ambition to become a novelist strike you?'

'I don't know that it has,' said Leo, fastening the lock on his briefcase. 'It's helping me make sense of what's happening, that's all. It's an outlet for my thoughts.'

'You have to be careful with that,' I said. 'You can't write about most of the things we are involved with.'

'I know that,' Leo almost shouted. 'It's not that kind of a book. It's about life and death, and how to create the meaning that goes in between. How to deal with love and loss, and get up and out every morning not knowing if this will be your last day on earth.' He ran his hand through his hair. 'Dammit, Hope. Why couldn't you leave well alone?'

'I'm sorry,' I faltered. I'd never seen Leo so upset. 'I didn't think . . .'

'No, you never do,' said Leo. He flung out of the room, only to return a few minutes later without the briefcase. 'I'll know if you open it,' he said. 'And I will never forgive you.' Then he left, slamming the front door behind him.

I sat down on the sofa. I found I was shivering. Leo could be grumpy, even angry, but I'd never seen him start to come apart at the seams like this. I told myself it was only to be expected that being at war would be mentally trying for everyone. My mother had told me even Fitzroy had had days of despair when they were working together. I was pretty sure I knew what Fitzroy had done to get himself out of the doldrums. He was, after all, a hedonist at heart, but there was a big difference, I realised, between Leo and my stepfather. Fitzroy didn't have a death wish, but he was not afraid of dying. My mother always said what he dreads most is dying of old age in his own bed. But that wasn't what I saw in Leo. I could see he was afraid. I was afraid sometimes. Probably not as often as I should be nor always of the right things. But somewhere along the way I had picked up my mother and Fitzroy's attitude of getting on with life. I could be scared out of my wits and still make jokes. I would act calm until I felt calm. I hadn't realised that this was a skill that not everyone had. I could still be overly emotional about things – Cole, Fitzroy, my mother and Fitzroy, Bernie's death – but I wasn't frightened. I had been trained all my life not to give in to fright, because fright affects your reasoning. Fear undermines all your skill and training. It leads to bad decisions. Impulsive, thoughtless decisions that can cost lives – yours and others'.

I had no idea what to do about Leo, so I made myself a fried-egg sandwich. The bread was going stale, so I toasted it, and slathered it in butter from White Orchards, and added far too much salt. It was delicious. I could feel my waistband stretching. Food makes me think, so I ate a couple of buns I'd been saving for good measure too. Which was just as well as I was sure they were on the verge of going stale. I even eked out a little of the jam Fitzroy's housekeeper had given me when we left.

Leo, I decided, needed a twenty-four-hour pass to vent the pressure he was clearly feeling. Normally, I would have asked Fitzroy to arrange this. As I generally didn't ask him for favours, he knew when I did that it was important and could be counted on to come up with something, no matter how impossible it often seemed.

But this time I didn't have a fairy godfather. I had a sudden mental image of Fitzroy in a ball gown and wings that made me laugh out loud. Although I knew if Fitzroy had ever, for some reason, to wear a damask gown and high heels he would carry it off with that unbounded arrogance of his and make every woman in the room look dowdy in comparison. I recalled him telling me once, when I was young, and my mother wasn't around, that some gentlemen enjoyed wearing women's clothes. I had been shocked, but he had merely shrugged and said, 'Where's the harm?' I'd asked him if he did, and he'd said no, he preferred more freedom of movement, and the ability to get out of his clothes quickly.

I smiled as I thought about this, and many other outrageous conversations we'd had. He'd always been of the mind that I could ask him anything, tell him anything, and really some of the things we talked about would have turned my mother's blood cold. It would definitely have killed my grandmother if she'd heard; a sort of dignity rupture of the soul.

It struck me then, as I was stirring some cocoa on the stove, how very hurt I still felt at their sudden departure after my father's funeral, and their lightning-fast wedding, to which I had not been invited.

An unearthly wailing interrupted my thoughts. Prentice had been right. The Germans were back. It was an air raid.

There was no one to make me go to the shelter this time. I moved away from the window. I decided to be sensible, but when I reached the ground floor I found myself heading for the entrance. As I opened the front door the noise grew to an almost painful intensity. The other half of the street lay in ruins but the piles of possessions had been removed. Despite this being a quiet street there were a number of people hurrying by. None of them paid me any attention. Their focus was entirely on getting to somewhere safe. I hesitated in the doorway. A young couple passed me. They couldn't have been more than sixteen and the girl was crying. My impulse was to invite them inside to the shelter, but I wasn't sure if Leo was in there, nor how they would react to my not following them in. It was in this moment that I realised I had no intention of ever going back there.

However, I wasn't completely devoid of reason, and I had no intention of standing in the middle of the street. Across from me I could see the stars shining through one of the roofless houses. It occurred to me that anyone, even a German bomber eager to drop his payload and return home, would not consider it worthwhile to bomb again something they had previously so well destroyed. I ran across the road, dodging a man who was pedalling furiously on his bicycle, and so beetroot red in the face I thought it more likely an apoplexy was liable to kill him before a bomb.

I had never been invited into any of the flats opposite, so it was with some curiosity that I edged past a door that was hanging squint. I didn't have a ceiling pike, but to my great luck someone had left a broom in the hall. It didn't look much like a broom any more. The bristles were burnt, but the charred handle seemed sturdy enough. I picked it up and darted back to the entrance. Then I poked the ceiling, half-heartedly. It seemed solid enough. I went through a fairly intact, but dusty, reception room. The only furniture left were larger pieces, a tall bookcase made of oak, and an enormous settle. I found a broken cup on the floor when I stepped on it. Next time I came out I needed to make myself up a kit, with a torch and a better stick. I moved through into what had been the dining room. I knew this because despite the fading light I could make out the stout mahogany legs of a Victorian table. I ran a finger along the dust on the top. It was so smooth I wondered if it was ebony.

I noticed the absence of the siren before I heard the planes. I sat down on the floor, but not under the table. I reckoned it must weigh more than I did. I had no desire for the coming commotion outside to bring it down on my head. Instead I leaned up against one of the legs and looked upwards through three storeys to the night sky.

I heard the drone of the incoming planes long before I saw them. I thought I knew what to expect. The bombers were like giant sharks swimming through the darkness, until they passed by the sliver of a moon that peeked between the clouds. Only then was their immensity and number truly realised. Even if someone had drawn a gun on me I wouldn't have been able to move. Instead I stared up at the squadron passing overhead as a rabbit stares motionlessly into a hunter's lamp. The night was cold, but the iciness I felt started inside my chest, and spread outwards through my bones. So many people were going to die tonight, and there was nothing anyone could do to prevent it. Oh, we could fight the enemy, and we would in many ways and in many arenas, but if you were under one of those bombs when it fell, then you were dead no matter who or what you were – king or commoner, trained espionage agent or milkman. Although no one could know until it was far too late, the moment those bombs had been loaded on those German planes, the lives of many British souls were forfeit.

The bombardment started and the noise was so loud, and so close, I thought my head would split open. I pressed my hands to my ears and folded myself over my knees. How long would it last? I felt the ground shake and shiver beneath me. It seemed the Germans weren't yet done with Kensington. I wondered if Leo was safe in a shelter somewhere. Then the noise grew so loud I could no longer think. I closed my eyes, but flashes of light burst through into my vision. I felt tears streaming down my face, but I hadn't realised I was crying. I gave up sitting against the table, and curled up into a ball. It gave an odd little bit of comfort.

It went on and on and on.

Chapter Thirteen

When it did stop, and I was still alive, it took me some time to realise both. The house around me was still standing as much as it had before, although I was now covered in enough dust that I was suitably camouflaged against the floor. I only realised this when someone bolted through the reception room and came to a stop by sliding under the table.

I shook myself and sat up. Under the table was a boy of around twelve years old, dressed in a saggy grey jumper and shorts. His face had soot and grime liberally smeared across it. He lay there, panting and cradling his left arm. There was a messenger bag over his shoulder. As I moved, he let out a loud yell. 'Bleeding hell! It's a ruddy ghost.'

'No,' I said, trying to keep my voice low, despite the ringing in my ears, 'I'm just a bit dusty.'

The boy sat up still cradling his arm. I moved closer and by the weak moonlight I could see it hung oddly, and the sleeve was bloody. However, he wasn't dripping blood, and he seemed quite conscious.

'Are you hurt?'

'Took a tumble going down some steps, didn't I? Fell on my shoulder. Think I fell on my head as well. But it's my bloody shoulder that hurts. Think I've bust my arm. Bloody Germans. Blew up the building behind me, they did. Sent me on a night flight. I fairly flew down those bloody steps. Just as well now though. There's no steps left. Just a ruddy great hole. Everything happens for a reason, or so my gran says.'

'You don't sound like you've got concussion to me,' I said. 'Let me have a look at your arm.'

'You a nurse?'

I shook my head and paused to swallow. The movement had disturbed my stomach, and my head was swimming. 'No, but I've been learning first aid with the ARP wardens.'

The boy squinted up his eyes at me. 'So where's your armband?' he said, and his voice was as full of suspicion as a child's can be.

'I'm going to get overalls when I've finished,' I said. 'I don't think your arm is broken. I think you've dislocated your shoulder.'

The boy inched away from me until he hit the far leg of the table. 'What does that mean? Will I lose my arm?'

I found myself smiling. It was a pleasant surprise. 'No, it means a bone has come out of a socket—'

'Now I know you're lying,' interrupted the boy. 'I ain't no mechanical person.'

'I didn't think you were,' I said in as gentle a voice as I could. 'It's just the term for where the shoulder and arm connect. It's called a ball and socket joint.' I mimed with my hands, although I was unsure he could see in the dark. 'It works like this.'

'Next you'll be asking me to take my bag off!'

The penny dropped. 'Oh, you think I'm a German spy. Hang on a minute.' I dug around in my pocket and produced my ID card. I handed it over to the boy. In his turn he, somewhat awkwardly, got a torch out of his pocket and shone it on both the card and my face. Eventually, he handed it back. 'Well, you might not be a German spy, but you still ain't getting my bag.'

'Fair enough,' I said. 'What's your name? Mine's Hope.'

'Like in the rhyme? Faith, Hope and Charity?'

I nodded, silently thanking fate that my mother had, out of three, chosen Hope. I've never liked it that much, but the other two were much worse.

'I'm Petey,' he said. 'You're only getting my first name.'

'Fine,' I said. 'You run messages for the ARP, don't you? I was down in the local post – or would you call it a bunker? – last night, and saw someone like you come running in. I didn't get a chance to ask because I went off with Warden Perkins to see how we could help.'

'You know Perkins?'

'Man with a face like a walnut,' I said, 'but jolly nice chap.'

'That's him,' said Petey. 'I suppose you're not likely to be a spy.'

'It's always best to be cautious,' I said. 'You're right not to trust strangers.' I took a deep breath. 'I should tell you, I'm out here because I can't take being shut up underground. I'd rather be blown to bits than buried alive.'

'You sound like me uncle Dickie. He used to be a miner. He can't bear it either. He was in a cave-in. Never been quite right since. They wouldn't let him sign up, so he was helping with stretchers and stuff at St Thomas' until it got bombed in. He's at Great Ormond Street now. But you couldn't have been a miner. What happened to you?'

'Nothing. I think some people might just be made this way.'

'You mean odd like?'

I laughed. 'I like you, Petey, you make me laugh, and not much else does at the moment.'

'That's what the wardens say,' said Petey giving a big grin. His teeth were luminous in the moonlight against his dirty face. 'They tell me to shut it, but I think they like me chatting really. Perkins said I always cheer him up.' He shifted a bit. The pain was clearly worse now he had moved back.

'Cradle your arm like this,' I said, showing him. 'It will hurt a bit less.'

'Like this? Yeah, that's not so smarting.'

'When the all-clear sounds,' I said, 'I'll find you a warden with an armband or official overalls to help.'

'I don't know why it's not sounded yet,' said Petey. 'I can't hear nothing else.'

'Neither can I. Maybe they're being cautious.'

Petey shook his head, and immediately winced. 'Nah, they want to get people out as soon as they can. Although the fire brigade go out during the bombing. My chum Davey saw them in the East End docks, climbing buildings and kicking off incendiaries as they fell.' Even in the starlight I could see his eyes shining. 'Ever so brave, that lot.'

'Is that what you want to do when you're older?'

'Yeah, I think so. Of course, I'll sign up if the war's still on when I'm fifteen.'

'Eighteen,' I corrected.

'One of my mates just signed up at sixteen, and I'm taller than him. If you tell them you're eighteen and look 'em in the eye when you say it, you're in. I'm not waiting five years. It might all be over by then.'

'I hope it is,' I said.

'Ha! Hope hoping!'

I smiled as if I hadn't heard the joke a thousand times before. I could see despite his chattiness, the pain was beginning to tire Petey. I ran my eyes quickly over him. As far as I could see he wasn't bleeding, but if he'd fallen down a long flight of steps, like he said, then he could have internal bleeding. The best I could do for now was to keep him conscious. 'So what's it like running the messages?' I asked.

'It's all right. Except for those bleeding steps. You get into the way of it. Ducking into buildings if you hear a plane coming. I think the people in charge thought they wouldn't gun down a child. But they have, and they will. We're carrying vital information and that's more important than how old we are.'

He sounded proud, so I held back my expression of horror. 'What's it like, when the bombing's on?'

Petey leaned back on to the floor. 'It's odd. Funny. Like a nightmare, sometimes. You see the oddest things. Davey once came across a pair of boots in the middle of a street, still had the feet in them, but no sign of the rest of him. His mum boxed his ears for not bringing good boots home, but I don't think I could have emptied out feet.'

'No, I couldn't have either.'

'But mostly it's things you see. All the stuff in the wrong places. A bed blown out of a window and landed in the front of a grocer's upside down. Or once I found a clock embedded in the side of a bus. Like it belonged there. Didn't half give me a fright. I thought it was some kind of bomb at first. It were still ticking.'

He closed his eyes, and slid further down on to the floor.

'Hey, Petey, what's the oddest thing you've seen?' I said, shaking him by his good arm.

'Couldn't tell you,' he muttered. 'You're a lady.'

'I've seen some odd stuff. I once found a group of people dead around a dinner table.'

'Any food on the table?'

'I didn't look,' I said. 'I don't think I would have fancied it.'

Petey laughed softly. 'Might have had a bit of eyeball in it. They pop out do eyeballs. Like shelled peas.'

He went quiet.

'Come on,' I said. 'Tell me.'

'Oh, all right,' he said, but his voice had taken a sleepy, singsong tone. 'I once spent – I don't know how long – digging out a hand during a raid.'

'A hand?'

'Yeah, I thought it still had a person attached,' he giggled, 'but turned out the person and the hand had got separated in the blast. Poor sod died of blood loss while I was digging like six feet away from where he was under some bricks. Firemen found him later. I saved the wrong bit.' He giggled again. 'Not that it's funny. The whole blimming world's all upside down, and I'm digging up some poor chump's hand. Don't do that any more. No matter what I see I keep going. That's what Warden Perkins told me.'

'He was right,' I said. 'It's too dangerous for you to stay in one place during a raid. Why did you volunteer to do this in the first place? Did you think it would be an adventure?'

'Nah, miss. My mum volunteered me. She gets a few bob for me doing it. We need the money. I even saw a gravedigger working once.'

The all-clear sounded. I sprang up. 'Right, I'm going to get help,' I said. 'You stay here and try to stay awake. I'll be back as soon as I can. And hold on to this for me, will you?' I slipped what silver change I had in my pockets into his good hand.

'Nah, miss, I can't take this . . .'

But I was already away and heading into the street looking for someone to help me get Petey out and into the hospital where he so clearly needed to be.

Chapter Fourteen

There was a man sitting in my kitchen feeding my cat. Ashes nibbled delicately at a piece of fish from one of the fine porcelain saucers Fitzroy had given me. I flicked on the light switch illuminating the man's profile. Cole didn't bat an eyelid at the change in environment. He said, 'You should carry a gun. You never know who you will find in your home.'

'No, you don't,' I said tartly, closing the front door behind me with more than necessary force. 'Is Leo here? Or have you tied him up somewhere? And I usually do carry a gun. It's been a difficult night.'

Cole did turn to face me at that, lifting one thin dark eyebrow. Now that I finally saw him clearly, I could tell he had aged even in the short time since we had been in the Highlands together – or rather not together. His close-cropped dark hair had more grey in it – although I supposed some could be dust from the bombings. He wore his long motorbike coat, and his goggles and gloves were on the table. His face showed more lines than I remembered, and for once I saw more than his usual coldness. He looked haunted.

'I take it you took yourself to a shelter and left the cat behind?' He stroked the cat's neck with his long, thin fingers. 'If you take responsibility for a living creature you should protect it.'

A variety of quips came to mind, but I knew I was irritable and snappy, and that Cole, who had showed me some . . . not kindness but consideration and tolerance in the past, was a man who enjoyed killing. So instead, I said, 'Were you looking for me in particular?'

'Well, I certainly didn't want to talk to your puppy-eyed boyfriend. I much prefer cats.' He stroked Ashes again. 'Perfect predators cats. Regardless of size.'

I walked over to the table and sat down. 'I took your advice.' Cole waited. I gave in. 'I stayed above ground during the bombing. It was – an experience.'

'You should have made the cat safe,' said Cole scowling.

I blinked. 'This isn't the single-minded cold-eyed killer Cole I am used to,' I said.

'I like cats.'

'Noted. Next time I'll put the cat in the shelter.'

'You don't need to go that far,' said Cole. 'He can find his own sanctuary. Cats are very capable. Just don't lock him into an upstairs flat during a raid.'

'I won't,' I said. 'What do you want?'

'Your parents will be returning early from Egypt, and I thought it likely you might discuss me with them. Especially now you know the man you killed was not one of our agents.'

'So you did mean me to think that—'

Cole waved aside my comment. 'It doesn't matter. They were bound to find out that you and I had been in contact at some point. I thought before you see Fitzroy I might tell you my side of the story.'

'You're both accomplished liars,' I said.

'Thank you,' said Cole. 'There should still be tea in the pot if you want some. I'd put sugar in it if you've got some.'

I did rather want tea, so I got a cup and poured myself some. Cole, it transpired, made tea as well as he handled a gun. In other words it was one of the best cups of tea I had had in a while.

'Carry my own,' he said. 'The stuff you have is more wood shavings than anything.'

I didn't rise to the remark. 'So what do you have to tell me that is so much more shocking than the allegation that Fitzroy is my father or that I will need sugar in my tea?'

Cole sat back in his chair and stretched out his long legs. 'It's funny,' he said, 'I never thought I would like you. With you looking so much like your mother, I thought . . . But you aren't like her. You don't have her fire. Much more of a slow burner. I'd like to see what it took to make you burst into flames.'

'If you're trying to make me feel uncomfortable, you are succeeding. Wait! What did you say? Why are my parents coming back?'

'Finally sunk in, has it? Well, Fitzroy hates the place and doesn't get on with the local man. That wouldn't be enough, but I hear your mother is unwell.'

'My mother? Is it serious?'

Cole shook his head. 'Not as far as my intelligence goes, but your father, now he's allowed to show it, is doting on her like some infatuated youth.' He gave a crack of laughter. 'She must hate that!'

I gritted my teeth, and kept my voice calm. 'So what do you want to tell me?'

'Right,' said Cole. He put his hands together and stretched out his arms, loudly cracking his knuckles. 'It's like this. I have something of a bone with Fitzroy.'

'I would never have known,' I said.

'Don't, Hope. Cheap hits don't suit you.'

I felt myself blushing, and tried to cover my face with the cup.

'Fitzroy and I knew each other when we were very young.'

'I knew you had worked together.'

'No, this goes back to when Fitzroy dropped out of university. He wasn't even officially a spy. My father asked him to do a couple of things as a favour to his father. As you may know, your father hated his father, and the feeling was mutual. My own father was surprised to find that Fitzroy had both potential and talent.'

'Goodness, it must hurt you to admit that.'

'Actually, in the beginning we were like brothers. My father welcomed him into our family – his mother was dead, and his father estranged – so my family took him under their wing. I've always told you that Fitzroy and I were more alike than either you or your mother ever realised. We're cut from the same cloth, trained the same way and were once important to each other.'

'What happened? Did he seduce your girlfriend?'

Cole shook his head. 'This was long before he got into all that. And no, I don't think that would have bothered me much. I haven't cared much for most of the women I've been involved with. They've served a function.'

'Done their duty by the crown,' I said sarcastically.

Cole shrugged. 'More or less. Although they rarely knew what I was.'

'I wasn't being serious!'

'No, well, it's irrelevant. As I said, Fitzroy became like family. He often stayed with us and he got to meet my sister, Rosamund.'

'If he was so close to all of you I can't believe he did anything—'

'He married her,' said Cole. 'With the family's blessing. Including mine.'

'Fitzroy was married before? He's never mentioned it.'

Cole's scowl deepened. 'He wouldn't. Ironically, rather like you left this cat shut in here with the bombing going on, he left her alone without protection when he went away on a mission.'

'I take it she wasn't in the espionage business?'

'No,' said Cole. 'She was quite innocent about what the men in the family did. She had no idea she would ever be in danger, but your father should have known that we have enemies. He had enemies. Enemies who couldn't get to him, so they got to Rosamund.'

'But couldn't you or your father—'

Cole stood up and banged his hand so hard on the table the teapot jumped, and his cup rolled over. The cat shot off leaving a sizeable portion of fish in the dish. I felt myself become very still. On the outside it might have looked as if I had frozen, but the reality was I was poised, coiled to react to whatever was coming.

'It was his duty to protect her, and he failed.'

'What happened to her?' I asked in a low voice.

'She was attacked and killed in her own home. Her marital home. Fitzroy couldn't be reached, so he didn't learn of it until two months later. The police had no idea who was responsible, and any leads were far too cold for him to follow. So do you know what he did?'

I shook my head.

'He took a mistress,' said Cole. 'And then another. He moved on without a care in the world. He became the louche degenerate your mother knew. What she saw in him I cannot imagine, but one thing I do admit, she has always brought out the best in him. I like your mother.'

'But not Fitzroy?'

'If I hadn't been expressly ordered not to kill him, he would be dead by now.'

'So your feud is well known?'

'Oh yes,' said Cole. 'But very few know why. Not only was it a very long time ago, anyone who mentioned my sister's name in my presence tended to lose teeth. So people stopped talking about it.'

'I see,' I said.

'I don't think you do,' said Cole. 'I could never have harmed your mother, but to discover Fitzroy had someone else he cared about – now that was an opportunity hard to resist. Your parents kept your existence very quiet. No one in our world knew. When I found out he had a child I finally saw my way forward. If I wasn't allowed to kill him, I thought I might hurt him through that child. I thought I might cut him to the quick as badly as he had hurt me.'

Cole took a pace towards me, looming over my chair; tall, broad and powerful. There had been an energy about him while he told his story, a passion I had not seen before, but now he was cold, calm, collected. He was like he always was when I saw him ready for the kill.

Chapter Fifteen

I wished I hadn't argued with Leo. I felt deep sorrow he was going to find my dead body after we had parted so badly. Still, I wasn't going to give up easily. I could never best Cole in a fight, but as long as I was alive there was hope. Did Leo carry a gun? I couldn't remember. If he did was he prepared to use it?

'But you saved me before? The attack here?'

'I arranged the attack,' said Cole. 'It seemed fitting to do to you what was done to Rosamund. But when it came to it, I realised if I wasn't there – if I didn't do it – it wasn't going to satisfy me. And then I saw you fight back, like a wild cat. You wouldn't give up even though it was clear from the start you would lose. I admit I felt a creeping respect, so I stopped it. I even punished him later for harming you.'

'Punished?'

'Killed. He shouldn't have touched you. He shouldn't have—'

'Cornered me in my bath?'

Cole's lips curled in disgust.

'So what happens now?'

'We are at war, and feuds, such as mine, must wait.'

'So you're telling me you will kill me later.'

Cole's face relaxed and he gave a genuine smile. 'No, I won't. I have decided not to harm you. I like you almost as much as I liked your mother. I thought I would give you my side of the story before Fitzroy told you his lies.'

'You want me to understand.'

'Exactly,' said Cole. 'My feud is not with you, and I will not take out any part of my revenge on you. I thought you would be more comfortable knowing that.' He said this as casually as he might mention he wasn't too keen on mushrooms in a pie. 'Fitzroy's stories might have worried you, but now you know you have no need to worry. That is as long as you look after the cat.'

'I will,' I said seriously. I had no idea if this was a real condition or not.

Cole picked up his goggles and gloves. 'You are likely to see me around. Don't let it worry you. I don't generally take to others, but you are different. We two, you and I, are more alike than you yet realise.' He left, flicking the light switch as he went and sending me back into darkness.

When Leo finally came back, shortly before dawn, he found me in the dark, still sitting at the kitchen table, my fingers grasping tightly at its edge. He turned on the light.

'Hope? Are you all right? Why are you sitting alone in the dark?' He knelt down in front of me. 'Are you in shock? Did something happen?'

'I had tea with a psychopath. Right here at this table.' Then I burst into tears.

It took quite a long time for Leo to calm me down. I think this was as much because he was worn out from whatever he had been doing, and because, perhaps, he had never had to deal with so much raw emotion being emitted by one person. So, I suppose it was hardly a surprise we ended up in bed together.

Afterwards, he made tea, and we sat and drank it in bed as if nothing unusual had passed between us. I noted that Cole was right – our tea did taste vile.

'Do you think we could go back to the start?' said Leo.

I glanced at the clock at the side of his bed. 'We have to get to work.'

Leo blushed a fiery red, which was surprising considering what we had just been doing. 'No, I meant are you in danger? Do you really think Cole is a deluded psychopath?'

'I don't know if he is deluded, and I don't know if he is actually a psychopath. It seemed he cared about his sister. Psychopaths don't care about anyone, do they?'

Leo shrugged, spilling tea into his saucer. 'I have no idea. I associate the word with someone who would kill for . . . well, for fun.'

I put my tea down on his bedside table. 'No, I don't think he intends to harm me. I think after being outside in the raid, and with everything that's been happening recently, I overreacted to being in the company of a man I found threatening, and who I thought could overwhelm me – even kill me.'

'That's very considered,' said Leo. 'I don't think I would be so calm in your situation.'

I pushed back the blankets and got out of bed. Over my shoulder, I said, 'Thank you. Thank you for looking after me.' Then I scuttled back to my room without a backward glance. I encountered Leo next at the front door. We were both dressed in uniform. 'Thank you,' I said again.

Leo shifted from foot to foot. 'Please stop doing that!'

'Thanking you?'

'Yes. Damn, this is awkward!' He opened the door. 'We'd better look lively if we're not to be late.'

We took a fast pace to the office. It was fast enough that neither of us had breath to talk. When we got there, Leo gave me a curt nod and headed off to the studio. I went to my desk. Captain Masterton spoke to me, so I apologised automatically without registering what she had said, and sat down to work. A minute or so later I was aware she was still standing in front of my desk. 'Is there something I can do for you, ma'am?' I asked.

She gave me the strangest look and turned on her heel. I watched her walk away, and then turned my attention back to the wretched files that were already stacked high on my desk. I knew at some point I needed to think about what Leo and I had done, and reflect on it for myself. I had no intention of discussing it with anyone, including Leo. It was down to me to order my thoughts, and decide if my affections were in the least involved. Only when I had decided that, might I even consider discussing the night's events with Leo.

Any awkwardness in avoiding him was helped by his being called away from the studio for the afternoon. I spent some time working through scripts and talking with Dashwood, who told me the most outrageous stories of his younger thespian days. I got home in the early evening. The flat was empty except for Ashes, who mewed piteously at me the moment I stepped through the door. I found him some milk and a little bit of cheese, and was soon listening to his happy purrs. I had gone into my bedroom to change when I heard the front door open. A moment later, there was a knock on my door.

'I'm changing,' I called.

'Could you stop?' said Leo. 'There's something I need to request you to do for me?'

I opened the door a crack and peeked out. Leo stood there looking handsome, smart and clearly embarrassed. 'Would you mind awfully coming to a party with me tonight? Only I don't know who else I can ask.'

'It's not the nicest invitation I've ever received,' I said, attempting to keep the tone light. 'But really, a party? A party during the Blitz?'

Leo produced a dress from behind his back and held it up. 'This would suit you, I think. I got it from the studio wardrobe.' It was a low-cut black and sparkly thing that would either fit me like a glove or make me look like an overstuffed chair. 'All right,' I said, reaching out to take it. 'How long do I have?'

Leo glanced at his watch. 'Fifteen minutes. I've got a car.'

I nodded, and retreated back into my room. Leo didn't usually have a car, so this had to be some kind of undercover operation, and for whatever reason he had yet to tell me the details. I put on the dress, did my hair, and put on a little make-up. I glanced in the mirror and decided I would pass as a human being rather than a piece of furniture.

Leo's face, when I joined him in the front room, suggested that he liked the dress on me. He gave a low whistle. 'I'm not used to seeing you in evening dress. You look lovely.'

'You're looking quite dapper yourself,' I said, because in evening dress he did scrub up nicely. 'Are you going to tell me what's going on?'

'You're my girlfriend,' said Leo. 'You can use your real name. I'm Leo Gordon. We've been seeing each other for a couple of months. We met at a dance. You know I'm in some kind of reserved occupation, and have a vague idea that I might have connections to the black market.'

'Is the relationship going well?' I asked with a smile.

'I'm afraid you are very much here to support my op. Don't add in any extra colour. I don't want anything to distract from the mission.'

'Which is?'

Leo shook his head. 'I can't tell you.'

'Fair enough,' I said. 'I shall act as normal.'

Leo looked faintly alarmed. 'Maybe you could dial that down a notch or two?'

Chapter Sixteen

If the long drive up to the house hadn't been a clue that our host was someone rich, and thus probably important, the servant who offered to park our car clinched the matter. The house was slightly outside London by a few miles, but it was keeping to blackout rules. Gravel crunched under my shoes, and I got the impression from the darker outline of the building against the night sky that this was likely to be Georgian. However, as soon as I was through the front door, and into the main reception room, I realised my mistake. The blacked-out windows ran from near the floor to the high ceilings. This was an Elizabethan building, and one in very fine condition.

We were in what was effectively a great hall. At the opposite end of the room I could see flickering flames that seemed to dance between the mingled throng, and were being emitted from a roaring fire in a hearth taller than myself. Leo tucked my arm into his and advanced into the room with a cocky confidence that was new to me. He nodded to people right and left as he led me towards a table laden with champagne bottles. A butler, who looked as if he suffered from chronic indigestion, served us two glasses with a flourish. He bowed slightly when I thanked him. Leo didn't so much as look him in the eye, but whisked me away to meet Anselm Fernsby, a rake-thin individual with azure-blue eyes, a mop of blond hair, and a barely noticeable stutter. I judged him to be in his late thirties or early forties, and this only due to the state of his skin, which was a leathery combination of sunspots and lines.

'So, Fernsby, this is the little lady I was telling you about,' said Leo, shaking him heartily by the hand.

The man looked me over. 'Pretty little thing,' he said in an adenoidal voice. 'Does she think what you tell her?'

Leo had his arm around my waist, and he nipped me sharply at the top of my buttocks. I squirmed slightly, but took the hint and didn't do more than flash a swift, unfeeling smile.

A woman slid into view. I would have said glided for she was also svelte and clad in gloriously draped pale green silk, but there was something oozy about her. She didn't walk as much as flow. Her hair was the same shade of blond, and her nose shared the pinched fineness of Fernsby's. Although, of the two of them, she had the stronger build. 'Now, Anselm, that is no way to talk to a lady.' She held out her hand to me. Her wrist was almost indecently limp. 'I'm Ottiline, and I have the misfortune to be Anselm's sister.'

'Hope Stapleford,' I said, shaking her hand gently.

'Title?' asked Ottiline.

I smiled. 'Only an honourable.'

'Me too,' she said. 'So much easier for the boys. Most of them here,' she glanced around the room, 'were born with half a dozen. So overblown. You'd think the families could have shared them out.'

'Women have their place,' said Anselm. 'Well bred, better breeding. One can see that Hope here has excellent birthing hips.'

No one had ever said anything like this to me in polite company. I didn't know whether to laugh or punch him. Leo broke in. 'Oh, we're a long way from going there,' he said. 'Still getting to know each other.'

'What's there to know?' asked Anselm. His expression chilled me. It appeared to be genuine bemusement.

Ottiline took me by the wrist, in a surprisingly strong grip.

'Oh, come and have a chat with me and my pals,' she said. 'The men are so boring when they get together.'

I glanced at Leo out of the corner of my eye, and saw his slight nod. Clearly, I was here as window dressing and no more.

'Do you like actors?' said Ottiline. 'I think they're marvellous! Just imagine playing a different person each night!'

She was still towing me like a small craft across the room. While my new friend could weave in and between the other guests, I invariably, having birthing hips, had to ask them to move. 'Yes, very interesting,' I managed to say as I grazed the foot of an older man with a ferocious moustache. He muttered something quite unrepeatable, and I could only smile and apologise. Still this rapid movement through the length of the room was giving me a good idea of the types of guests there. All the women were young, well dressed and attractive. The men ranged in age from thirties to older types who must have fought in the last war. These elders had in common luxurious facial hair and wandering hands. My behind was pinched at least three times during our passage. It took enormous force of mind not to jerk Ottiline to a halt and deal with these gropers in a suitably painful manner. If I hadn't been introduced to Anselm's sister, I might have thought this was the kind of party where the women were, shall we say, available. Although I did give Leo credit enough not to knowingly bring me to one of those.

Ottiline stopped by a door, released my hand, and tidied her hair. 'Did we go fast enough? Or did any of those rotters get their mitts on you?'

'I got pinched,' I managed to say between clenched teeth.

'Well, never mind that, come through here and meet a real gentleman.' She opened the door and I saw Dashwood enthroned in a central wingback chair holding court to a bevy of young women. It forcibly reminded me of my stepfather – at least how my stepfather used to behave before he married my mother.

'Darling Hope,' called out Dashwood. 'A friendly face. What terrible wind has blown you to these wretched shores?'

This was greeted by a gale of girlish laughter, which Dashwood graciously acknowledged, but I thought I caught a flicker of desperation in his eyes.

'Ottiline, I must tell you,' began a girl with washed-out blue eyes and wispy blond hair, 'it's so terribly, terribly . . .'

I never got to know what was so terribly, terribly something. Dashwood took the current diversion as an opportunity to break away from his audience, pleading the necessity of drink. I still had a glass of champagne clutched in my hand, miraculously unspilt, and he took it off me. 'God, I need this,' he said quietly.

'You're welcome to it,' I said. 'I'm starving. Got dragged out without having any supper.'

'Well, that really will not do!' He downed the rest of the drink in one and took me by the hand. 'To the kitchens!'

The girls were still clustered around Ottiline discussing whatever disaster had befallen them – I suspected either a broken nail or a broken engagement. From the demeanour of the group I imagined a broken nail would cause more consternation. They reminded me of the girls invited to the Varsity balls that I had attended, all fluttery nonsense and powdered faces. Whatever they were up to it allowed Dashwood and me to get out through a side door and then nip down a servants' backstairs. We emerged into a large, old-fashioned kitchen to the surprise of several men, who were unpacking yet more champagne, and an older women in an apron, who was watching them with a beady eye.

'Greetings, Mrs Grovener! Are the invaders behaving themselves? No broken dishes I hope.'

'None as yet, Mr Dashwood,' answered the woman. 'But they know I've got my eye on them.' One of the footmen turned away from her and gave me a cheeky wink. I had a sudden memory of the first time I met Harvey.

'Now, my dear Mrs Grovener, I am aware this is not a properly catered event, as you would have thought proper, but I do wonder if you might have a cold piece of pie somewhere for my friend here. She too was scooped up and brought to this party, but unlike myself she did not have a moment to grab a bite before she was unceremoniously transported here.' The cook gave a slight nod and bustled off. Dashwood turned his attention to me. 'Who did bring you, by the way, Hope?'

'The major,' I said.

'Well I never,' said Dashwood. 'It just goes to show you never can tell.' He addressed the cook once more. 'Hope works on the scripts at the production unit. Writes me some of my best lines, so I must see her strengths are kept up.'

'Not a friend of the Fernsbys then?' asked the cook, reappearing and passing me a plate of cold pie with a portion of sauce on the side. My stomach growled hungrily at the sight of it. Dashwood pulled up a stool for me and I already had a forkful in my mouth before I remembered she had asked me a question. I swallowed hastily. 'I met them briefly for the first time this evening. This is a wonderful pie.'

'Hunger makes the best sauce,' said the cook stoically, but I thought I saw a slight twinkle in her eye.

'I was hired for the event,' said Dashwood. 'Raconteur, dancer and entertainer!'

'I didn't hear any music,' I said through a mouthful of pie.

'No, I'm getting the impression business is done first. My job is to keep the ladies entertained while the men get on with it. Then there will be dancing.'

'And a cold collation,' said the cook with a strange vehemence.

'Is that a problem?' asked Dashwood. 'I'm sure it will be delicious if you made it – or have they used outside caterers?'

'Outside caterers over my dead body,' said the cook. 'I came with the house, I did, and once it's after two in the morning we always serves a hot breakfast. That's what the real ladies and gents want.' She looked quickly around to see if anyone had heard her other than us.

I had a brief image of her in Elizabethan dress, but I knew what she meant. 'It is certainly what my stepfather would order,' I said.

'Really, who is your stepfather?' asked Dashwood.

'Nobility,' I said. 'I don't usually mention him. I'm only an honourable by birth. I don't want to give people the wrong idea.'

'You can tell proper class,' said the cook, 'and you have it, miss. You're not bad yourself, Mr Dashwood, but—'

'I know,' said the actor, 'I'm not top drawer like our Hope here.'

I could feel myself blushing. 'It all seems rather foolish. A bomb doesn't discriminate on who it explodes.'

Dashwood nodded.

'Don't think standards don't matter, miss,' said the cook. 'You carry yourself like a person of breeding, and that makes others look up to you. We all fit into our own position. The Fernsbys. They might have inherited the place, but they're new money through and through. This whole evening is about them trying to prove they belong among their so-called betters. Betters! No decent man or woman would have anything to do with them.'

'Oh, I don't know,' said Dashwood, appeasingly. 'Ottiline doesn't seem too bad. She's the one who first directed me to your gracious abode, Mrs Grovener.'

'Pah,' said the cook, putting her hands on her hips. 'I wouldn't trust either of them further than I could spit 'em!'

Chapter Seventeen

By the time we got back to the flat it was almost three o'clock in the morning. I sat down heavily on the settee, and eased my poor aching feet out of my shoes. Behind me Leo closed the front door and locked it.

I flopped back and closed my eyes. I felt too exhausted to crawl the last few feet to my bedroom, let alone get out of this dress.

'Hope?' I opened my eyes to see a glass on brandy being held out to me. 'You dosed off. I didn't want to leave you there to get a pain in your neck. Besides, we have things to talk about.'

'Now?' I said. 'Leo, I'm dead on my feet – or rather dead on this seat. It's all right for you. You don't have to report to Masterton first thing tomorrow.' I sighed. 'Or rather today. Can't it wait?'

'It would be helpful to have your thoughts while they're fresh,' said Leo. 'Drink up. It will give you a bit of a boost, and then later you'll sleep more deeply.'

I sipped my drink. 'I don't know how people are doing this. I thought I'd get used to the routine but I keep feeling worse and worse.'

Leo nodded. He got up and fetched a small pillbox from his briefcase. He stood there tossing it from side to side and frowning. 'This is the stuff they've been giving our airmen to keep them going. There's some thoughts about giving it to other operatives. If you are really having trouble . . . I don't like using it myself, but I've had to recently. I can leave this lot with you, but really, Hope, only use it in case of emergency.'

'What is it?'

'A new thing. Revs you up and keeps you going. Not as bad as the stuff they used in the last war but—'

'Stuff?'

'Heroin – got its name from the hero it makes you feel like. Nasty stuff.'

'I don't believe anyone I know used or uses anything. Although Fitzroy sometimes seems as if he never needs sleep, so maybe—'

'No,' said Leo. 'I know he doesn't. I've read reports in which he is ferociously against this kind of thing.' He sat down next to me, placing the pillbox on the table. 'So, your impressions of the night?'

For an awful moment I thought he was asking me about last night, and it must have shown on my face, because he went pink and dropped his gaze. 'The Fernsbys' affair.'

'I got shuffled off with the other women pretty fast,' I said, staring straight ahead, and trying not to show I knew he realised I had thought he was talking about our night together. 'Dashwood said he was hired to entertain them.'

'Yes, I'll be talking to him tomorrow. Leo Gordon and Major Leo don't quite add up. I'm going to try and get him to keep quiet and tell him as little as possible about what I was doing. I suggest you do the same. It's always harder dealing with civilians.'

'As I have no idea what you were working on, are working on, I'm hardly likely to discuss anything with him.'

'I don't know,' said Leo, and this time he scowled rather than frowned, 'he seems rather taken with you. I came looking for you at one point and was told you'd gone off on your own with him.'

'To the kitchen to inveigle pie out of the cook. You rushed me out before I had a chance to eat a bite.'

The scowl faded. 'I forget you share your stepfather's legendary appetite.' He saw the surprise on my face. 'For food!'

'Leo, maybe we should talk about last night,' I said. 'Especially if it's going to get in the way of work.'

Leo shook his head. 'I don't have time to think about

relationships. I'm up to my neck in stuff – and not the stuff I thought I was going to be doing. It's a very steep learning curve for me, and I don't have the energy, let alone the time, to deal with emotions right now. It happened. We were both highly stressed. We'd been through yet another air raid. The service was always dangerous, but now we might die at any time. We have to live in the moment. That was all it was, wasn't it?'

'Of course,' I said. 'You're quite right.' I could feel a lump rising in my throat. I wanted to tell him he was the first man I had ever been with and that it meant a lot to me. I didn't. Instead I hurried on. 'The women were all remarkably young compared to the average age of the men. I didn't get the impression any of them were . . . er . . . being paid for their companionship, except in the way that some girls tend to go for rich men. And, of course, most of the younger men are overseas. There was a sprinkling of wedding rings, but more engagement rings, I would have said. Ottiline was very efficient at keeping them out of the main hall until the band started. A lot of the girls . . . I suppose they might have been playing a part but I got the impression they were rather empty-headed. Not her though. I was a little surprised she allowed herself to be sidelined.'

'You didn't hear them talking about anything in particular? The war? Politics?'

I shook my head and took another sip of brandy. It slid warm and comforting down my throat. Although I would rather have had a hug. 'Where to get stockings. What shade of red lipstick was acceptable to wear when you had blond hair.'

'I see,' said Leo. 'Well, thank you for coming with me. It was a great help.' He got up as if he was about to go to bed.

'Is that all you can tell me?' I asked.

'It's not like you to ask . . .'

'I know I shouldn't ask for extra information, but if you're ever going to ask me to pick . . . besides, you said you felt out of your depth. I have a very high security clearance. Maybe I could help you talk things out.'

Leo sat down again. 'Don't think I don't appreciate the offer, Hope. The thing is, not everyone approves of the security clearance you've got. If you were working directly for Fitzroy it wouldn't be anyone's business, but—'

'I'm always working for him,' I said coldly.

Leo pulled a face. 'Okay, if I don't tell you this you'll probably dig it out for yourself. The Fernsbys are half-siblings to Rafe Warren.'

'I don't know who that is.'

'He's in our line of work, so he needs to be above reproach. Let's just say the Fernsbys are drawing unwanted attention to themselves. So far Rafe has kept himself apart, but it has to be watched.'

'The watchers watching the watchers – I'm familiar with the procedure. Most of my work has been counter-espionage, and centred around our own.'

Leo's head sank lower. 'I'm all too aware this is the kind of thing you should be doing. Gubbins never trained me for this. He never expected me to need this skill set. I get the distinct impression that there is another game being played here, and it's to do with your stepfather. Do you know what is going on?'

This made me laugh. 'Hardly ever. I usually only understand once things are over.'

'And this Cole chap?'

I blinked at the fast change of subject. 'He trained with Fitzroy. Excellent sniper. Adaptable morals, but as far as I can tell, highly rated for his ability to get the job done.'

'Does he have a relationship with you?'

'Leo! He's old enough to be my father!'

'I meant how are you and he connected?'

'We're not really. He thinks I show promise as an agent – or to be an agent like him.'

Leo looked, if anything, more bemused than when we had begun. 'Right, I'm going to bed to sleep. I'm thinking of sleeping in the shelter in case there is a raid. Do you want to come down with me?'

'No,' I said. 'I'd prefer not to spend any more time than I must there.' What I really meant was I had no intention of spending any more time down there ever.

'Well, maybe I'll stay up here then,' said Leo.

I didn't argue. I merely nodded and headed to my room. I fell into bed without even bothering to undress, and was quickly fast asleep. I dreamed of clouds and iced buns. It was all very pleasant.

The next morning, I had barely sat down at my desk when Masterton called me over. 'I understand you will be having a forty-eight-hour pass,' she said. 'Let me be clear this will be your only pass in the next three months.'

This pass, of which I as yet knew nothing, had clearly got her hackles up, so I merely said, 'Yes, ma'am, understood.' I waited for the day to reveal what on earth was going on. As it turned out, things only became more confusing. On the way down to lunch I caught sight of Leo walking upstairs. He didn't have his hands on the woman he was walking next to, but you could barely see any light between them. It was not the same blonde woman I had seen him run across the road to meet a day or so ago. He didn't see me, but I saw his face, and it looked lit from within. He was clearly delighted to be with her. She was very pretty in a kittenish sort of way and, unlike me, seductively slender. She looked like the kind of girl who appealed to men for help. Again totally unlike me. I had thought Leo favoured independent women, but then our intimate time together had come on the back of my tears. Maybe I had him all wrong. I turned back, partly so we would not pass each other on the stairs, but also because I had lost my appetite. Leo, I told myself, flirted as part of his work. He had been tasked with reeling in potential candidates for the SOE. That he was looking at some girl as if she was all the light in his world didn't have to mean a thing. There was no reason for me to feel so low. Even if it was a real interest, hadn't he said he had no time for emotions right now? He was absolutely right, of course.

There was a war on and I had no time to pine like a wallflower at a party.

I went outside and down the steps. There was a little park where I could sit for the few minutes remaining of my lunchtime. I wished I had brought a book. I determined to practise my skills at sizing up people from passing impressions. I was in the midst of deciding if a young woman might be a waitress or governess, when a voice called my name. I turned awkwardly on the bench and found myself looking up at the tall, slim figure of Harvey.

Chapter Eighteen

'Good heavens!' I said. 'I thought I was daydreaming when I saw you the other day. But here you are in the flesh, and in an army uniform. I thought you'd be in the clouds by now.'

Harvey, my erstwhile asset, had shown a great deal of enthusiasm and ability as an aeroplane mechanic during my previous mission. He had also talked his way into spending time on the flight simulator and to everyone's surprise had turned out to have a natural ability as a pilot. An old injury from our earliest mission had meant that he could not serve in the infantry, so the RAF's decision to let anyone in, 'not just toffs', as Harvey had said, had seen him apply and be admitted to pilot training.

Harvey's handsome face scrunched up in a scowl. 'Can I sit?' he said curtly. I nodded and moved up the bench to make room for him. 'It was all going so very well when I was pulled from the pilots programme.'

'But why?'

'I don't know,' said Harvey. He scuffed a boot along the ground like a naughty child. 'I might know, but I can't prove anything.'

'It's not got anything to do with Fitzroy, has it?' I said, feeling my heart sink. 'He's in Cairo right now. I can't—'

'No,' said Harvey. 'At least I don't think so.' He scuffed his shoes some more. I waited. Eventually he said, 'Seems like one of the officers heard how I wasn't always on the straight and narrow and decided I couldn't be trusted with anything as valuable as an aircraft!'

'What? That's ridiculous!'

'I know,' said Harvey. 'What did he think I was going to do? Break it up and sell it down the Roman Road market? Hey, guv'nor, fancy a real bit of a fighter aircraft? Makes a nice lean-to kennel for the dog. That is if people even keep dogs still. I heard some people were putting their pets down.'

'Oh, how awful! On both counts. I've just got a cat.'

'Typical upper classes. Everyone else is getting rid of theirs and you buy a cat.'

'Can you buy cats? I never thought about it. There just always were cats around White Orchards. But no, I haven't been buying a pet. I found him – or he found me – in a bomb site. I'm calling him Ash or Ashes. I've not decided.'

'Ash,' said Harvey decidedly. 'Sorry to be so grumpy. It really is good to see you again, Hope. I take it you're working round the corner?' He jerked his head in the direction of the office.

'Yes. You too?'

'Yeah,' said Harvey. 'It's all right. Some of it is quite interesting. There's a lot I'd like to tell you, but I can't. I suppose I can say I fit in better with some of the lot here. What about you?'

'Typing,' I said. 'Lots of typing.'

'Cor! What a waste.'

'I'm training to be an ARP warden in the evenings.'

'I joined up with the fire guards. The SFP. Speaking of which, I'd like to talk to you about something.'

'I have to go back,' I said looking at my watch. 'Come visit me?'

'Same flat?'

'Yes.'

His eyes grew sad. 'I miss Bernie.'

'Me too.'

'I can't believe she's gone. I didn't even get to go to her funeral.'

'Neither did I.' I stood up. 'This evening? Six o'clock? You can have supper with us before I head out to the ARP?'

'It's a date,' said Harvey. It was only when I was walking away that I heard him say, 'Us?'

I pretended not to hear. After all, I didn't know if Leo would even come back for supper. The unspoken rule seemed to be if no one said anything, whichever of us got home first would cook and leave some in the oven to be heated later if the other wasn't present. As I went back to the office, I wondered if I had to give the dress from last night back. Maybe if I didn't mention it . . .

I spent the afternoon going over scripts for the next two shoots. One of which was causing great excitement as it was going to be done outside. This one had to be very carefully broken down into scenes, so Leo could then choose how to shoot it. I couldn't see why I couldn't decide that too. I would have simplified the process, but according to Dashwood, who still came by to keep me up to speed with the job, that was not how it was done.

'When did you get away from the Fernsbys?' I asked.

'I ended up staying the night,' he said with a grimace. 'They put me in a decent room with horrid sheets, and I ate breakfast in the kitchen.'

'Neither a guest nor a servant,' I said.

'Exactly, my dear. But the breakfast was spiffing. They have their own pigs! The cook is a bit of a marvel as well.'

'I can't see the Fernsbys valuing that. They seemed thin as rakes. How do you know them?'

'Ah,' said Dashwood, coming to sit on the side of my desk, 'it's a bit complicated. Have you come across Major Warren yet?'

'I don't think so. Is he in—' I stopped, lost for words.

'He works in Whitehall,' said Dashwood, 'but I thought you might have met him through your stepfather.'

I shook my head.

'The Fernsbys are his step-siblings. He's the one with the blue blood. They're the ones who ended up with all the money. Anyway, it doesn't seem to have damaged the relationship too badly. They knew about the film unit, and they asked Warren if he could drum up some entertainment suitable for the ladies, while the men were doing business.'

'I don't know that I'm surprised,' I said, thinking of what Cole had told me. 'Everyone in this business is connected to everyone else.'

'In show business?' asked Dashwood raising an eyebrow.

'In London,' I said quickly. I had meant espionage, but I caught myself just in time. Dashwood knew I worked in a high-security building, but he didn't know I was anything more than a typist and gifted editor.

I say gifted, because he was being particularly praising about my efforts this afternoon. 'You've really brought life into this dull little story,' he said. 'Lucy is going to love her new lines.'

'Lucy?'

'New girl taking over from Nel. The major brought her in. One of those candyfloss blondes you could knock down with a feather. She will look marvellous on screen. Film adds so much weight, she'll look almost normal.'

'You don't like her?'

'I don't know her.' He looked away for a moment and then back at me. 'I may have got this all wrong, and it isn't really any of my business, but I had the impression that you and the major were an item. You can tell a lot from watching people dance, and you and he the other night . . . well, let's only say it was clear you'd been more than friends.'

I put my cold hands up to my cheeks in a futile attempt to stop the blush rising in my cheeks. Dashwood again looked away. 'Anyway, Lucy's clearly set her cap at the major. It's the sort of thing the less talented often do. I wouldn't have thought much of it. The major seemed to have a firm head on his shoulders, but from what I saw in the canteen today, he is clearly taken with her.' He got up. 'Anyway, if I have to choose sides, I'm on yours. I thought you should know that.' He left, closing the door quietly behind him.

I admit a couple of tears might have fallen on my typewriter. I told myself I was severely deprived of sleep, and I had missed luncheon. It was no wonder I felt a bit weepy. Besides, in London, with Fitzroy and my mother away, I was the most on my own I had been since college. But then I had had Bernie – and later Bernie and Harvey. At least I would be seeing Harvey tonight. That was something to look forward to, so why did I still feel so down?

Chapter Nineteen

The doorbell rang as I was taking the cottage pie out of the oven. I put it down on the side and ran to open the door. Harvey stood there awkwardly clutching a rather thin bunch of flowers. 'Oh, freesias, my favourite,' I said, taking them off him. 'They smell so wonderful. Much better than plants twice their size. Come through. You know where to put your coat. I've only this moment taken the cottage pie out of the oven.'

Harvey hung up his coat and grinned. 'I can smell it. My mother used to say that food talked to you when it was ready, and I can tell you that pie and my stomach have already set up a communication station!'

I laughed. 'I've got beer and wine. Though I won't be drinking, but you're welcome.'

'No, I'm on fire watch tonight. I take it you're on ARP training. Isn't that a bit dangerous? You can be outside when the raids happen.'

'It's more dangerous than being a typist,' I said. 'Which is mostly what I'm doing now.'

Harvey pulled up a chair and I served us both a good portion. I put the flowers in a vase, and put them up on the side beside us. They did add a welcome splash of colour, as well as a fragrance strong enough to compete with the food. I got a water jug and a couple of glasses. I hadn't set another place, but Harvey asked, 'Is anyone else joining us? You said "us" earlier.'

'It's complicated,' I said, trying to get my brain into order.

A wave of fatigue washed over me so intense I almost dropped my fork.

'Are you all right?'

'I'm tired,' I said. 'I know everyone is with the raids, but I'm not used to it yet.'

'Tell me about it,' said Harvey. 'I was walking down the long corridor at the top of the building, and one minute I was at one end, and the next I was at the other. I am so tired I reckon I fell asleep while walking, and only woke up when I got to the door. It seems even my brain knows I can't sleepwalk through a door.'

I ate some food and felt some of my strength returning. 'I've heard people can do all sorts of things when asleep. My father once told me that we had a shepherd who would get up in the middle of the night and start herding his sheep up the hill only to awaken confused and cold in a field with no memory of how he got there.'

Harvey laughed. 'Actually, Hope, though it is great to see you, I wonder if I could pick your brains?'

'Pick away,' I said, considering whether or not I had to leave any food for Leo. This supper had come out rather well, if I said so myself.

Harvey rolled his lips together, and ran his tongue around them. 'Thing is . . . I think there's something funny going on.'

'You're going to have to be more specific,' I said. 'In my world there's always something funny going on. That is, unless you mean, it's something that makes people laugh.'

'No, very much the other kind of funny.' He took a drink of water. 'I was on duty the other night, and it was raining incendiaries. When that happens it's not unusual for blokes to climb up on to the buildings and kick them off the roofs into the street.'

'What?'

'The streets are empty, and either a warden or a fire person can put out the blaze. They're really hot, but they burn so quickly some of them go out by themselves. Besides, putting them out on a road is better than trying to put out a building.'

'I can see that. Do you want some more pie?' I asked. Leo was probably out for dinner with that blonde.

Harvey nodded so hard I could almost see his scalp ripple through his close-shaved hair. After I'd shared the rest of the pie between us, he continued. 'Anyway, I was up on a roof imagining I was kicking these things in through Hitler's bedroom window. It was dark and even with the searchlights going over I couldn't see too well but I'd been fairly successful. Then I see one land on the building next to mine. You see them raining down. A lot of them bounced off into the street, but some stuck and began to burn.'

'But the noise – the planes, the explosions,' I said.

'Oh, it's not that bad. Unless they're landing right on top of you, you tend to tune it out. And if it does land right on top of you then you don't have anything more to worry about.'

'Don't!'

'Sorry. Gallows humour, they call it, don't they? No idea who the bloke Gallows was or what he did . . . Anyway, I decide that I'm going to leap across to get the other incendiaries off this roof. I was pretty high up, but as I said, I couldn't see properly. I've been back and seen it in daylight, and I'll tell you there's no way I would attempt it when I could see the drop. I reckon it was more than fifty feet. Thing is, when you're caught up with it all you don't think about how high you're climbing. So, I took a running leap, and blow me if I didn't make it clean across.'

My heart was beating very fast in my chest, but I managed to say with a mildly ironic air, 'I guessed that.'

'So, I lands on the other side, but I don't land lightly like a cat might. Say, where is your cat?'

'Around. Continue the story.'

'Bossy,' said Harvey with a genuine smile. 'So I lands with an almighty thump, and I'm congratulating myself on having made it, when the floor, I mean roof, sort of sags beneath my feet.'

'Oh no!' I said.

'Oh yes! It gives way and I'm falling down into the blackness. I fall for long enough to think I'm going to die, and then I land on something soft. Not soft enough I don't have the breath knocked out of me. I lay there for a minute, before I see another one of those bloody bombs coming straight towards me through the hole I made in the roof. That got me going. It was like I didn't need oxygen any more. Once you've seen one sod dead in a burnt-out building you know that's not how you want to go. I pushed myself to my feet with a strength I didn't know I had, and bolted for the exit. Ran straight into the wall, I did. But I managed to feel my way around it till I got to the door. It wasn't far, thank goodness, and then I was down the stairs and out into the street quicker than you can say, "How's your father?"'

I reached out a hand and laid it on his. 'I'm very glad you made it out.'

'Yeah, me too,' said Harvey. 'But that's not what I wanted to tell you. It was what I landed on. I think it was a body. I think I saw more than one in there.'

'The building was on fire,' I said. 'The smoke—'

'No. No, that's the thing. The fire hadn't started. There was no reason anyone should be dead in there, but they were.'

'Are you sure?' I said.

'Do you mean was my mind playing tricks on me?'

He stopped as the flat door opened, and a very weary Leo walked in. He threw his briefcase down on the settle before he looked up and saw us sitting at the table, eating his dinner, and holding hands.

'Goodness, Hope,' he said. 'If I'd known we were having company I would have come back earlier.'

Both Harvey and I shot to our feet. 'No need to stand to attention,' said Leo. 'We're not on duty.' He came over and looked into the pot. Then he looked pointedly at me.

'Leo, you remember Harvey from up north?'

'The aeroplane mechanic,' said Leo.

'My asset,' I said. 'Harvey is far more than merely a mechanic.'

'So I saw,' said Leo. 'If you'll excuse me, I'm going to change out of uniform and rustle myself up a sandwich. If there's any bread and cheese left?'

'There's plenty of bread,' I said in a quiet voice. 'I did put rather a lot of cheese in the topping, but there's jam. Strawberry.'

'Excellent. Strawberry jam sandwiches for dinner. The perfect end to a perfect day.' He stormed off.

'Should I go?' said Harvey.

'You should finish the food on your plate,' I said. 'I've no idea why he's being so—'

'I wouldn't like to see my girl holding hands with another man,' said Harvey.

'You know full well I didn't mean it like that. We're comrades. We've been through a lot together. Besides, I am not Leo's girl. I have it on excellent authority he is dating a wispy blonde called Lucy.'

Harvey gave me an odd look, but sat down again. 'How did you both end up here?'

Behind us, Leo had come back and started to noisily make himself a sandwich. 'We both thought we were heading for Scotland. Fitzroy had had us delivered to the train. We'd been staying with him and Mother. Did I tell you he married my mother?'

'Yes, and took her to live in a castle, I expect.'

'Yes,' I said.

'Really?' said Harvey with his eyes bulging. 'A real castle? Are you a princess now or something?'

'I'm an "or something",' I said smiling. 'My mother's a duchess, but it doesn't change who I am. You have to be a blood relative to have a title.'

'Does this mean Fitzroy is a duke?' asked Harvey. His voice ended in a squeaky tone of surprise.

'Are you really surprised?' I said. 'My stepfather always gets what he wants.'

'But he put you on the wrong train?'

'No, he'd made other arrangements. These arrangements. For us to end up in London.'

'Why?' asked Harvey.

'That's a very good question,' I said. 'A very good question indeed.'

Chapter Twenty

Harvey left not long after Leo sat down at the table and began to eat his sandwich angrily. I hadn't known it was possible to eat a sandwich with malice, but Leo achieved this. It was annoying because I wanted to talk to Harvey about what he'd seen in the building. Once he'd left I asked Leo if there was a problem.

'Other than my coming home tired and hungry to discover you'd given my dinner to someone else.'

Ash took this moment to reappear and jump on to Leo's lap. He immediately sneezed.

'Are you allergic to cats?'

'I have no idea. I've only ever had—' He sneezed again.

'Dogs,' I finished for him. 'Ash, come over here.' To my surprise the cat came and curled up on my lap. 'I'm sorry about dinner,' I said. 'We did leave some for you, but when you didn't turn up—'

'You ate it,' said Leo. 'I suppose that's fair enough. I might have done the same. I was more annoyed seeing you with Harvey. Your stepfather asked me to keep him away from you.'

'He what?'

'As I thought we were going to the SEO training house I didn't think that would be a problem, but if you think he always knew where we would end up, I suppose he might have had an operational reason.'

'Oh God,' I said, burying my head in my hands. 'Nothing is ever straightforward with that man. Just for once I'd like someone to give me my mission in honest and simple language.'

'You mean you don't know if you're working for him at the moment?'

'I'm always working for him,' I said. 'Even when I'm working for someone else.'

'Am I working for him?' asked Leo.

'I haven't the faintest idea,' I said. 'Can you see Fitzroy getting into the movies? No, wait. Don't answer that.'

I got up and made some coffee. 'Have you seen Rafe Warren recently?'

Leo looked up startled. 'Why on earth would you ask me that?'

'It's a simple question,' I said.

'It's not one I can answer,' said Leo. 'Sorry, Hope.'

'Well, at least can I keep the dress?'

'Dress? Oh that. Certainly. Lucy would be swallowed by it.' Leo flinched. He must have read my expression. 'Are you training tonight? If there's a raid you will go into a proper shelter, won't you?'

'What else would I do?' I said, and went off to get ready to go out.

In fact when I got to the church hall all I found was a notice saying that due to illness tonight's session was cancelled. Perkins had told me there was some kind of a bug going round. It had laid his partner low on the night we'd gone out together. I stopped by the ARP station and was told I was welcome to help with any casualties that turned up, but I was not allowed to go out on patrol. It seemed either Perkins or Prentice had decided I wasn't to be trusted to behave sensibly under fire.

As it was, it was turning out to be a fairly quiet night, and I managed to get some sleep on a cot. At least no one told me to head down into a shelter, and that kept me happy. Petey came by with a message and waved at me, but he didn't have time to stop and talk. A thirteen-year-old boy was being more use in this war than I was.

It was shortly before dawn, when everyone was winding down, that all hell broke loose. I'll never know why the planes weren't spotted earlier, but the sirens had barely begun to wail before the first bombs dropped. I stood watching helplessly as the bombs fell across the city. The noise and force of the explosions had me dodging behind the sandbags of the ARP station, but I could easily see from the horizon turning orange that Kensington was not getting the worst of it.

Even with this being the case there was a steady flow of walking wounded seeking help from the station. Far too many people had presumed with dawn almost nigh there wouldn't be another raid, and had been caught out in the open when it began. All the injuries I saw were from flying glass and splintered wood. People who had been on the very edge of explosions. I wasn't foolish enough to think these would be the only injuries. The rest were liable to be far worse.

I unrolled bandages, splinted legs, mopped blood from minor head injuries, all while the bombs were still falling. The flow of injured civilians seemed never ending. Adrenaline and the shock of seeing so many wounded meant that I could no longer feel my own fatigue. Not, that is, until my legs folded underneath me.

'You're wrung out, girl,' said Perkins, who had the presence of mind to catch me before I hit the ground and became a casualty at my own station. 'Get some tea down your neck. You're no good to man or beast in this state. Here's a spare pair of overalls. Your clothes are torn and bloody.' I slipped behind some of the sandbags further away and changed quickly. He was right. My own clothes were as ragged, bloody and torn as if I had been caught in the raid. It felt good to peel them away from my skin. I used the less dirty parts of them to wipe myself down, and got into the fresh overalls. I threw my old clothes in one of the small fires we kept for warmth. There was no point trying to save them, and they might as well keep someone warm tonight. The sirens were sounding the all-clear, so I took my tea and sat on the kerb outside, sipping my drink and watching London burn. I must have nodded off for a moment, as I was startled awake by a prod in the arm. 'Oi, miss! You alive?' said Petey.

He sat next to me on the kerb, his face covered in its normal patchwork of soot. I wondered what he looked like without it.

'Having a busy night?' I asked.

'You could say that,' said Petey, pulling a biscuit out of his pocket. 'It's a bit covered in fluff, but I'll give you half if you want.'

I shook my head. 'Couldn't eat a thing,' I said.

'My gran says tea is too wet without a biscuit,' said Petey.

'I'm sure she's right,' I said, 'but I've had to patch up a lot of people tonight. I'm not usually squeamish—'

'But it's the number of them, isn't it? It's like the whole blimming world is bleeding. There's so much of it – that and all the other stuff.' He looked askance at me.

'Indeed, the other stuff,' I said. 'Smelly.'

Petey laughed. 'I can't smell nothing except the burning. It's a bad 'un tonight. I'm glad I'm done now.'

'Hang on a moment,' I said, getting up. I returned shortly and handed him a cup of sugared tea.

'Cor,' he said. 'Ain't this bliss.'

'I was afraid your biscuit might be too dry without it.'

Petey laughed loudly enough that heads turned. He lowered it to a chuckle but the damage was done, and we ended up giggling together like schoolchildren, for which he at least had an excuse. When I finally managed to wipe my eyes and was managing to drink my tea once more, Petey lowered his voice and said, ''Ere, miss, we're friends, aren't we?'

I almost gave a humorous response, but there was something in the way he had suddenly become tense that stopped me, so I just nodded.

'So I can tell you something I ain't told a living soul. I don't know what I should do.'

'Of course,' I said.

'It's not the first time it's happened, mind, so there has to be a reason. Cos odd things don't just keep happening on their own, do they?'

'No,' I said. 'What's been happening?'

'It's a bit scary like, but . . .'

He hesitated and I waited.

'Some people die before the bombs fall.' I must have frowned because he said, 'I wouldn't lie to you, miss. I wouldn't.'

'I know,' I said calmly. 'Tell me about what you've seen.' I was thinking that he had seen people who had killed themselves rather than sit through the raid. Although I hadn't heard of such a thing.

'You know how you get these half-bombed-out buildings? Well, when I'm running, you get to know the ones that are still standing. You know, less likely to fall down. Anyway, I was running through one, and there was all these people lying on the ground inside. I'd been through before and never seen anything.'

'Are you sure they weren't hiding? Sheltering there?'

'They weren't moving, and some of 'em lay funny like. It didn't look comfortable. And there was blood. I'm fairly sure they was dead. I couldn't stop as I had a message to get through – and they drill it into you that you have to go as fast as you possibly can. So I thought I'd tell them at the station.'

'Well, that is very odd,' I said.

Petey nodded. 'No bombs went down in that street that night, so I went back home that way. The building was all burnt out. Like it had been bombed, but it hadn't. It's not the only time I've seen things like that.' He took a big gulp of tea. 'I mean, sometimes I see people climbing out of windas, carrying a pillowcase or a bag, and I know they've been up to no good. I look the other way. It's a bit more than some folk can manage, losing everything and knowing there's big houses with . . . with, like, sellable stuff inside.'

'It's called looting,' I said. 'It's very serious. People who do that can be shot.'

'I don't have any truck with 'em, miss. I do me job. But the dead people . . . and then there's the gravedigger. I've seen him more than—'

‘Petey,’ said Prentice’s voice from behind us. ‘Come here, boy. I need you to run a message.’

I started. With all the other noise I hadn’t heard him come up behind us.

‘I’m finished, Mr Prentice. I’m right done in!’

‘There’s a war on, Petey. We all have to do our bit.’

‘Sorry, miss. I’ll see you later.’

‘Yes,’ I said. ‘We can talk again then.’

Petey nodded and disappeared into the station. The next I saw of him was him running off with his bag flapping at his side, one sock up and one sock down. It seemed wrong to be using children this way.

I was thinking over what he’d told me. I’d almost convinced myself that the people I’d seen around the table had been my mind playing tricks on me. I’d assumed something smouldering had caught. Yes, Harvey had told me about landing on a body, but he’d also been in a highly stressful situation, and I’d told myself it had to be someone overcome by smoke. But what if someone was setting fires to cover up murders? Blackouts and bomb sites could be a good way to get rid of victims. You’d have to be sure the bodies were burnt. Then no one would look twice. I shook my head. Not now. Not in a time of war. We were all pulling together against the Germans. There had to be another explanation. Neither Harvey nor I were fanciful people, but anyone could make a mistake, and in the chaos that reigned in London, it was hardly surprising we’d got confused. As for Petey, he was a child with a child’s imagination.

Chapter Twenty-one

I had barely finished my tea when I heard the ringing of an ambulance bell. A moment later a vehicle tore round the corner in front of me. It screeched to a halt, and the back door opened.

''Ere, you! Do you know any first aid?' shouted a young woman.

I nodded.

'Well, get your arse in here! We're three nurses down and we're on our way to a bad 'un.'

I wanted to say I was so tired I could hardly stand, but before I knew what I was doing I'd put my tin cup down on the kerb and staggered over to the vehicle. Two strong arms hauled me in, and the ambulance roared off with me inside it.

'Looks like you've been having a nice quiet time,' said the nurse. 'I'm Maggie. Have you got any first-aid training?'

'Yes,' I said. 'This overall is fresh on. I've been patching up people at the station. My own clothes got soaked through.'

The ambulance veered sharply around a corner. 'Watch it, Gladys,' shouted Maggie to the driver, as she clutched on to a stretcher to keep it in place. 'Well, I guess you're not a loafer then. Are you good enough to triage for me?'

'Yes,' I said. 'I've been trained in emergency first aid for this sort of thing.'

'Have you really,' said Maggie, giving me an odd look.

The ambulance swung around the other way, and I barely braced myself in time.

'She gets a bit carried away, does our Gladys. Not thrown anyone out the back yet.'

'Always a first time,' I said, clinging grimly to the edge of my seat.

Maggie laughed. 'Makes you feel like you're really alive, doesn't it?'

I wanted to respond that I had until that moment felt more than adequately alive, but the noise levels were rising outside. Over the creaking and frankly alarming squeaking of the ambulance's axles, we could hear shouts and screams from all around us, and the occasional crash of falling masonry.

'What's the bad one?' I managed to shout.

'Unexploded bomb exploded,' said Maggie. 'Got a lot of us!'

'Out!' yelled Gladys as she hauled on the brake, and I swear the ambulance fishtailed.

Maggie and I jumped out. Maggie thrust a small first-aid kit at me. 'We'll bring the worst back here. I only hope . . .'

I didn't get to hear what she hoped as both of us were struck dumb by what we saw. The grey early morning sky was still criss-crossed with vapour trails of the departed craft and below us yawned a crater about fifteen feet across. Gladys had stopped some twenty feet or so in front of it. Between us and it lay the twisted shell of a fire engine, and another of an ambulance. Smoke obscured the scene, but an early morning breeze was already beginning to shift it. Behind us our ambulance moved aside for another fire engine to get through. People were already swarming across the scene, but lying among the debris we could see were the rescuers who had been first on the scene. Behind me a man's voice, roughened by smoke, yelled, 'Get the civilians away from here!'

'Get on it,' said Gladys, as she ran to kneel by the nearest body.

I moved on to the next. It was a young man, maybe twenty, dressed in a fireman's jacket that was much too large for his skinny frame. His hair was unusually long, and a lock fell over his left eye. His other eye was a startling blue, and looked far beyond me.

I couldn't see any evidence of an injury, so I checked for a pulse and found nothing. His flesh remained warm to the touch, so his death could only have happened moments ago. I had no idea what had killed him. I closed his eyes and moved to the next. This time it was an ARP warden. He was lying on his front as if he had been thrown forward. I wondered if the men in the crater had been able to sound an alarm before the explosion. They would have known they were dead men, but could still have tried to give a warning. Or maybe it had been too sudden.

The warden had a shard of glass some six inches long sticking out of his back. It had come from a windowpane. A piece of white painted wood stuck to one edge of the glass. From under the back of his helmet I saw a curl of grey hair. As I felt his weak and thready pulse, he gave a half-cough, half-choke. Very gently I turned him on to his side.

'It's all right,' I said. 'We'll get you out of here.'

His eyes focused slowly on me. 'No point,' he said in a faint voice. 'Goner.'

I couldn't take off his jacket, so I pulled the one off the fireman and rolled it up to wedge him on his side. 'I'm going to get the ambulance,' I said.

As I stood, his hand snatched weakly at me. I stood and ran back. 'Maggie, I've got a man who needs to get to the hospital.'

Maggie appeared from the side of the van. 'No way, love. I've already eight on board. I'll be back as soon as I can.' With that she clambered back into the driver's seat.

When I got back to the ARP man he was already dead. I was aware of the arrival of more ambulances and of more people helping as I worked my way through what felt like endless rows of bodies. No one close to the explosion had survived. I learned later about internal injuries due to blasts, but at the time it was eerily as though some people had merely lain down and died. One chap, further out, had had his head taken clean off by flying debris. An enormous amount of blood spread out from around him, covering not only the ground but the people he was near. His wife sat next to him, shaking and making nonsensical sounds. She had no injuries, but had lost touch totally with reality. By now the wardens were marking people for transportation, and I put her down for the tea wagon, and one of the shelters for the bombed-out. I had to trust someone would take care of her. There were too many wounded for her to be taken to hospital. Besides, I wasn't convinced the doctors would have been able to do anything for her.

I joined up with Gladys briefly, who told me Maggie was on her seventh trip. 'It's grim,' she said. 'I thought I'd got used to it, but when you see people you know – every third body seems to be a rescuer from my section – then it's bloody hard. Don't think I will ever get used to seeing someone I knew dead.'

'You don't want to,' I said.

'Maybe not,' said Gladys, 'but I'd like to turn off my feelings right now. Listen, the fire service has said the buildings on the right are stable. I'm going to start making my way through. Want to come with me? It'll be easier with two if we have to pull anyone out.'

'Won't the fire service have done that?'

Gladys shook her head. 'There's fires cropping up everywhere tonight. They want us and the home guard to clear out the wounded.'

We were put with a pair of old servicemen, Syd and George. Syd kept muttering, 'It ain't right. Killing civilians. It ain't right. This isn't war. This is slaughter.' I paid no heed as we clambered down into the cellar of the first building. It wasn't doing me any harm, and if talking to himself got him through this then who was I to complain? George didn't take it so well. He kept telling him to shut up. Gladys winked at me, and I found myself suppressing a smile. It was like a vaudeville comedy duo act. The first building was clear, but I noticed a beam against a cellar door. 'We should check behind that,' I said. George and Syd complained even more as we heaved it away. Inside was a middle-aged woman, pinned under a pile of wood.

'Thank goodness,' she said. 'I kept calling, but no one could hear me. I thought I'd be safe here. John put a new heavy door on before he went off. Said it would protect me here. Almost had me killed. No one hearing my shouts.'

She rambled on and on in a cheerful voice as we pulled the wood off of her. Gladys was working at the end near her feet. I heard her sudden intake of breath. 'Go get a cloth. A big one from the house, if you can find it. We need something to wrap her legs.' I looked at her quizzically. Gladys was as white as milk. She told George and Syd to stop, while she did a bit of bandaging.

I found a tablecloth blown off on to a fence and took that. The woman protested it was her Sunday best, but I took it over to Gladys. It was then I saw that while one of the woman's legs was slightly bruised, the other had been severed at the knee. From the calf down it was still in its stocking and even had the shoe neatly tied, but it was no longer part of her. The pressure from the wood pile had suppressed the bleeding to a degree and Gladys now had a tourniquet on it. She wrapped the cloth around the woman's lower half so she wouldn't see and had Syd and George lift her on to the stretcher. 'I need to go with her,' she said. 'I'll be back. Have a peak in next door, but don't go in without me.' Her voice sounded calm, but I could see the horror in her eyes. If the patient hadn't still been alive I think she would have screamed.

I waited in the cellar with the woman's leg, gathering my breath, for a few moments. I looked down at the leg as it lay there. I don't know what I expected. But if it had suddenly stood up and hopped after the stretcher I wouldn't have been surprised. Being surrounded by dead bodies, by the maimed and by pieces of meat that had once been attached to a human being, gives everything a sense of unreality. My brain kept telling me this couldn't be happening. This couldn't be real. Suddenly I had to get away from the leg. I clambered out of the cellar and across some debris. It was grey and sharp and square. A larger building had come down. I was slightly below street level, and with my abominable sense of direction, I had lost all idea of where I was.

I came across a door that had been blown open. Behind it I could see a staircase going up. I made my way to it, thinking I could get my bearings if I went up to street level again. Through the door were the remnants of a grand stairway. I could tell by the parts of the ebony curling banisters that remained. They went both up and down. My instincts told me to go up to the street, but seeing how large the building must have been made me fear there might still be people trapped below. I headed down the steps.

A passageway ran under the house, but instead of being straight, it was now turned at an angle. Little bits of light bled through from openings in the ceiling, but it stretched off into darkness. I got out my torch and headed in, stopping and calling 'Hello?' every few feet.

Then, a few steps into the darkest part, my torch showed me the floor had fallen away and stretched down into an even deeper darkness. I stopped a few inches short, and took a few breaths. If I had taken another step . . . It was then I felt a hard shove in the small of my back.

I fell. All thoughts vanished into fear.

Chapter Twenty-two

I woke up in a hospital bed. I knew immediately where I was because the bed felt hard, and the sheets were shiny with starch and cleanliness. I couldn't recall when I had last had my sheets washed at the flat. I wasn't even sure if the laundry was still standing. And if there wasn't a laundry or a housekeeper how did one get one's sheets cleaned?

I asked the next nurse who came to check on me, and she told me I had a concussion. I said this was ridiculous and then was promptly sick over her and the bed. After they'd cleaned me up and moved me to another bed, I fell straight back to sleep.

When I woke again it was early evening, and the nurses were putting the ward to bed. A woman with a trolley was piling up empty plates with quiet efficiency. Nurses were tucking patients into bed and the lights were being lowered. I managed to catch the attention of one as she bustled by.

'Awake again?' she said. 'Feeling sick?'

'No,' I said. 'Where is this?'

She came over and took my wrist. Two fingers found my pulse. 'Ssh,' she said, and flipped up her watch to count. I bit my tongue and waited. 'A bit fast and thready,' she said. I peered up at her name band.

'Can I get something to eat, Nurse Hamilton?'

'I don't think so,' she said. 'I'll ask Matron, but I think she'll advise water till morning. Let your insides settle a bit. Did you see the lovely flowers your young man left?' I looked over at my bedside cabinet and saw an odd arrangement of flowers in a glass jar. It was far from being a professional bouquet, but the bright colours lifted my spirits.

'What did the doctor say?'

'He's not been on the ward today. We're a recuperation ward. Doctors come by when they can.'

'Of course,' I said. 'It's just that I'm very hungry. Isn't a good appetite a sign of recovery?'

Hamilton gave a brief smile, but her eyes were steely. My stomach gave a hopeful growl. The nurse nodded to me and stepped away. I still had some hope she would return with a morsel, but as I watched the sky grow dark she didn't reappear, and I was left to wonder which young man had left my flowers.

I awoke in the middle of a nightmare when someone sat heavily on the edge of my bed. Masterton looked down at me, and for a moment I thought I was still dreaming. When she smiled, I was certain I was, but then I saw the smile didn't quite reach her eyes. I sat up and tried to salute. I wasn't in the habit of doing this. I wasn't sure I had ever seen Fitzroy salute anyone. I got somewhat entangled in the sheets. My limbs felt heavy and uncooperative.

'Settle down, Stapleford. I'm here to give you this.' She handed me an envelope. 'There's a travel warrant inside. And you certainly have serious connections as there is a leave pass for three weeks. If you're lucky maybe the war will be over by then. It's a much bigger deal than the forty-eight-hour pass that had been put aside for you.'

'I doubt it will, ma'am,' I said before I realised she was joking. 'I expect my typing pile will decrease.'

'I will ensure there is plenty for you when you return,' said Masterton.

'It was good of you to come yourself, ma'am. I appreciate it.'

'Yes.' She looked down at her lap. 'I've been hearing reports about you, Stapleford, and I don't like what I am hearing. You've got yourself involved with the ARP, and frankly you can't work all day and all night. I know there are some whose duties demand . . . well, more, but yours don't. They have help to do what they do.'

'You mean the drugs.'

She spoke over me. 'And there have been reports of you wandering around above ground during a raid when you frankly had no reason to be there. Can you explain why?'

'I was looking for Leo,' I lied.

'The major is more than capable of looking after himself. Or do you mean you have feelings for him, and in a rush of emotion ran out into the night raid?'

'No,' I said.

'Good. Because that would not be the mindset we need in an intelligence officer.'

This time I kept my mouth shut.

'Yes, I am aware that you work in intelligence. From what I can currently discover you have been placed in a clerical role as a working sabbatical after your last two assignments. Most of the details are above my security clearance, but I did manage to glean that there were fatalities among own during both missions. I assume your stepfather decided to give you a quieter role to allow you to recuperate.'

'I don't think—'

'It's either that or he used his position to place his little stepdaughter as far away from harm as he could?'

'You mean abused, and Fitzroy would never do that. Besides, I wouldn't exactly have called London safe.'

'Safer if you had stayed within that shelter he had built for you.'

'I'm sorry, I am feeling tired,' I said.

'Very well. If that is how you want it.' She stood up. 'Take care of yourself, Hope. I will see you when you return.'

Suddenly I felt all too awake. However, I feigned sleep, closing my eyes until I heard her footsteps fade completely. I had the distinct impression I had not made a friend.

*

Two days later I used the travel warrant to take me to Fitzroy's castle. I had finally been fed in the hospital, but the food was particularly bad, and I had been eating MOI canteen food! All the patients made a great show of saying how good it was. Presumably they thought they were showing wartime spirit, but I suspected the quality of the catering was of a level where they could, as the old adage goes, burn water. I was looking forward to some proper food at the castle. I knew the estate grew a great deal of produce. Although Fitzroy had barely inherited it, he seemed from my last fleeting visit to have whipped it into shape.

The taxi from the station dropped me at the end of the drive. I had protested I could walk, but the driver, once he learned who I was, would have none of it. I stepped out of the car with my kitbag over my shoulder. It contained a clean uniform and a few personal items, but little else. Last time I was here, both my mother and Fitzroy had insisted I set up a wardrobe as they did wherever they frequently visited. Mine did include evening dresses, stout walking shoes and the like, but it also contained climbing kit, black night-manoeuvre clothing, and various other spy-ish things. I couldn't imagine using them here, but it was a relief to only bring a light bag with me. If I was honest, I was still feeling rather out of sorts. I hadn't managed to see Leo before I left. But I had seen various discarded evening jackets thrown about the place. He was clearly burning the candle at both ends. He'd better not think I would forget that he had got me into trouble with Masterton.

I rang the large bell by the very large, and slightly intimidating, door. I rather think you have to be brought up in a castle not to feel a little awed. Fitzroy liked his family home, but he thought nothing of it being extremely large and extremely old. In fact, growing up in such a place could almost explain his preternatural confidence.

The bell rope had barely returned to its original place before the door opened and Griffin greeted me with a warm smile.

'Welcome home, Miss Hope,' he said. Or at least I think that was what he was saying. His welcome speech was lost under the yapping of a small English bull terrier.

'Jack!' I said, dropping my bag and kneeling down to greet him. 'I thought you would have gone with them.'

The small dog, who wasn't yet full grown, bounced around me. He alternately barked loudly and jumped up to lick my face. I was covered in grime from the journey so I wasn't bothered.

'I am so sorry, Miss Hope. It was like he knew you were at the door. I did attempt to close him in the pantry, but he is very wily. Please be careful. He does tend to nip when he is overexcited.'

I fussed Jack, who looked up at me with eyes filled with total adoration. 'I imagine he is missing his master,' I said. 'I thought they would have taken him?'

'There were concerns over the length of the flight, and his ability to co-exist with Egyptian dogs.'

I stood up. 'You mean if my mother had not interceded he would have taken the dog.' Griffin bowed his head in acknowledgement. 'It's very good to see you, Griffin. I'm not entirely sure why my travel pass was issued to here rather than White Orchards. I hope you don't mind me popping up like this, disturbing your peace. They're not due back for at least another month, are they?'

Griffin ushered me through the door, and insisted on taking my kitbag himself. 'I think originally,' he said, 'that the trip was meant to be of at least two months' duration, possibly longer. Communication between Cairo and here is much more efficient than one would have imagined.' He led me towards the main staircase.

'There's no need to show me to my room, unless they've moved it,' I said.

'You have been unwell. I shall carry your bag,' said Griffin. 'But no, the room you chose has had a fresh coat of paint, and the duke has had a small bathroom made out of the space by the wardrobe. I think you will like it.'

'Fitzroy has been redecorating during a war?'

'Estate people,' said Griffin. 'Those too old to go to war, and a number of rather nice young ladies, who have been learning all aspects of estate management.'

I raised an eyebrow.

We reached my room, and as he opened the door, I saw it had indeed been made over. It was much the same as when I had chosen it, but upgraded. Same style, same colours, but it was luxurious. 'I feel a little embarrassed,' I said, looking around. 'It's rather a lot.'

'People say many things about your stepfather,' said Griffin, 'but no one has ever said that he is ungenerous to those close to him.'

I peeked into the chic washroom. 'I suppose it's good that there aren't many of those or he'd go bankrupt.'

'I doubt it,' said Griffin. 'He is a remarkably rich gentleman.'

I felt uncomfortable discussing Fitzroy behind his back. 'Well, I hope I might get to see them at the end of my stay here. In the meantime, I shall be as quiet as a mouse and no trouble to anyone. I shall rest, read in the library, and walk in the grounds. When this horrid lethargy leaves me I am happy to volunteer to help in any way I can.'

Griffin put my bag down. 'Oh no, that wouldn't do at all. And don't even think of unpacking. I shall send a maid to do that.'

'I can manage,' I said. 'I'm only a little under par.'

'Actually, Miss Hope, you are looking extremely pale. If you would permit me I would like to examine you later – I have had my medical licence temporarily restored. It seems that the war has led to the short-term forgiveness of my previous misdeeds.' Which was a nice way of putting that he had killed a man he believed responsible for his wife's death. In his defence, he had surrendered himself immediately to the police. But the fact that he was free now was a minor miracle. And it could be due to only one individual.

'Fitzroy?'

Griffin nodded. 'Quite a feat. I am grateful. But as to unpacking for yourself, miss. You don't seem to appreciate you are family.'

'You don't have to call Miss Hope.'

'That is precisely my point. The difference in our stations is now much increased.'

'You've known me from a child,' I protested. 'Besides, I am not Fitzroy's daughter.'

'But you are Euphemia's and she is now a duchess.'

I sat down on the bed. 'I don't like this sort thing. Does my mother?'

'I cannot speak for her feelings, but she gives every appearance of enjoying being a duchess.'

'Does it mean I can't have meals in my room?'

'You could dine in the Great Hall, or, as you are convalescing perhaps the small red salon would be more appropriate.'

'Yes. Definitely. Will you dine with me?' Griffin pulled a face. 'You are more Fitzroy's major-domo, and an acting GP, what could be more respectable? I'd rather not be alone,' I ended rather pathetically.

'I don't think there is any danger of that, miss. Until his master returns I think Jack will cleave only unto you. I shall send a maid to run you a bath, and see dinner is served in an hour. If that suits?' He gave me a small smile. 'Actually, I am very glad you are here now. I have never seen eye to eye with either Jack I or Jack II, and this Jack, though young, already shows a distinct penchant for my flesh. You will be doing me a great service by allowing him to accompany you while you are here.'

As if there was a secret signal, Jack leapt up on to my lap, and curled up neatly as if to show he was the most perfectly behaved dog in the world.

Once I had bathed and dressed, I went down to the red salon, where I found Griffin waiting with the oddest look on his face. 'Is something wrong?' I asked, my heart racing. 'Are they in trouble?'

'Not at all,' said Griffin. 'I have just received a telegram informing me that the duke and duchess will be back at the castle much earlier than expected.'

Chapter Twenty-three

By the time my mother and her husband arrived I was looking and feeling very much better. Apart from a certain queasiness when I woke, a hangover from the concussion, I was only a slightly reduced version of myself.

I knew the second Fitzroy had walked into the castle. Although we had had no warning of their actual time of arrival, the entire atmosphere changed. It was like even the castle walls straightened themselves and stood to attention. Servants scurried everywhere at the sound of the honking of his car on the driveway, so that by the time he entered the hall and declaimed, 'Greetings, all! Your lord and master is returned!' there was a long line of servants to greet him. However, he ran past these when he saw me and scooped me up in a big hug. 'Little Hope! What have you been up to?' he said. For a moment I was enclosed in a very masculine embrace, smelling of cologne and tweed. It felt enormously comforting and safe. But he put me down before I could answer and went back to the servants. Whereupon he greeted them all by name, made some joke or complimented them on looking after the estate. Each and every one of them displayed an almost slavish affection. Fitzroy, loud as he was, always treated people with the respect due to them, regardless of station and, of course, he would have no one on his staff who wasn't excellent.

I was looking for my mother when she appeared by my side. She didn't embrace me like Fitzroy, but took both my hands. 'I am so glad to see you,' she said. 'I understand we will have two weeks together?'

'Slightly longer, if I take all my leave.'

'You'll go back when you are fully recovered,' said my mother, 'no earlier and no later.' She smiled warmly at me. 'Shall we go in and find some coffee?' she suggested. 'Eric very much enjoys being a duke. He is devoted to the various duties. I, on the other hand, feel a little fatigued after the journey, and I shall speak to the servants later. Besides,' she looked over her shoulder, 'I feel they have had more than enough ducal attention for the present. He's rather like an over-friendly bouncy tiger, isn't he?'

'He's certainly full of energy,' I said.

'He's glad to be home,' said my mother. 'It was not a wholly successful trip. Ah, here he comes. Make time to speak with me in private later, please, Hope. Now shh!'

Fitzroy's expression changed to one of concern when he saw my mother. 'You should not be standing, Alice.' He looked around. 'Where is the housekeeper? She needs to take you to your room.'

'I want my coat taken and I want coffee,' said my mother firmly.

Fitzroy looked for a moment as if he would argue, but he capitulated with grace and took my mother's coat. 'Your mother has been feeling a bit under the weather,' he said. 'Cairo did not agree with her – well, either of us.'

'I quite liked Cairo,' said my mother. 'It was full of the most interesting people. Work out there is very different.'

'An unholy combination of fantasy and butchery,' said Fitzroy as he took my mother's arm. 'Red salon? Coffee? Cake? Come with us, Hope!'

It was definitely a command and I followed obediently in their wake, while Fitzroy called out what sounded very much like military commands to his staff, except he added 'please' to them. My head was spinning. Clearly they, or Fitzroy, were going to ask me what I had been up to, and I had no idea who I was talking to – my commanding officer or my stepfather. It didn't help one bit that my mother always called Fitzroy by his real name, Eric, and he in turn preferred to call her by her spy moniker, Alice. At least neither of them had started using my moniker, which I truly hated. I decided as I was out of uniform I was stepdaughter rather than wayward subordinate.

Once coffee was poured, and Fitzroy had fussed over my mother to the extent that she threatened to slap him if he didn't stop, he turned his attention back to me. 'Can't get used to your mother being ill,' he said. 'She's always fighting fit.' He gave a wry smile. 'Literally.'

'I will let Griffin check me over later.'

'Pah! We need to get a decent London doctor for you!'

'There's a war going on, Eric. Griffin will do in the first instance. So, Hope, how are things with you?'

I realised then that I was being used as a deflective shield by both of them. It didn't make me doubt their affection. In fact, in an odd sort of way it made me feel more at home. It reminded me of my childhood growing up in their world.

'London is terribly affected by the Blitz,' I said, joining in the deflection game. 'I don't know how the people in the East End keep going.'

'I've read some reports,' said my mother. 'I should have more waiting for me here. But the very fact that the newspapers are having both their copy and photographs so heavily censored made me fear the worst.'

'That's the new Ministry of Information,' said Fitzroy. 'Part of the reason I got Hope in there. I want eyes and ears—'

'Everywhere,' said my mother. 'I am aware.' She looked at me. 'Counter-espionage has never been so important,' she said. 'We will win this war only if we keep up the morale of the people, and our enemies know this. A panicking public would topple the government and force surrender.'

'Unthinkable,' said Fitzroy, crunching a shortbread biscuit with such ferocity that crumbs went everywhere. He swept the offending crumbs off himself with angry flicks of his hand. He reminded me of a big cat. I wondered why I had never seen it before.

'Right,' he said, getting up, 'we'll have plenty of time for chat later. Alice, you need your rest. Don't argue! You've had your coffee. Go and lie down. I shall amuse myself by combing through a junior officer's verbal report.'

'He means you, dear,' said my mother, rising. 'Don't let him bully you.'

'I wouldn't bully Hope!' exclaimed my stepfather.

Mother left without reply, but she winked at me as she passed by.

'Let's adjourn to my office,' said Fitzroy. 'It has thicker walls. I've ordered them to light a fire and bring sandwiches. It must still be hours till dinner.'

'At least two,' I said, and watched him wince.

One of the few things Fitzroy and I had in common was our appetite. Although on him, it never seemed to show in his waistline. Mine was less forgiving. Two beef and mustard sandwiches in, I asked, 'Mother doesn't look ill. Is it serious?'

'I shouldn't think so,' said Fitzroy. 'But I'm not taking any chances. As soon as I noticed she was not her usual self I made arrangements to get home as fast as we could.' He paused. 'It's perfectly true what she said about me not getting on with people out there. Your mother has a more stoic attitude to war. She says I'm a romantic. The only hurtful thing I can think that she's said to me since we married.'

'What does that mean?'

'I suppose,' began Fitzroy. He broke off to examine his sandwich. 'What's in this? Cheese and pickle? I hope it's got relish.' He bit into it. 'Hmm. Yes. Nothing beats a good Gentleman's Relish. I should have ordered beers with this. Do you want a beer?'

'I'd rather have tea.'

Fitzroy rang the bell and gave the order. 'So what's this I hear about you not using the shelter I set up for you? And I hear you've got some older man tagging along after you. Apparently, you've fallen in with the filming crowd, and then there's some rumour you've joined the ARP. Are you really writing the new propaganda movies? How is Leo taking all this? Your mother likes Leo. You'd better tell me all before your mother gets into this.'

'It doesn't sound as if there is much to tell you,' I said. 'You've clearly had people watching me.'

'Naturally. You're not only one of my agents, but you're a member of my family.'

'Only by marriage,' I said.

'Don't be silly, Hope. Or should I call you Sunflower?' He broke off to crack a laugh. 'How much you must hate that. I didn't know Gubbins was so insightful. Oh, don't scowl, it makes you look like a petulant teenager. You look so much younger than your years.'

Attack, I decided, was going to be my only form of defence. 'Have you told mother about Rosa yet?'

Fitzroy frowned. 'Rosa? What nonsense is this? Your mother is the only woman for me now. You should know there will always be rumours about me. I have a large reputation.'

'Your first wife.'

Fitzroy paled and stood up.

At this, the door opened with a maid bringing the requested refreshments. When she left, Fitzroy was standing with his back to me by the window.

'Who told you about Rosamund?' he asked. 'That was her full name. Rose of all the world.'

'Cole.'

'Ah. Did he tell you she was his sister?'

'Yes.'

Fitzroy came back to his seat and opened a beer. He took a sip from the bottle. 'You and Cole have clearly become good friends in my absence.'

'Is it true? About Rosamund?'

'I don't know what he told you. When I was – I think – twenty,

I married Rosa. Shortly afterwards I left on a mission. I returned some months later to hear she had been murdered. It's not the kind of thing they inform you of when you're in the field. They worry you'll take your eye off the ball.'

'Is that why you helped Griffin?'

Fitzroy paused with the bottle lifted to his lips. 'You know, I hadn't thought about that, but maybe. Both of our wives were murdered, true. I think more than anything I understand the desire for revenge, and of course it was an opportunity. But no, I don't think I thought about Rosa at the time. I'm afraid I've had to put the dear girl out of my mind. By the time I got back, and the police had failed, rather messily, to find her killer, the trail was distinctly cold. Of course, I tried to find him. I tried desperately to get justice for the poor girl, but I couldn't. I had to let it go or it would have driven me quite mad.'

'You loved her that much?'

'No. I was fond of her, and I thought we might be happy. Her father was a senior officer in the department, so she understood all about the job – not in the way Alice does – but she knew what it would require from me, that I would often be away and that I wouldn't be able to tell her much, if anything. She knew exactly what sort of life she was getting into.' He sighed. 'I cannot tell you the guilt I felt, still feel, that I didn't protect her. She entrusted herself to me and I let her down in the worst way possible.' He took a breath. 'Have I already said how much I dislike your friendship with Cole? He's a cunning beast and he will do anything to hurt me. You must be very careful around him.'

'He told me he was trying to hurt you through me, but he has recognised that I am a significant asset to the department. He thinks I am like him.'

'Dear God, I hope not.'

'He let me use his sniper rifle. He says I have an aptitude.'

'Thankfully, long gone are the days when one's fundamental training was to be an assassin.'

'Like you?'

'I have no intention of repeating myself,' said Fitzroy, and this time there was steel in his voice.

'Is my mother in danger because of you?'

'If Germany had any idea of your mother's abilities and fortitude they'd surrender now.' He smiled. 'Your mother is capable of looking after herself if she has to. Rosa was not. She was a sweet, gentle girl, who had been trained to be a nice little wife to some fortunate gentleman. What made her different was that she was also intelligent. Her wit could be razor sharp, but her family never saw her in that light. I did. We would have been happy. At least I think I could have made her happy. Now, with your mother it's quite different. As you know, and perhaps now understand why, I've had many lovers during my life. But no one has ever come within a mile of what I feel for Alice. She is without doubt the love of my life – and I have enough experience, you can be assured, to know.'

'The only night I spent in the shelter below the flat,' I said, returning honesty for honesty, 'I thought I would go mad. I could hardly bear it. The sound of the bombs outside. The earth shaken loose from the walls. The feeling of powerlessness. Knowing that it was possible I could be buried alive. Having to stay there—'

'While you were under attack?' said Fitzroy. 'I can understand that feeling, but not why it was so extreme. Was Leo there?'

'He went to sleep.'

'And they say chivalry is dead. I will have to think about why your response was so intense, and we will then come up with a solution. Having you as a rogue ARP warden who goes in alone to bombed-out buildings, is not an option. So far I've managed to keep that report off your mother's desk, but if she sees it we will both be for it. That kind of wanton self-endangerment is not on, Hope. Do you understand?'

Chapter Twenty-four

The conversation I had later that night, after dinner with my mother, was even more disturbing, but for reasons I couldn't ever have imagined. I was summoned to her bedroom. I knocked on the door.

'It's all right, Hope,' said my mother's voice. 'You can come in.'

What had been the duchess's bedroom, doubtlessly for generations, had become a working office. My mother was seated at a round table covered with files. The grand canopied bed had been pushed into a corner. My mother gestured for me to draw up a seat near her. 'It's all right. We don't sleep in here,' she said. 'It's a lovely room with lots of light, and of course there is the safe his father put in for the late duchess's jewels. It comes in very handy for reports.'

'I thought you would share an office?'

'Like when he was at White Orchards? Oh, that was far too difficult. I like to concentrate. Eric is very distracting. And this way the servants understand why we share the same bedroom. It's really not the done thing in these exalted circles, but Eric and I wouldn't have it any other way.'

I poured myself a cup of tea, leaning over the table to mask my reddened face.

'Oh, Hope, don't be prudish,' said my mother. 'It's this sort of thing I wanted to talk to you about. Do you have a lover?'

'Mother!'

'It's perfectly fine if you don't want to tell me. Although I did rather like Leo. I thought he would suit you. Intelligent, gentlemanly without being too . . . you know what I mean, and at heart the kind of man who both respects women and wants to look after them. And believe me, there are times when we all want to be looked after.' At this point she whipped a handkerchief from her sleeve and had to dab at her eyes.

'Should I get Fitzroy,' I asked, half-rising in my seat.

'There is no need to panic. I am a little emotional at present. I know you know how to take care of yourself, but this dreadful war makes everything uncertain, doesn't it? I wanted to say that if you fell in love I wouldn't judge you if you took things further than girls in my day did.' She looked away, and said, half to herself, 'When things are very dark I can't believe it is ever wrong to reach out for love.'

'I've never seen you cry before – except when . . .'

'Your father died. Of course. It's what persuaded Eric to come back, I think. I burst into tears in Cairo and couldn't tell him why. Scared the life out of the poor man. I'm not a crier.'

'No.'

'But,' she reached out her hand to grasp mine, 'the thing is, I started being sick in Cairo. I thought it was the water, or the food. I can't say foreign food had ever troubled me before, but I am getting older. But then I realised I only felt sick in the morning, and I'd missed my menses. I thought I was coming to that time of life, but there was a little voice inside that wondered if I might be pregnant.'

'No!' I said.

'Don't sound so horrified. It is a natural course of events between a husband and wife.'

I clasped her hand with both of mine. 'No, I'm not horrified. I'm amazed. I think it's wonderful. I'm surprised, that's all.'

My mother pulled her hand away to make use of her hankie again. 'Who knows, I might even get the mothering bit right this time. I know I spent far too much time away for work when you were young. Eric always tried to convince me I'd regret it. But I didn't feel, at the time, that I could allow myself to become smaller again – to live an entirely ordinary life. Even with your father. I thought it would make me bitter and resentful.'

'It doesn't matter now. How is Fitzroy about this? I know he likes children, but I don't think he ever thought—'

'No, if he wanted an heir he should have married someone much younger. And it could be another girl. The ducal estate is obviously entailed.'

'What has he said?'

'Nothing yet. I haven't told him. I wanted Griffin to confirm it first – and he has. I will be telling Fitzroy tomorrow at breakfast. That's usually when he's most vulnerable, so I can see what he really thinks. I know he'll be pleased for my sake . . .'

'But you want to know what he really feels.'

'Exactly. But I wanted to tell you first. I was your mother before I married Eric, and it seemed right you knew first. I hope you'll want to be involved with the baby. I realise you may feel more of an aunt as the baby will be so much younger than you.'

'I would love to help out in any way I can. I always wanted a sibling, and I don't mind if it's a boy or a girl. As long as I'm alive I will be there for them when they need me.'

'Thank you, Hope,' said my mother, with tears running down her face. 'I needed to hear that. I'm in my forties, you know. So I won't be around for ever. Knowing you . . .'

The conversation became even more emotional after that. I almost cried myself. My mother opened up to me much more about my childhood, and even how much of an emotional support Fitzroy had been to her when my father's health started its downward path. By the end, I understood more. Not entirely, perhaps, all her choices, but my mother is an odd combination of passion and stoicism. She is far braver than me, but I could see she was genuinely concerned how Fitzroy might take the news.

That night I lay awake thinking about what I hadn't been able to bring myself to say. My mother's symptoms sounded uncannily like what I had been experiencing. It also made me realise my own period was late. I had put everything down to my recent experiences – except I hadn't taken into account my night with Leo. Was it possible that I too might be with child?

The next morning I managed to capture Griffin between tasks. 'Anything I say to you as a doctor is confidential, isn't it?'

'Yes,' said Griffin warily.

'Can I consult you? It's important.'

My tone must have convinced him. When I told him I feared I might be pregnant he looked somewhat taken aback, but he didn't criticise me. Instead, he conducted a gentle and thorough examination. At the end, he said, 'I cannot be a hundred per cent sure with the equipment available to me here. This would still be very early stages, wouldn't it? Certainly less than three months?'

'Less than two.'

'But,' said Griffin, 'I think it unlikely. You are probably right in thinking your body is responding to stress and trauma. If you haven't seen blood in two weeks then I would consult with a doctor again. To me you seem healthy, if slightly above what one might consider a good weight for a serving officer, but still in recovery. I certainly wouldn't want you to go back on duty yet.'

'Thank you,' I said. 'Please don't tell my parents!' Then I burst into tears for the second time this year. It was something of a record. Griffin was very understanding, and he talked very sweetly and in a highly embarrassed manner about what I might do to prevent myself getting in this quandary again.

'It was only once,' I told him. 'I'd seen some terrible things in the air raid . . .'

'I feel quite strongly that women should not be exposed to the rigours of war, but Herr Hitler has very different ideas.'

This made me laugh. 'You know my mother and you think women aren't strong enough to face war?'

'Your mother is the strongest person I know,' he said seriously. 'But I believe, and call this chauvinistic if you will, that women are also the stronger in empathy, and putting them into battle is wrong.'

Dinner that night dispelled any doubts that Fitzroy was not pleased about his impending fatherhood. Although my mother refused to have any, he opened the biggest bottle of champagne I have ever seen. He kept calling in servants to come and drink a glass to my mother's health. In the end he was still standing, but quite the most inebriated I had ever seen him. He even demonstrated, and at some length, that he has a fine baritone voice.

Chapter Twenty-five

In the end I did spend the rest of my leave at the castle. My period finally arrived a week late, and I was glad I hadn't mentioned anything to anyone other than Griffin. This was one aspect of my life I could control in future. To discover I wasn't about to give birth at the same time as my mother lifted a huge weight from my shoulders and I began to really enjoy being with my parents.

I did feel guilty that London was still being hammered by the Luftwaffe, and I was luxuriating at Fitzroy's expense. But I knew I needed to heal in mind and body. I spent a lot of time thinking about what Fitzroy had said about something triggering my fear of being underground. In fact, I had now been trapped twice in actual underground buildings, but that was after the fear manifested. Even I knew phobias were not meant to work like that.

The truth was that although we sometimes heard a plane overhead this little bit of the countryside was well and truly cut off from the horrors of the war. I foresaw that this would be likely to cause a lot of argument between my mother and Fitzroy. Both would want to be at the heart of the action, and from the way Fitzroy kept pulling out chairs for my mother and ordering her more tea, I could tell that his over-solicitousness was on the way to achieving two things. Firstly, my mother would shortly erupt. She could never stand being coddled. Although occasionally she did now shed a tear or two that always brought Fitzroy running to her side. She was grateful then, but the chair-pulling and cushion-plumping was getting to her. Fitzroy, who had only managed to work out that she sometimes needed him, was completely confused. The second thing he would achieve would be her determination to go to London and work from the heart of things. I didn't want to be around for that argument.

It was towards the end of my time at the castle that I awoke in the middle of the night with the strong sensation that I was not alone. I sat up in bed and looked around. I had grown used to the shapes of the room. My windows were completely blacked out, but light from the hallway tended to trickle under the door and give a subtle illumination. Fitzroy had told me he left passageway lights that could not be seen from outside on, in case there ever was an emergency. He'd also had ladder boxes added to all the bedrooms. These were iron chests that had a sturdy wire ladder welded to the bottom. The idea was you opened the window, threw the coil of ladder out and climbed down it. It all seemed very sensible to me, but by the time I left he was muttering about setting up castle wardens, and reinforcing the cellars further. No one was in any doubt that he was doing this all to protect my mother and her unborn child.

So you will understand that security in the castle was taken most seriously. The chance of an intruder was extremely remote, and the servants were loyal to the point of idiocy (in my view). Despite this, I was certain someone was with me. The door had the usual crack of light around it. I hadn't locked it, but it wasn't standing open. I reached under my pillow for the knife I kept there. (One cannot assume anywhere is totally safe and old habits die hard.)

My kitbag was standing packed and ready for my departure tomorrow. As I watched, it shivered slightly and then slid to the floor. 'Pepper,' I called, addressing the kitchen cat, 'you know you're not allowed upstairs.'

My voice alerted Jack who was sleeping on the end of my bed. He pulled himself up on his front paws to peer across the room. His ears pricked when I mentioned the cat's name. Pepper was his nemesis. Jack was strongly of the belief that any kitchen scraps should be given to him and not shared with a cat.

'It's fine, Jack,' I said. 'I'll get her out.'

I pulled the blankets back and was about to get out of bed, when Jack's ears went back as far as his anatomy would allow, and he bared his teeth in a low growl. I followed the direction of his gaze, but could see nothing but dark shadow.

'If there's anyone there,' I said in a steady, strong voice. 'You should know I am armed with a knife and know how to use it.' Much good that will be if they have a gun, I thought. I couldn't see anyone, but I still couldn't shake the feeling there was someone there.

'I'm warning you,' I said, getting up. 'Don't make me come and find you.'

I held the knife defensively and began to advance slowly towards the corner. I had barely taken two steps before Jack launched himself off the bed, and ran towards the shadows barking loudly. I sprinted for the light switch by the door.

But as I flooded the room with light I saw it was empty except for Jack and me. The door had remained closed, so if it was the cat she was still in here. I began a search of all cat-sized spaces, with Jack following me. He was calm now, and clearly thought we were playing some new kind of game. He didn't understand the rules, but was quite happy to join in by licking my face every time I crawled under furniture to check for Pepper.

'What are you doing?' Fitzroy stood in the doorway.

'My kitbag fell over. I thought the cat had got in. Is everything all right? Shouldn't you be asleep?'

'You sound like your mother,' said Fitzroy, bending down to pet Jack. 'Everything is fine. I was going over some files. I heard this one barking and thought I would check on you. The castle is very quiet at night. Sound travels a long way.'

'I noticed everyone does tend to move very quietly after dinner,' I said. 'I thought you'd been training them.'

Fitzroy laughed and gestured to me to get back into bed. 'No need. There are lots of old ghosts here. Not that I believe in ghosts in general, but the castle has a few residents who are less than corporeal. As far as I know, they've only ever been seen by family, but the servants are always primed. I rather think they all want to be the first. Besides, there were obviously dukes who were a little more friendly with the servants and tenants on their estates, so all of them hope they have a bit of blue blood. Seeing a ghost would prove it.' He sat down on the end of my bed. Jack snuggled up to him.

'Have you seen one?'

Fitzroy shrugged. 'On occasion. They just need a firm telling-off to go back to the crypt.'

'I don't know whether you're joking or not,' I said. 'Has my mother seen any?'

'I think your mother is much more open to seeing ghosts than I, but no. She's family by marriage. They wouldn't appear to her. Now, go back to sleep. I've decided with your mother's blessing that I will run you back to London tomorrow.'

I lay back down. 'Thank you,' I said. It would be infinitely better travelling with him than going by troupe train. 'I didn't think Mother would spare you.'

'She was the one who insisted. I'll leave this dog with you to scare away any other ghosts, shall I?' He chuckled. He turned out the light, and I half sat up to say a final goodnight, when my attention was caught by the mirror over my dressing table. I could see the vague, misty outlines of a face. 'Oh, very funny,' I said, sitting up.

Fitzroy popped his head back round the door. 'What was that?' he said.

I pointed to the mirror, but it showed only the reflection of the room.

'Nothing,' I said. 'I must have been talking in my sleep. I'm so tired.'

He nodded and closed the door. I lay awake, looking at the ceiling and thinking. Jack crawled into bed with me. I don't normally allow him to do this, but that night I held him tight until morning.

Chapter Twenty-six

'I have promised to drive reasonably,' said Fitzroy as I climbed into the car.

'Do you know what that word means?' I asked.

'I feel it's a matter of interpretation,' he said. He turned the car to face the driveway, and with one last look over his shoulder, drove us forward.

'She did say she wouldn't be coming to the window,' I said. 'I don't think she wanted you to see she was upset at you going.'

'I know,' said Fitzroy. 'I feel like a cad going away at a time like this, but we both need you to get to London safely.'

'How long are you staying up?'

'Only a couple of nights.'

'So this is very different from being a father-to-be who is being sent abroad to fight, isn't it?'

'Well, yes,' said Fitzroy. 'But your mother and I have always gone through everything together.'

'Oh, come on, that isn't true. You went off on solo missions when I was very young, she told me.'

'Yes, well, perhaps.' He sighed and settled down in his seat. My mother had always said he had a sulky side, but this was the first time I was seeing any trace of it. 'I hope you will be more respectful when we get to the city. You are in uniform.'

'Can I ask you something then? Something as my commanding officer – I have the feeling no matter where I end up I'm actually always working for you?'

'Correct.'

I told him then about seeing the dead bodies around the table and what Harvey had told me. 'I'm not sure what to make of it all. Harvey's could be someone overcome by smoke, and—'

'He saw it differently because he was panicking trying to get out?' said Fitzroy. 'But you . . .'

'Either saw something awful or I'm hallucinating.'

'Stress can do strange things to the mind,' said Fitzroy quietly. We had pulled out on to the country roads, which without their signposts would have quickly had me quite lost. 'I am worried about you. Your missions have come too closely together, and have been demanding.'

'Isn't that part of a war?'

'Your main use to the department is your ability to observe and analyse without getting hurt. You are not trained as an assassin nor as a soldier. You might wear an army uniform. You may have learned self-defence at college, but you have never undergone basic army training.'

'You mean I am only where I am because of you?'

Fitzroy turned down what appeared to resemble a forest tunnel. I was totally lost.

'Yes and no. I would not put you in a position you couldn't do. I have tried to choose operations for you that utilise the assets that I listed. Except you keep digging yourself further in, and taking risks I never imagined you would have to take. I would never stop you doing your bit for the war, but I fear you aren't as mentally strong as you need to be with the things you are facing.'

'None of the ARP or the fire service expected to see what they did.'

'That's different. You are a trained asset. I need you to do things for me that are vital to the war.'

'These are?'

'You know very well that I can't always tell you. Sometimes I need to put you in places or with people so you can assess them without bias – or without my bias at least. You are extremely acute. I'm afraid I need to call a halt to your ARP pretensions.'

'But what if there is something going on?'

'I'm sure you are more than capable of working out that the blackouts and the raids give people an opportunity to dispose of bodies or to burgle. The war has not stopped people from doing all the bad things they did before.'

'So what I saw might have been real?'

'Remind me when you saw it?'

I told him.

'Right, this goes no further than you and me, you understand?' He pulled over into a clearing and got out of the car and shone a torch around. Even when he climbed back into his seat he kept his voice so low I had to strain to hear it. 'There was an Operation Matchbook. You might hear about an Operation Matchbox, but this is different: Matchbook. Remember the difference.'

'Got it,' I said, as he seemed to be waiting for a response.

'Operation Matchbook was closed within weeks of it starting. It was to do exactly what you describe – get rid of bodies in the raid. Before you ask who, let me say undesirables. People who were a threat to national security. However, the operation got leaked to some minister or other and they put the kibosh on it. Undesirables had to be treated as we would in peacetime and incarcerated until the war was over.'

'Resources,' I said.

'Yes, from an intelligence point of view it is a drain on the country's resources. But to be honest, I didn't like it. It's too neat a solution. I worried about some departments cutting corners.'

'Would that be what Cole was doing out and about in the Blitz?'

'Almost certainly. The man relishes his role as an assassin.'

'But . . .'

'Hope, our world has much darker paths than your mother and I have ever shown you. After the war it will be entirely your choice how you pursue your career, but I wouldn't ask my people to do something I considered fundamentally immoral. Yes, sometimes there are people who need to be removed, but this should be the exception rather than the way of things. Operation Matchbook offered far too carte blanche a way of getting rid of people, in my opinion.'

'Is this why my mother calls you a romantic?'

'Touché. In part. I have been, in the past, shall we say, on the naughtier side of things, but I have never, according to what I believe, been dishonourable.'

'And my mother is?' I said, sitting up rather straighter.

'My wife,' said Fitzroy, looking me directly in the eye, 'will do whatever is necessary to achieve her mission or protect her loved ones.' He paused. 'We see things a little differently.'

'You discovered this in Cairo,' I said.

Fitzroy looked away. 'The point is, Operation Matchbook was taken down before your incident. Why Cole was still riding around London during a bombing, I can't say. He may merely have been enjoying the action. He is that kind of man. So your memory, and possibly your mind, is at fault, or someone is continuing the operation.'

'So I either submit myself to psychiatric assessment . . .'

'I really wouldn't do that,' said Fitzroy, his eyebrows rising in alarm.

'Or I continue to investigate as an ARP warden.'

'You will be unable to do that. You have been assigned elsewhere at night.'

'What?'

'Until you understand why you can't stay in a shelter, I'm placing you on night shift elsewhere.'

'You can't!'

'You are too much of a risk not only to yourself, but to those who might have to rescue you.'

That brought me to silence. That consequence of my conduct had finally sunk in.

'What you can do,' said Fitzroy, after he had let his previous comment strike home, 'is question Harvey again, and then very carefully build up information about other occurrences, if they exist, using sources that do not lead back to you. Harvey can help you there. Don't ask questions directly. If someone is still operating then they will be merciless in dealing with you.'

'You mean Cole?'

'I would have thought it unlikely that Cole would disobey a direct order. I may be wrong. Or there may still be a deeper operation going on. Whatever he is into I would stay away from him.'

I opened my mouth to speak. Fitzroy interrupted. 'Even if he has appeared to be friendly towards you, he is someone who always puts his own self-interest first. He is the epitome of ruthlessness.'

'But you were friends?'

'When we were friendly he was a very different person.'

He started the car. 'Now, this has taken so long I shall have to drive unreasonably.'

'And that bothers you?'

'Not in the slightest. But it may bother you. I want to get to London after the raids have finished but before the day starts. I have people to visit and faces to punch.'

'Why?'

'Oh, the general stupidity of some people. Can you believe they won't open the underground as shelters in case it disrupts the working of the city? There'll be no one working in the city if there are no people left. Bureaucratic idiots.'

Fitzroy put his foot down and the road began to rush past at alarming speed. He was, of course, not using headlights.

'Can you really see in this?' I asked.

'Mostly,' he said.

'How reassuring.'

He gave a crack of laughter. 'By the way, Hope, I didn't bring you anything back from Cairo, but I have arranged for a present to be delivered to your flat. I advise you not to let Leo play with it.'

Chapter Twenty-seven

I decided the best way to endure my stepfather's driving was to close my eyes. Much to my surprise I fell asleep, only waking when he pulled up by my flat.

'Out you hop!' he said, shaking me gently. 'Doesn't look as if this was one of the worst nights, but I think I'll have to spend more time here than I hoped. Don't be surprised if I turn up at the oddest times to take you to dinner and debrief you.'

'Is Leo working for you?' I asked.

Fitzroy got my kitbag for me. 'Not exactly. I thought he would be company for you. He would have been wasted in Scotland, and it would have made him even more neurotic. He clearly has the knack of being charming, so I pointed him out to a colleague and suggested he was just what they needed for their current operation. I believe he is doing quite well, but no real results yet. But then he's new to our world. You should let me know in a few weeks if we should keep him in counter-intelligence or throw him back into the general pool.'

'He outranks me.'

'I can change that if you want.'

'No, don't do that,' I said.

Fitzroy climbed back into the car. 'Which worries you more? That I might demote him or that I might promote you?'

'Both!'

He honked his horn twice and drove off.

It was odd coming back from the country. I'd been cocooned

in a safe little world where it felt as if the war couldn't touch us. Now, I was back in a city reeking of smoke and devastation. My side of the street remained unscathed, and frankly I still couldn't see why they bothered bombing Kensington at all. I could hear bells from fire engines and ambulances. I could understand Fitzroy saying he would have to be in town more. Although I doubted even he thought he could end the war alone, I knew his reaction to the ruin of London would be the same as my own, he wanted to do more to help.

When I walked into the flat, Leo was sitting in the kitchen still wearing his evening suit. I turned on the light, and he winced. His face looked haggard and there were deep shadows around his eyes. I walked in and put my kitbag down. My anger at him dissipated into concern. It seemed to be more than simply exhaustion. 'Are you all right?' I asked. 'You look dreadful.'

'I know. Perhaps I should ask for a pass to the country. You look smashing.'

I laughed. 'I slept all the way up in the car. I've also been so fattened up by home cooking that I had to get a maid to let my uniforms out.'

'Don't talk to me about food,' said Leo. 'I can't remember the last time I had a sit-down meal.'

'You could have made yourself breakfast,' I said.

'I barely had the energy to make coffee, and I needed the coffee.'

'I'll make something for us both,' I said. 'Let me put my kit away. I'll be back in two shakes.'

Leo practically dived into the plate when I set it before him. I had barely eaten one sausage before he was eyeing up my plate.

'I fed your cat,' he said.

My hand flew to my mouth. 'Oh crikey! I forgot all about Ash! How could I do that?'

'He's a wily stray,' said Leo as he used his fingers to swipe one of my sausages. I jabbed menacing at his hand with my fork.

'What?' he said. 'You said you'd put on too much weight.'

'I meant to miss . . . that time . . .' I said, slitting my eyes.

Leo laughed again. He stood up. 'It's good to have you back, Hope. Even if you are walking into hell. Your friend Harvey has called for you a few times. He seems eager to talk. Wouldn't say a thing to me. Anyway, I need to get in. Hopefully see you later. I'm not sure if I'm getting to keep you on scripts yet. And the raw dialogue I've been getting could have been written by a primary school child. Probably was, considering our budget.'

'You need to change.'

'Oh botheration!' said Leo. 'Thanks.' He ran into his room, the door slamming behind him. I heard the sound of things being moved around none too gently, before he emerged minutes later in uniform.

'Cap,' I said.

This time he swore obscenely before going back into his room and thumping around some more. He fairly ran out and was gone with only a quick wave of his hand.

I sat back and finished what remained of my breakfast. It was odd seeing him again like this. That we had slept together seemed to have left little impression on him. He was more friendly than when I'd been working for him at the SOE. He'd been very much the commanding officer then. But he had tried to recruit me at a dinner for the SOE only to be told it was not possible. Then I had ended up his adjunct, which had felt more like his secretary, and he had been on his high horse until I caught him with a hangover. We'd sort of rubbed along after that. Then we'd almost kissed, but Fitzroy caught us. At the castle I realised now Fitzroy had been watching us both intently. Leo had become quite distant under his gaze. I could chalk that up to self-preservation. But since then, we had made love and I had almost died – and he was treating me like what? An old but not close friend? A comrade? I hadn't expected we'd sleep together again. I might have hoped, but I realised we had both been under a lot of pressure, and it had been like the release of a steam safety valve. But somehow I had still expected more than this. It didn't help that I didn't know what. I grew angry at the thought that it had never occurred to him to enquire if I'd become pregnant. Surely the man should take some responsibility for that too?

I washed the things up rather roughly and chipped a plate. I was already missing life at the castle.

Fitzroy had given me sealed orders, which I now opened. They told me to report with the filming department at the Ministry of Information at two p.m. It also added, somewhat mysteriously, when I had finished my duty there I was to find room 7C, which was in Basement Three. I hadn't the faintest idea what this was, but I assumed it was all part of my stepfather's plan to keep me off the streets at night. As far as I was aware, Basement Three was the lowest level of the ministry.

The moment I came through the ministry's doors it felt different. There was always a charge in the air. People moved swiftly with the air of needing to get things done. But it was something more. I made my way down to the studio and found the cast in full rehearsal. Leo was sitting in a chair watching them with an expression close to despair on his face. I stopped at the back, behind him, and behind the lights, to get a sense of what was happening. I quickly realised that part of the problem was the actors were miming building an Anderson shelter, and they weren't very good at it. Too much time was being spent on the construction, unless this was meant to be a film on how to build one. I thought this unlikely, as the films were never that long. The script was trying to get across how important it was to build the thing, how easy it was and how snug it could be made. I walked up to Leo and tapped him on the shoulder. He jumped in his seat.

'Good God, Lieutenant! Don't do that!'

'The scene needs to be set more inside the shelter with the mother making it homely. There's too much earth being thrown around and too much poor dialogue. The little boy saying, "Oh gosh, Daddy, I saw a worm," is neither endearing nor useful. Much better to see him being happily tucked up for bed inside when the thing is done. You could give him a teddy bear. He's quite a photogenic child when he's not picking his nose.'

All this time Leo stared up at me without speaking. I wondered if I had overstepped my role. 'It's just an idea . . .' I began.

Leo leapt up and came towards me. For a moment I thought he was going to hug me, but he stepped back again. 'That sounds like a much better script, Stapleford. How long before you could rustle it up for us?'

'Forty-five minutes? Half an hour?' I said, guessing. 'I assume it's the usual two minutes?'

'Two and a half,' said Leo. Then he called out to the cast, 'Take a break. Back here in fifty.' There was some muttering and mumbling as the cast attempted to conceal their eagerness to get away. All except the little boy, who dug his heels in when the woman looking after him said this would be the perfect time to do his schoolwork. Eventually she managed to pry his fingers off the edge of the seat and dragged him away.

'Little horror,' said Leo, lighting a cigarette. He offered me one.

'I didn't know you smoked,' I said.

Leo raised an eyebrow at me. 'I didn't before I was sent here.' He looked less exhausted than when I had seen him earlier. Presumably, he'd managed to get lunch too. He remained one of the best-looking men I had ever met. I realised I was staring when Leo broke my gaze and turned away. He took a couple of drags then turned around on his heel. 'It's a pity you weren't here earlier. I've been looking at this dreadful thing for so long that I couldn't see any way out. No matter what direction I gave them, it turned out awful. I should have realised it was the script. Amazing how one simply accepts the lines that are written and tries to do something with them. It took you seeing the devastation to realise the whole thing needed to be torn up and started again.'

'Hang on a minute,' I said. 'I didn't say I'd rewrite the entire thing in less than an hour!'

'Hang on a minute, *sir.*'

'There's no one here but us,' I said. Even the lighting and sound crew had taken the opportunity to grab a cup of tea.

'We're both in uniform and we are on duty, Lieutenant,' said Leo firmly.

'Of course,' I said, ducking my head so he wouldn't see that his reproof had affected me so strongly. 'I'll get on with it now, sir,' and I scuttled back to my office like a whipped dog with its tail between its legs. Fortunately someone had filed a copy of the script, so I didn't have to swallow my pride and go back out and ask for one. I knew I was being too emotional. I put paper and carbons in my typewriter and pulled back the carriage return. Then I threw myself into the rigours of taming the monstrosity before me.

It took me one hour and ten minutes. The cast were back sitting and smoking on the set when I finally came out and began to distribute the copies. I handed them out in order of seniority of the cast. I had already comprehended the fragility of the actors' egos. 'One for me?' asked Leo.

I turned quickly, realising now I should have sought his approval before handing them out to the staff. As I did so, my left foot came down into a tangle of cables. They shouldn't have been there, but I regained my balance quickly. 'Sorry, sir,' I said, handing him a copy. 'Of course I'll make any changes you see fit.'

I turned away hastily, intending to retreat quickly to my office, but somehow another cable caught me by the ankle and sent me tumbling towards the big lights. One of the first things you learn in ju-jitsu is how to fall. This is the one and only reason I am not dead. If I had stumbled into the giant studio lights, the resulting smash would have cut me to pieces. As it was, I displayed my underwear to all present, but managed to avoid fatality. I stood up and swayed slightly.

'Bloody hell! How did that happen?' shouted Leo. He ran over to me. 'Are you all right, Hope?' he asked quietly. 'That could have been . . . thank goodness you didn't end up . . .' He yelled to the cast to take twenty and then led me into his own office, which was slightly further down the corridor. He had a very young-looking secretary, who he sent scurrying off for hot tea and biscuits. He handed me into a chair as if I was made of glass.

'What happened?'

'The cables. I tripped. I think someone pulled at them.'

'Some idiot who clearly realised they shouldn't have been where they were. I am so sorry, Hope. I will ensure the crew are censured for this, and things are kept tidier in future. There was no reason for those cables to be where they were except for sheer bloody untidiness. When I get those men to myself, I will give them a piece of my mind. They're not military, so I'm limited in what I can do, but by the time I've finished yelling at them they'll wish they'd never been born. You could have died!'

Chapter Twenty-eight

Leo wanted to send me home, but I told him I had another shift after dinner. I felt washed out by the whole thing. 'I don't think I've got the energy to go running back and forth tonight,' I said. 'It's better I stay here.'

I rather liked that he was so upset, but to give him credit, he was a kind enough man who would have been appalled at any of his cast or crew having such a near mishap. At least he had called me Hope when he comforted me and not Lieutenant. Of course, even in the safety of his office it wouldn't have been proper to hug me in uniform. Although I couldn't help feeling if the situation had been reversed, I would have clung to him like a limpet if he had barely escaped death. But then it hadn't occurred to Leo it could be anything but an accident. I felt Fitzroy was right when he suggested Leo was somewhat naive when it came to counter terrorism matters. I suspected everyone was, except for a small inner circle.

He did sit with me for some of dinner in the canteen. He was eating out later that night, so he heroically drank a cup of the swill that passed for coffee at the ministry.

'Going anywhere special?' I asked.

'Another party,' said Leo.

'Fitzroy told me you're not working for him,' I kept my voice low, 'but he pointed you at somewhere where he thought your talents would be appreciated. From something else he said I got the distinct impression you're still with counter terrorism. Are you enjoying it?'

'I would enjoy the parties or the film direction,' said Leo. 'It's both that's killing me. It's like I'm not expected to get any sleep.'

I grinned. 'Don't you know there's a war on.'

'Even during the last war they rotated the men from the front lines every week.'

'Are you seriously comparing drinking champagne to being in the front line?'

'No, I suppose not. But at least in the trenches the men knew who was shooting at them!' He got up before I could ask if anyone had fired a gun at him. 'I have to get back to the flat and change.'

'Wouldn't it be easier to keep an evening suit here?'

'Oh yes, then I would have no need to ever see my bed again. I think not. Besides, the car usually picks me up from the flat.'

I stood up so I could speak softly. 'Have fun, and try not to get shot! Thank you for looking after me.' Without thinking I gave him a quick kiss on the cheek. He recoiled in horror. 'We are in uniform,' he hissed. 'I am your superior officer!'

I thought about saying Fitzroy had offered to promote me, but settled for sitting back down meekly and looking at my plate. I did have a couple of potatoes left.

'Good evening, Stapleford,' Leo said loud enough for people to hear his stern response. The canteen was at the tail end of serving supper. After this there were only sandwiches and hot drinks on offer. Few people were still eating, so I was able to watch Leo walk away with a ramrod stiff back. He was seriously displeased.

I sighed. I wondered if I had done enough recently to be promoted. A jump to major seemed a bit much. I ate the last two potatoes wondering how the cooking here could destroy so utterly my favourite food. Maybe we should think about parachuting British undercover cooks into Nazi Germany. A few meals like this and morale amongst the troops would falter.

When I had finished and cleared my plate, I took the lift down to the Third Basement and went looking for room 7C. I guessed that Fitzroy was putting me at some kind of overnight intelligence hub. Maybe a place where reports from all over London were brought together, so a report could be awaiting the PM on his desk first thing. I only hoped my role in all this was not to type the wretched thing. It was a maze of corridors on this level. I did try looking for someone to ask the way, but most of the rooms were locked or empty. I did walk into one with a gigantic model of central London set up on a surface the size of a billiards table. Everything looked very realistic and made to scale. There were even little red buses. It was in a large room and surrounded by desks and telephones. However, there was no one present, and much as I would have liked to stay and examine the model I had an uncomfortable feeling that being caught in the room, snooping, would not be good for my career and possibly my freedom.

Eventually I found 7C at the end of a long narrow corridor. This did not bode well. I could hear no noise coming from the room or any of the other doors on either side of the passageway. How big was room 7C? I tried to imagine the building from outside, but I was so turned around I had no idea whether I was near the front or the back. Besides, they could have excavated what they liked underground. No, I would knock on the door and discover a bustling hive of activity where work of extreme importance was happening for the war.

The door opened on the echo of my knock. Standing in front of me was a man in an army major's uniform. He looked to be even younger than me. He had one of those well-bred faces that is pleasant enough if you are able to overlook the lack of chin. He had a lanky frame and a certain awkwardness of movement – like a puppy that hasn't grown into its paws, but far less attractive. His Adam's apple was bobbing like mad as he spoke, which meant that between some of the words he made an odd 'glumpf' noise. 'Thank goodness (glumpf),' he said. 'I was afraid you'd (glumpf) get lost. Have you brought your (glumpf) supplies?'

I was barely listening. Instead I was looking past him to a room that was so small it could have been, and probably had been at some point in the past, a broom cupboard. I could see a chair and the edge of a desk.

'I usually wedge myself between the two walls (glumpf) and get a bit of kip,' said the major. 'Nothing much else to do unless you've brought a (glumpf) book. You are allowed to leave to go to the (glumpf) latrine at two a.m. and five a.m. You get (glumpf!) five minutes. I'm afraid you'll have to use the men's one (glumpf). The one for women is too far away.' He opened a door on the right revealing a basic toilet and sink. It was one of those ones with the incredibly high cisterns. It was old and did not look to be either particularly clean or reliable. He must have seen my expression. 'We call it Old Sir John. You might have to pull on the chain a few times. Can be a bit fussy. So allow for that in your (glumpf) timings.'

'I don't understand,' I said. 'What am I meant to do? Just sit here?'

'Oh goodness, no. You're here (glumpf) to watch the telephone line. If it rings you have to answer it. It's vital the line isn't left (glumpf) unattended.'

'Oh,' I said. 'Will whoever rings give me instructions? Can I leave my room to carry them out or do I have to ring someone else?'

'Buggered if I know,' said the major. 'Never rung while I've been on duty. I reckon you get your instructions (glumpf) from whoever is on the other end.'

'But what's it for? Who is likely to call and about what?'

'No idea. Above my pay grade. If you don't mind me asking, how did you end up on this (glumpf) assignment?'

'I was assigned in the normal way,' I said.

'Never good. Better forgotten anyway, I suspect. I'll see you (glumpf) in the morning.' He pushed past me and walked, almost ran, down the corridor. He clearly couldn't get away fast enough.

I ventured into the room. It was slightly larger than the desk. There was a simple seat. On the desk sat an orange telephone. There was nothing else in the room. The door swung shut behind me and I heard a locking mechanism activate. In a bit of a panic I fiddled with the door and managed to work out that I could open it from the inside. It was set up so no one could open it from the outside. This made me think that I should have been given either a code word or at least a time to answer it.

As I sat in the little room, I discovered it quickly grew very hot with the door closed. It also currently smelled of sharp, pungent male sweat. From what the major had said, I got the distinct impression this was a punishment duty of sorts. What on earth had I done to deserve this? Or was it simply that Fitzroy had been determined to keep me away from the raids and this was all he could come up with in short order.

I had, in effect, been kennelled.

Chapter Twenty-nine

When one is very tired it is surprising where one can sleep and at what angle. Overnight I managed to concertina myself into a position where I did drop off. I did so with my ear inches from the telephone, so there was no way I would not awaken when it rang.

I was woken the next morning by a rat-a-tat at the door. 'Who's there?' I called. I couldn't quite make out the responses, but I did hear a few glumpfs. I also discovered my bladder was bursting. I opened the door, and said, 'All yours. It didn't ring,' and legged it for the loo. Behind me I heard, 'It's not your (glumpf) time to use it!' I ignored him as I imagined most people did.

After I had seen to my personal needs, the fury that had been building last night flooded through me. It was all very well for Fitzroy to say I couldn't be an ARP warden – although whether is was quite legitimate considering it was in my own time and contributed to the war effort, I didn't know – but I didn't need to be shut in like some wayward dog. I would always have obeyed a direct order.

I assumed he had spent the night at his flat in town, but by now he'd probably be in his office. He was desperate to get back to my mother, so I couldn't see him sleeping in. He was more likely to have demanded his entire staff came in at the crack of dawn. The building this was in wasn't far away. I decided to pay him a visit and give him a piece of my mind.

I was storming across the road when I heard someone shout

my name. I turned to see Harvey waving at me. 'Whatcha!' he said. 'You look in an awful mess. You weren't caught in a raid were you?'

'Mess?' I said, blinking at him.

'You look like you've fought with several dozen rose bushes and lost. And your uniform looks like you've slept in it. It's not like you.'

'Drat! I hadn't thought how I looked. I can hardly go storming in and demand to see Fitzroy like this. He'll skin me alive.'

'Any officer catching sight of you like that is bound to be a bit shirty. Morale and keeping the side up, don't you know!' He said the last sentence in a faux posh voice that sounded both like some of the officers I knew and equally ridiculous.

I giggled.

'That's more like it. You had a face like a thunderstorm on you. What's the old boy done this time?'

'Old boy? Oh, Fitzroy. Just put me in an impossible position. I shouldn't give you details.'

'Yes. The less I know the happier I am,' said Harvey with a grin.

'Come into the park,' I said, 'before anyone spots me'. We detoured around the corner to the little park the local nannies had always used. Although there were less of them day by day as more people moved their families out of the city. Or at least those that could afford to did.

'Can't spend long,' said Harvey. 'I'm due in. I get a bit of flexibility, but I can't take liberties.'

I scoffed at this. 'You?'

'Nah, the people I'm working with are nice. I don't want to let them down.' He found a park bench and pulled me down to sit beside him. 'I don't suppose you know who I'm working for, do you?'

'No,' I said.

'Well, if you don't know there's no way I can tell you.'

'Oh,' I said. 'You mean if you're still on Fitzroy's staff. He did take you over as an asset, didn't he?'

'Yes, but I'd rather not be,' said Harvey with an unusual intensity. 'I'd really like to stay out of all that stuff.'

'What about the strange incident with you and the building – and the body,' I added when he looked a bit blank.

'Oh that. Smoke inhalation. I was in a bit of a funk. Not thinking clearly. I expect the same happened to you, with what you thought you saw. I mean it's not unreasonable. Every morning we're seeing bodies on the street after the raids. That's not normal. It's not surprising our minds are playing tricks on us.'

I leaned back in the seat and frowned at him. 'Really. You seemed intrigued before. You wanted to look into things with me.'

'Well, I don't, Hope. I don't think there is anything odd happening, and no offence, but I like what I'm doing. I'm working on the MO during the day and with the fire service at night – that's more than enough for me. I don't want any doings with the funny stuff you lot deal with.'

'Fair enough,' I said lightly. 'If you change your mind you know where I am. You came round to see me a few times, when I was on leave. Did you need me for something?'

'I'd heard through the grapevine you'd had a bit of bother. I didn't know it was serious enough for you to take leave until Leo told me. He didn't know when you were coming back, and I didn't fancy getting in touch with Fitzroy to ask him, so I popped round a few times to see if you were back. Leo seemed to think you would be fine after some recovery time. He's not a bad bloke, Leo, for all he sounds like a posh ninnie.'

'I'm fine,' I said grasping his arm in a friendly, sisterly sort of way. 'I'd better get back and get brushed up. I'm back on duty in a few hours.'

'Not going to see the boss then?'

'No. You've made me rethink that.'

'Good idea. The less you see him the less he can get you into trouble. I'm hoping if I stay low, he'll forget about me entirely.'

We said our goodbyes, and Harvey said he would pop round again when he had time. I couldn't promise to be in, but then neither of us expected to be able to make firm plans with the way the world was at the moment. I said he was welcome anytime. 'Cheerio, Hope. If you're not in, Leo's been stocking up on beer, so it won't be a wasted journey, and I like Lucy.'

He walked off before I could gather my wits to ask who Lucy was and what she was doing in my flat. I took a way back through the side roads in an attempt to avoid meeting anyone who would discipline me for the state of my appearance. It meant it took me longer to get home, as more than once I had to turn back because the road had been bombed. It gave me plenty of time to think. I'd failed to ask him what MO was. Military Operations? I could imagine Harvey in his element as a quartermaster. Although he was a fool if he thought that once Fitzroy had his claws into someone he'd ever let them go. He'd done Harvey more than one good turn – clearing his police record at least twice. I knew as far as my stepfather was concerned Harvey remained in his debt.

The entire side of my street remained standing. It was only as I finally turned into the road it occurred to me that I could have come back to find a hole in the ground, as so many others had done. But there the building stood, a little smutty, but still white in the sunshine. I noticed the blackout curtains had been opened upstairs. If Leo and I were out for the day we tended to leave them shut, to ensure they were closed by nightfall. I wasn't aware he had any time off. I trotted up the stairs and opened my front door with a cheery greeting on my lips.

It was at that moment I realised I was indeed losing my mind. There, sitting at my kitchen table, was Bernie. Her hair was dark now, but it was without doubt my very best friend, who was dead. I slumped down to the floor as the door closed behind me. Harvey was right – I was seeing things.

Chapter Thirty

'I have to say, Hope, I thought you'd be delighted to see me,' said Bernie as she held the foul-smelling salts under my nose. 'This is not the reaction I'd hoped for.'

'But you're dead,' I said, pushing the vial away.

'Yes, well, Bernie is dead. Such a shame! I always liked that name. I am now Ingrid Moreau. Come into the kitchen and I'll make you a cuppa. You seem to have a well-stocked larder. I'm afraid I've been nibbling, but I'm sure Fitzy keeps you well stocked.'

'But how?' I said weakly. I pushed against the door to get to my feet. 'How?'

Bernie, who was wearing a most becoming pencil skirt, slitted at the back, a severe white blouse and tottering heels, paused in her click-clacking across the floor. 'How? Why Fitzy, of course.'

'You call him Fitzy?'

'Well, not to his face.'

Later, when the tea was made, and she'd toasted some teacakes, Bernie explained more fully. 'As you know, a ruddy great bomb came down on our London place. Hubby dearest wasn't there, but he thought I was.'

'But you weren't?'

'No, I was visiting a friend. An incognito kind of friend, if you know what I mean.'

'Oh, Bernie!'

'Ingrid, please. So you could have knocked me down with a

feather when I came home and found a damned big hole instead. But you know me, I'm good at thinking on my feet.'

'No,' I said. 'You were impetuous. I used to be the one that cleared up your messes at college.'

'I suppose so. But since life has got a bit – spicier – I've had to do a lot of my own thinking. It was something about that time we all got shot at – you, me and Harvey – that sort of determined me to grab control of my life.'

'By getting married to an awful man?'

'I admit it wasn't the best step I could have taken, but it got me out of my parents' control.'

'Said the sausage jumping from the frying pan into the fire!'

'Honestly, Hope, do you want to hear my story or not?'

I put my hands up to my mouth miming dumbness.

'So, after a few pangs for my lost jewels and clothes, I realised what an opportunity this was for me. I'd already asked your step-father for help getting out of my marriage, and he'd said that I needed either a court judge or an archbishop, and he was neither. He was rather snippy about it. Though to give him his due, he did warn me against the marriage. Although I got the impression at the time that your mother had put him up to it. He was terribly self-conscious about it. I could tell he didn't want to do it.'

I waited.

'What do you think?' said Bernie, thrusting her hands out at me.

'I don't have a clue,' I said. 'What happens between my mother and Fitzroy has nothing to do with me.'

'You are so not good at gossip. How on earth can you be a spy?'

'It's a requirement of the job – not to gossip.'

'But spying on your parents is like covert surveillance. Besides, everyone does it.'

I shook my head. The thought of spying on what my mother and Fitzroy got up to frankly gave me the willies.

'Right. To continue, I had been dressed to conceal my identity anyway, so I high-tailed it to Fitzy's office, blagged my way in and asked if he could kill me off.'

'I'd love to have seen the expression on his face,' I said, suppressing a laugh.

'He really didn't tell you any of this?'

I shook my head again.

'His face went through quite a lot of expressions as I recall, but when I explained it all to him, he could see it was my way out. I don't think he would have gone for it though if I hadn't told him that my husband beat me.'

'That's what Harvey was afraid of.'

'It's true. I always fought back, but I was lucky if I got a scratch in. He was much bigger than me, terribly jealous and terribly controlling.' She paused for a moment to sip some tea. Her eyes sparkled, but she blinked back the tears. 'I know I can be flirty, but honestly, when we were first married I gave him no reason at all to be jealous. He was suspicious of every man I ever spoke to right from the start. I had to tell him at breakfast each morning where I wanted to go and who I wanted to see, and then he'd decide if I was allowed to go.' She gave a shuddering sigh. 'The thing is, sometimes he could still be the charming, attentive man he was before we married. Usually when we'd . . . we'd come to blows, the next day it would be all about making it up to me, and promising it would never happen again, but it always did. So I did start looking for love and kindness elsewhere, but I was terrified he'd find out and what he would do when he did. There had already been times I had been convinced he was going to kill me when I'd done nothing wrong. Fitzroy made me tell him everything, and he went over and over it. I think he thought I was lying at first or maybe exaggerating, but I managed to convince him of the truth. It was only then he said he would help me, but I'd need to give up everything I had and everyone I had ever known. I hated the thought I would never see you or Harvey again, but I couldn't go back. I knew one day he would kill me.'

I reached out a hand to her. 'I am so sorry. Several times I tried to see you, and to telephone you, but I was never allowed access.'

'You wouldn't have been. He thought you were a terrible influence on me.'

'Ha!' I said, smiling at her. 'If he'd only known how you behaved in college.'

'I did wonder if he'd found out. Searched out information on me. I suppose that could have explained it.'

'No, nothing explains or excuses his treatment of you,' I said.

'That's what Fitzroy said. By the time he knew the whole story I'd never seen him so angry. I'm afraid I cowered away from him. He said later that was what had shocked him the most. That I was afraid he might strike me. Of course, I know him better now, and I know he'd never strike anyone he perceived as being inferior in strength, and never a woman. He's actually quite a romantic, isn't he? I'm glad he has your mother to protect him from female assassins!'

'But why let me in on the secret now?'

'I'm going to be deployed by the SOE soon. I've trained as a radio operator in Scotland.'

'So that's why he wouldn't let me go to Scotland,' I said. 'I'd have recognised you at once. Even with your hair dyed. Looks nice by the way.'

'Can't stand it myself. Blondes definitely have more fun,' said Bernie. 'I don't think he would have told you, but he said you'd been in a few scrapes recently, which I took as him meaning you'd been nearly killed during operations. I got the impression that he felt he owed us a chance to say goodbye.'

'Does it have to be goodbye?'

'I can stay for a few days, if you'll let me.'

'Of course.'

'Thing is, Hope, the life expectancy for radio operators isn't expected to be . . . well, let's just say I don't expect I will be a grandmother. I think I probably won't end up coming back at all. Don't mistake me, I'm going to do my darnedest to survive, and to help the Resistance give Hitler and his chums hell, but I'm under no illusions about how dangerous this is.'

'You can still say no,' I said. 'I worked on the recruitment process. Right up until deployment you can withdraw, no questions asked.'

'Oh, Hope. Don't you understand? I'm already dead. I have nowhere to go. If my husband ever found out about me being alive, he'd kill me.'

'There has to be another way,' I said.

'At least this way I'll go out doing something that counts.'

'You've changed,' I said.

'Yes, I think I have.' She gave me a sudden radiant smile. 'Not that I don't intend to have a little fun before I go!'

Chapter Thirty-one

'We've got a guest,' I told Leo when I saw him at the studio.

He drew me to one side. 'I take it you're not referring to the cat?'

'No. I can't tell you here.'

'Is it Harvey? Cole?'

'I thought I had made myself clear,' I said. 'Sorry, Leo. I mean sorry, sir. I've had very little sleep and what's happened has put me a bit on edge. Is it all right if I keep out of the way and work on scripts?'

'It's what you're mainly here for,' said Leo frowning.

'Can you tell me what MO is?'

'Mass Observation.'

'Do you know where it is? I need to get a message to Harvey.'

'This all sounds a bit sticky,' said Leo. 'What do you need to tell him?'

'It's about the guest.'

'The one you can't tell me about?'

Leo ran his hand through his hair, ruffling it badly. It made him look both more attractive and less severe. I had a sudden memory of the time we had spent under the covers when he had been so sweet, and felt my face grow red. I stared down at my shoes. 'I need to polish these.'

'Yes, you do, Lieutenant. You need to smarten yourself up,' said Leo slightly louder. 'I don't care what is happening in your personal life, you have the reputation of the Army to uphold.'

Then he added under his breath, 'I got permission to take you off whatever you're doing tonight. I need you.'

My eyes flicked up to his face. It was his turn to blush. He caught me by the elbow, and turned us so the crew couldn't see our faces. 'Stop it,' he said. 'You can't look at me like that here.'

'Like what?' I said.

'You know damn well like what. We can talk over dinner tonight. We'll walk home together. You also need to go to costume and get a dress for tonight. You know the kind of thing. If anyone asks, you're going to dinner with your stepfather.'

'Is he involved?'

'Peripherally.'

'Isn't he always?' I said, and gave Leo a small smart salute. He gave me a look of horror in return. I headed off to costume where I found a dress that fitted me. It was silver lamé with slits in all the right places, and ample fabric to drape over all the right bits. I wondered if I would get to keep this one as well.

I spent the afternoon trying to write a script that convinced the average British person that a meal without meat was as good as one with meat. It was a nigh on impossible task. I heard the crew striking the set, and in short order Leo came into the room, shutting the door firmly behind him. He had regained his hat and his serious look.

'We are in one of the most secure buildings in the city and you can't tell me what is going on?'

'No,' I said. 'Sorry. It's bigger than that.'

'I wondered why Fitzroy didn't make a fuss about letting you off whatever you were supposed to be doing tonight. It is to do with him, isn't it?'

'Look, let's just go home, and you can see for yourself.'

He opened the door for me. 'Hope, you have to stop looking at me that way when we're at work.'

'How do you mean?'

Leo sighed. 'You look at me as if you know me.'

'I do know you.'

'Intimately,' said Leo.

'Oh,' I said, ducking my head. 'I'll do my best.'

We walked home briskly, but with a more than decent space between us. 'Don't people know we share the same billet?' I asked when we were further away from the ministry.

'I haven't made it general knowledge. Have you?'

'No, of course not. Besides, you're the only superior officer I now report to. The night shift duty has me on my own.'

'What are you doing on night shift?'

'I wish I knew,' I said. 'It's very odd. I don't know what I'm allowed to say.'

'Then you had better not,' he said.

'You're about to be let in on something that pushes your security clearance through the roof, so I can't think it matters much.'

Leo stopped and turned me towards him. 'I am?'

'You are. But I suppose there is compartmentalisation to consider. I don't think it does any harm to tell you that I'm waiting all night in case something happens.'

'Waiting for what?'

'I'm not entirely sure. I think if it happens I will be told what to do. At least I hope so. Anyway, let's get on. I'd like to grab something to eat before we head out tonight.'

'Do you want me to carry the bag for you?'

'No, majors aren't allowed to carry things. You know that.'

'Yes,' said Leo, 'but friends are.' And he took the heavy dress bag from me. 'I'm curious to see what you picked. Was it the green chiffon? That would have gone with your eyes.'

'I didn't know you took such an interest in dresses,' I teased, starting to walk again.

'Costume. I have to know what costume we have available. So is it?'

'You'll have to wait and see,' I said.

'Minx,' said Leo, half under his breath.

When I opened the flat door I was greeted with the most marvellous cooking aroma. 'This smells wonderful!' I called out. 'Do tell me you made enough for three?'

'Three?' said Bernie, popping her head out from the kitchen. 'Hello! You must be Leo. Hope has told me terrible things about you.' She flashed him a smile. 'Hope, you didn't tell me he was dashing. He's definitely dashing. Can you open wine, dashing major? I've got a bottle out, but I'm useless at opening them.'

The door had closed automatically. I turned to see how Leo was taking this. I'd heard the expression 'his jaw was on the floor' and while it wasn't physically there, Leo looked stunned. 'I can't remember if you ever met my friend Bernie?' I said, allowing him a little time to pull himself together.

Leo almost jumped. 'The girl who died?'

'Yes, that's me,' called Bernie, from the kitchen. 'I'm dead. I'm Ingrid now. Can you please open the wine, Major? Fitzroy said it needs time to breathe.'

Leo turned on the spot. 'He's not here, is he?'

'I don't think so,' I said. 'Bernie, do you have a Fitzroy in there with you?'

'No, but he did drop off the wine. He wanted to know how you had taken my arrival.' She came back through carrying a large casserole. 'I think he wanted to know if you were cross with him. I said you were too delighted I was alive to be cross with anyone ever again.' She gave Leo a dazzling smile. He hadn't moved.

'I'll deal with the wine,' I said.

'Is he all right?' asked Bernie.

'Just a bit stunned,' I said and went through to the kitchen. Behind me I heard my stepfather's name being uttered in a frustrated tone. As there was nothing particularly unusual about this I didn't see the need to hurry back, and took a moment to brush my hair and wash my face after opening the wine.

When I returned, Leo and Bernie were chatting away happily. She had turned the coffee table into a makeshift dining table so we could all sit round it easily and informally, rather than staying in the kitchen. It wasn't long before Bernie gravitated to sitting on a cushion on the floor. I was aware she was doing this to show off her long legs. Leo, from the direction of his gaze, was also aware.

I wasn't entirely sure how I felt about seeing Leo so smitten. But watching them I realised I would rather have Bernie back than have Leo to myself and no Bernie. This struck me mid-sip of wine, and I choked slightly. To his credit Leo did pull himself away from his new infatuation to pat me on the back and ask, 'Are you all right, old thing?'

Yes, I thought, I am very much the old thing, but I didn't care. Bernie being alive was all that mattered.

'I'm sorry, we're going out tonight,' he said. 'We won't be back till late.'

'Where are you going?' asked Bernie.

'A party,' I said.

Bernie's eyes lit up. 'Can I come?'

Leo hesitated.

'Is there anyone connected with Naval Intelligence likely to be there?' I asked him.

Leo frowned and shook his head. 'No, nothing like that.'

I turned to Bernie. 'Leo took me to one of these parties before. No,' I said, seeing the glint in her eyes, 'it's not that kind of party. The men get together and consider how best to help Germany win the war.'

This time it was Leo's turn to choke on his wine.

'Of course I know what you're doing,' I said. 'I've been involved in infiltration before. Although I do wonder who Lucy is?'

'My cousin,' said Leo shortly.

'Ian Fleming asked me to sleep with him,' said Bernie.

'I hear he asks everyone,' I said.

Bernie nodded. 'That's what I said to him, and he said that about one in ten said yes. I didn't. He's a strange man. Apparently wants to be a writer.'

Having established she was used to men propositioning her and that she considered writers to be very odd people, Bernie went off to see if there was anything in the flat she could wear.

'I don't have to come as well,' I said to Leo.

He had the grace to blush slightly. 'I'd rather you did. I don't think I can handle her on my own. You haven't told her about my novel, have you?'

Maybe, I thought, she's not his type, after all.

Chapter Thirty-two

Fortunately, my gorgeous silver dress was much too short for Bernie, and she opted for one my mother had insisted I bring, and which I hated. It was scarlet and sleek, and didn't suit my curvier body. On Bernie, of course, it looked magnificent.

In the car, with the glass panel between us and the driver, she reminded us, 'Do call me Ingrid at the party. It's probably best if you don't use my second name unless you have to. It's Moreau,' she added for Leo's benefit.

'I won't introduce either of you,' said Leo. 'I'm going to be too busy watching the reactions of the other men when I walk in with a beautiful woman on each arm.'

The party was again being held outside London, and it was rather late by the time we arrived. I was only too glad I wasn't on shift until the afternoon tomorrow. We drove up a long drive, lined with trees, until we came to a gravel forecourt. The house was entirely blacked out. I saw a footman come out at the sound of our car with a small torch, which he kept well shielded. This time we were deep enough in the country, and there was little enough of the moon, that without his guidance we would have had trouble finding the house.

I knew a few of the big houses around London because of my time spent on the debutante circuit with Bernie back in '39, but I had no idea whose house this might be. However, I knew a lot of the families I'd got to know had let out their London houses and gone deeper into the country. At least the ones who weren't able to join up had done so. I did wonder, though, if any of them would willingly let their houses out to a Fascist sympathiser. I hadn't had a chance to discuss this with Leo, but I was more than aware that many among the nobility had been on side with Mosley and his lot. My first – and admittedly accidental – serious mission had led me into their circles, and allowed me to realise that Fascism was not dead in England. I didn't expect to see anyone I knew, but I reckoned I could pass myself off as interested if I did.

I hoped the men inside were more interested in getting Britain and Germany aligned than trying to achieve a British defeat. The spirit of elitism and classism, even with a fascist taint, was alive and well in the upper echelons of British high society. If they were after a German partnership then this lot would be no more than a talking shop, full of people trying to persuade other important people, to get politicians on their side. This made them despicable, an irritant, but essentially harmless. If they were trying to engineer Britain's demise it was a very different story, and they were far more dangerous.

I should mention at this time I knew of the harshness of the Gestapo, but I had no idea that the concentration camps existed. If I had, I would have happily set explosives all around the building and blown the lot of them to high heaven.

But I didn't. Instead I gave my coat to the footman, and looked around the lofty, wooden-panelled antechamber where we had been received. I noticed where there should have been a coat of arms, but it had been removed. I nudged Leo and indicated this. He gave me a quick scowl, and held out an arm to each of us. 'Come, ladies, time to find the champagne.'

I took his arm, telling myself he knew nothing of my previous operation, and I really knew nothing about his. Fitzroy had said it wasn't one of his, so I supposed I should keep my nose well out of it. But as two footmen opened the door into the great hall, where the party was being held, I saw a vast number of well-heeled, black-suited gentlemen with young women flitting between them like gaudy dragonflies, and all my intelligence instincts began to itch.

A wave of warmth rolled over us as we made our way into the throng, and I was glad for the low-cut neckline and slits in my dress. A marble hearth the size of two men had a veritable bonfire blazing within. Along the left wall ran a series of tables laden with small bites of everything from lobster to caviar, and with tiny little sweetmeats for the ladies to nibble. The high-beamed arched roof overhead should have kept the heat down, but the blacked-out windows increased the temperature enormously. I could already feel sweat beading in the small of my back. I looked around to see if the guests were circulating anywhere else. There were several doors off the hall that were all closed. At the far end rose an impressive wooden staircase that divided into two and led to another floor.

Leo had released us to track down champagne. As I watched the stairs, Bernie nudged me. 'You said it wasn't that kind of a party. Don't look!' There were three couples separately making their way up the stairs. The men were all older than their companions, who were doing a lot of laughing and head tossing with their hair cascading down their backs. Not how one should dress for the evening.

'Oh,' I said. 'That's new. Or at least I didn't see it at the last party.'

'Naughty Leo bringing us here,' said Bernie with saucy delight.

'I'm not sure he knew.'

'Nonsense,' said Bernie. 'He's a man of the world, I'm sure.'

I felt sick. 'It's too hot in here,' I said. 'Do you think there's anywhere else we can go?'

'I think we should wait for Leo,' said Bernie. 'This isn't the kind of party where you wander off on your own, Hope.'

'No,' I said. 'But it smells awful in here. Sweaty and smoky and cheap varnish.'

Bernie wrinkled her nose. 'It is quite nasty,' she said. 'Look, there's Leo. Once you've got the champagne down you, you'll start to feel much better. I do hope it's decent – and cold!'

I took a glass from Leo and had to force myself not to down it in one. It was perfectly chilled and a wonderful contrast to the room.

Leo steered our small group to one side. 'I didn't know it was going to be like this,' he said. Outwardly he was smiling and had placed an arm around Bernie's waist, so our actions looked in keeping with the rest of the party. 'I wouldn't have brought you if I'd known. I'm afraid we're going to have to stick it out. It would look odd if I left now. The thing is, there are a number of people I need to talk to, and they won't talk in front of you. Last time, Ingrid, there was entertainment for the ladies while the gentleman talked, and then there was dancing.'

'Whereas this time,' said Bernie, 'it looks like the ladies are the entertainment.'

'Yes, quite,' said Leo.

'Not all of them,' I said. 'I can see Ottiline over there.'

Leo turned to look. 'Thank goodness. I can hand you over to her. I'd stick together though. She's prone to wander off in the middle of conversations.' He raised his hand to signal to her.

'Oh well, if we're being sidelined,' said Bernie, 'don't do anything I wouldn't do, Leo!'

Leo retreated as Ottiline approached. 'Oh, how lovely to see you again,' she said kissing me on both cheeks. 'Who is this?'

'I'm Ingrid,' said Bernie holding out her hand. Ottiline gave it the tiniest of shakes. 'How nice,' she said. 'So what are you two up to?'

'Leo Gordon dragged us along,' I said. 'But he's already disappeared. He said there would be dancing.' I gave a little pout.

Ottiline patted my arm. 'Oh, there will be, darling, once they've got all the silly business out of the way. Do I take it that politics doesn't interest you much?'

I thought frantically. What should I say. Leo and I had never discussed what role I was going to play. Before I could answer, Bernie spoke up. 'I like a man who has power,' she said. 'If they haven't got money then they at least have to be a political force. That way I know they'll have money later.' She gave a cold smile.

'Indeed,' said Ottiline. 'I can't say I've thought about it like that before, but I see your point. I take it that's why Gordon is here? Unless he's the go-between for someone else.'

'Is there anything for us to do while he talks?' I interrupted.

'Well, there is Dashwood doing his usual entertaining for the wives and daughters. I think he's doing a set in half an hour or so. It'll be in the library upstairs.' She sighed. 'I suppose I had better take you up to make sure you get there all right. Really, Gordon should be doing this himself. But then, as I told Anselm, hiring such a big house with so many bedrooms is such an enticement to the kind of man who attends.'

'What kind of man is that?' asked Bernie. She placed one hand on her hip and adopted a vaguely predatory smile.

'Rich and powerful,' said Ottiline. 'Just the kind I imagine you like.'

'Then you should take her to the library. I'll stay down here and mingle.' She drew out the last word in a highly suggestive manner. I looked at her horrified.

'Whatever you want,' said Ottiline. Then she slipped her arm through mine. 'Come along, dear. Let's find you a safe haven.'

Chapter Thirty-three

There was nothing I could do without causing a scene. I threw a beseeching look at Bernie over my shoulder, but she was already walking away, swinging her hips so widely I thought she was in danger of dislocating them. Ottiline had me firmly by the arm, so I had to go along with her. I chatted airy nonsense about the house and the gowns I saw. By the time we reached the library she must have thought me utterly empty-headed. If this had been my operation I would have tried to befriend her and learn some of the secrets here, but it wasn't. More than anything I didn't want her asking questions about me. Although when I saw Dashwood sitting in the corner in a wingback chair, smoking a cigar, with no care given to the books that lined the shelves around him, I realised he knew exactly who I was. Whether he had told our hostess I didn't know.

'Good evening, young lady,' he said rising from his seat.

'Look after her, will you?' said Ottiline. 'Her young man's gone off for now.'

Dashwood pulled up another chair for me. 'Gone off where, I wonder?' he said. 'I wouldn't have thought this was the kind of party to interest the major, and yet here he is again.'

I sat down with an exaggerated sigh. 'I don't know what he's up to. He asked me to come with him as a favour and promised me a dance. Last time it was a bit odd, but we had a lovely dance later. I feel less comfortable here.'

'You're soft on the major, aren't you?'

I shrugged. 'A bit, I guess. We've worked together before – twice actually. I like him.' I looked off into the distance. 'There was a pilot I was fond of, but he died.' I looked directly at Dashwood. 'I think in these times it's better to keep it light, don't you? And Leo is a very handsome man.'

'Does he also work in counter-intelligence, like you?'

I smiled, trying not to let the cold feeling seeping through me show. 'I don't know about anything Leo is involved in apart from the studio.'

'You're working in the studio,' pointed out Dashwood.

'Yes, because you got me the job. I am enormously relieved to be out of clerical. I owe you for that.'

'Did Fitzroy put Leo in the studio? As far as I can tell he's never directed before. Although he's been a fast learner, I'll give him that.'

'You'd need to ask my stepfather,' I said. 'You said you knew him, so I imagine you'll know what your chances of success are.'

Dashwood smiled. 'I do like you, Hope. I also think you are far brighter than you are letting on. You must have picked up by now that a lot of the people here have unpopular political beliefs.'

'As I said, I am here as a favour to Leo.'

'You're trying to tell me you haven't attempted to pick up any information for your godfather?'

'Stepfather,' I corrected. 'If there is something going on here, then I'm keeping my fingers out of it. It does no good to go messing around in other people's missions. It's liable to get someone killed.'

'Indeed,' said Dashwood. 'That would be my concern. If you are really here for no other reason, perhaps you can keep me company until my next turn. I'm doing a comedy routine tonight. We can sit and talk about what other films the studio should do. No problem with anyone overhearing that.'

'I'd be glad to,' I said seriously. And I was. I had said I had no intention of interfering with whatever Leo was doing and I meant it. I didn't want to mess up his cover or get in the way. As for Bernie, the fewer people who saw us together the better. She looked different, and no one was expecting to see Bernie, but if we stayed together it was possible someone might work out who she was. Even if this was for no other reason than we were clearly good friends.

I had qualms about what she might get up to, but she'd been trained by the SOE and, I suspected, to a degree by Fitzroy. Besides, I couldn't see how it was any more dangerous for her here than it might be in France. At least at this party she knew enough of the language to talk herself out of trouble. I had no idea what she was going to do in France.

'You're miles away,' said Dashwood. 'Penny for your thoughts?'

'No different to anyone else's, I expect. I have friends and family who are contributing to the war effort in a way that puts them in danger – and I worry for them.'

'That I understand,' said Dashwood. 'My daughter is currently overseas. I'm hoping she will shortly get back, but I worry.'

'What is she doing? Can you say?'

'She's a medical doctor,' said Dashwood. 'She specialises in what they call "internal medicine". I know very little about it. I would have thought all medicine was internal.'

'You must be proud of her?'

Dashwood picked up his whisky glass and took a good slug. 'She is the most important person in the world to me. My wife died during the first raid. My son is in the RAF. So she will be the only family I have here.'

'I'm sorry to hear that,' I said.

'By the time this is over, my story will be common enough. Everyone will have lost someone they care about. That's the nature of war.'

'Yes. I always think when it comes to war both sides have already lost. It is only left to decide who loses the most.'

Dashwood put down his glass and gave me a strange look. 'Are you repeating something your stepfather says?'

'No, my own thoughts only. I try not to guess what other people are thinking, and I rarely take anyone's word at face value.'

'A hazard of your job, I assume. So what do you think should be our next script? Should we extol the virtues of this awful vegetable pie the government wants people to eat. Have you tried it?'

I nodded. 'I have. And even made by someone who knows what they're doing, it's vile.'

'I don't think you can put that in the script. It would be unpatriotic.'

'It will also taste better and better the hungrier people get,' I said, looking mournfully at my empty glass.

Dashwood gave me an odd look. He summoned a waiter to get us fresh drinks. 'You are an odd young woman,' he said. 'So wise and yet so naive.'

'I will attempt to take that as a compliment!'

He smiled and handed me the drink from the footman's tray. 'I certainly didn't mean to insult you. Looks can deceive, and you are a very beautiful young woman.'

'Perhaps we should persist in discussing the studio,' I said.

'As you wish.'

Half an hour later, I followed him into a medium-sized salon, and watched him do a comedy song and dance act. He was surprisingly good. His imitations of Churchill got the biggest laughs. However, he stayed just shy of lampooning Britain's leaders too severely. Most of his comedy was observational, and could have applied as well before the war as now. I think that was the point. There were certainly no crude salutations to Germany or its ideologies.

It was towards the end of his turn, when he was singing a popular pre-war song I vaguely remembered, when Leo slipped into the seat beside me.

'Having fun?' he asked in a low voice.

'It's not my kind of party,' I answered equally softly, 'but Dashwood is better, much better than I expected.'

Leo nodded. 'I'd heard he was good, but this is certainly above the level he has delivered to me. I'd thought him rather washed-up, but he still has it when he wants, doesn't he?'

'It makes you wonder why he never became a bigger star,' I said.

'Luck, I expect. From what I've heard from these showbiz types, it's all about being in the right place at the right time. It's no wonder they're all so superstitious.'

'Has your evening gone well?'

'When I saw what kind of party it was I thought I was sunk, but it's gone all right. I am sorry about dragging you and B— Ingrid into this. I wouldn't have brought you if I'd known how louche it was going to be.'

'Ottiline helped me stay out of trouble.'

'I hoped she would. Where is Ingrid now? Powdering her nose?'

'I have no idea. She went off on her own.'

'And you didn't stop her?' hissed Leo.

'She's her own person,' I said. 'I have no authority over her.'

'God, I'd better go and look for her. You stay with Dashwood,' he said and left.

By the time Dashwood finished it was close on three a.m., and I hadn't seen Leo for an hour. Dashwood had gone down well and performed several encores. I was close enough I could see he was not only pale, but his skin looked stretched taut across his cheeks. His eyes had sunk into shade. He was clearly exhausted. Finally, he got the audience to release him and left. I followed him into the library, where he went straight for the nearest whisky decanter and poured himself a large drink. He downed it in one before he saw me. 'Did you like it?' he asked.

'You were very good,' I said. 'Most entertaining.'

He smiled. 'Still got it. But I tell you, Hope, I don't have the stamina. I am absolutely whacked. I can't imagine how I will make it to the studio in time. I'm meant to be staying here for what remains of the night.'

'Do you want to come back to town in our car?' I asked. 'It's big enough to take all of us.'

'Do you know, that would be awfully kind, dear girl, but would your companions mind?'

'I don't see why,' I said. 'Let me go and find them. You wait here.'

The party was ending and people were leaving, so I felt no qualms about looking for Bernie and Leo alone. I imagined they would be in search of me, and hopefully we would meet in the middle. Unless, that is, Bernie had got herself into some terrible mischief.

I was trotting down the big stairway, holding my dress above my ankles, when I felt a sudden shove in the small of my back. Instinctively, I dropped the material I was holding and attempted to roll. It was no good. I was too tangled up. I collided with one man, who let out a cry of horror, and tumbled down. I tried to shield my head with my hands and I thought I was going to be all right, if very undignified, when I caught the edge of a stair and went full force into the panelled way. I barely had time to think 'Damn, not again!' before everything went black.

Chapter Thirty-four

I came to in the car outside with Leo and Dashwood bending over me. I was lying on the back seat and they were standing in the open doorways on either side. It was extremely cold, and there was something foul in my face.

'Not again,' I said, picking up the thought I'd had before I lost consciousness.

'Is she awake?' cried Bernie's voice from the front of the car. She appeared over the back of the seat. 'Thank goodness. You gave us all a terrible fright.'

'What happened?' I asked. I tried sitting up, but my head throbbed with pain and I lay back again with a little cry.

'We should take her to a hospital,' said Bernie.

'I'm not sure there is much point,' said Dashwood. 'If the raids are continuing tonight I doubt they would be able to see her.'

'That's ridiculous,' said Bernie. 'Isn't there a doctor here?'

'I'll go back in and see if I can find someone,' said Dashwood.

Very gently Leo helped me to sit up in the back of the car. 'I think you're going to have a whacking great bruise on the back of your head,' he said softly. 'The thing is, Hope, you were out for quite a while and we're afraid you might have an internal injury.'

'In my head?' I said. 'I'm always bashing it off things. I even flew with concussion once. Please tell me what happened?'

'You fell down the stairs.'

I frowned, trying to remember. 'No, I didn't. Someone pushed me. I distinctly felt a push in the small of my back.'

'Are you sure?' asked Leo. 'It was a bad fall.'

I looked down at the gorgeous dress. 'This kind of clothing isn't designed to let you roll properly.'

'No,' said Bernie. 'We almost had to cut it off you, you were so tied up at the bottom. Only Leo thought you'd rather not have your birthday suit displayed at the party if we could prevent it.'

'Thank you,' I said to Leo. 'That would have been awful.'

'I would have done it if it meant saving your life,' said Leo, 'but apart from the bang to the head there doesn't seem to be anything else wrong with you.'

'Leo felt all your bones very thoroughly,' said Bernie with a dash of her old spirit.

Leo looked pleadingly at me. 'It's fine,' I said. 'I would have done the same for you.' This made Bernie laugh far too hard, so by the time a doctor was found I'm sure he thought we were all off our heads on drink and cocaine. However, he did confirm that I could go home. I should be treated gently he said, and not allowed to sleep for another eight hours. He also recommended I was not given anything else to eat until then at least. Although I could have some water in the meantime. I was more upset about this than the pain in my head. He gave me a couple of pills for it, and when he'd gone I washed them down with some brandy from Bernie's hip flask.

'I'm not sure the doctor would approve,' said Leo.

Dashwood laughed. 'I've seen far worse things backstage.'

Leo had sent our driver to make his own way back. 'A bit harsh,' he admitted, 'but we need the room should Hope need to lie down again.'

'You should have sent me off,' said Dashwood.

'Nonsense, old chap,' said Leo. 'We'll drop you off on the way. I'm perfectly capable of driving. I wasn't drinking this evening, and I certainly didn't touch the other stuff that was going around.' Bernie looked pointedly in the other direction when he said this, but Leo was still watching me closely.

He drove back at a reasonable speed, but with a smoothness I hadn't anticipated. I had been all set for experiencing all the bumps of country roads we had endured on the way there. When we dropped Dashwood on the edge of town, he commented, 'Rather superb driving, Major. If I didn't know better I would say you'd worked as a chauffeur. Please let me know if there is anything I can do, Hope.'

Once we three were alone in the car Leo drove off saying, 'I didn't want to say anything in front of Dashwood, not that I suspect him, of course, but these actors can be terrible gossips. Anyway, the point is, Hope, are you sure someone pushed you?'

Bernie was sitting up front, so I stretched out on the back seat, and lay back. I felt much better lying down. 'Yes,' I said. 'I absolutely am. It's not the kind of thing I would imagine.'

'It might not be some interesting conspiracy,' said Bernie. 'You looked utterly amazing in that dress, Hope. It might have been a drunken rival. Don't you agree, Leo?'

'Rival?' asked Leo.

'I meant,' persisted Bernie, 'don't you agree about the dress.'

'Yes,' said Leo. 'You looked very nice, Hope.' He paused. 'Do other women do things like that?'

'She looked beautiful,' said Bernie with a touch of anger. 'But, yes, women can be jealous. There was enough snow and booze going around that one of them might have got a bit amped up. Did any of them in particular try to come on to you, Leo?'

'Me?' said Leo, failing to avoid a pothole for the first time in this journey. 'Me? Are you saying this is somehow my fault?'

'Ouch,' I said loudly in an attempt to forestall the brewing argument.

'Oh my God,' said Bernie, looking ahead, 'isn't that your street, Hope?'

I struggled to sit up. The dawn sky as we came into London was lit yet again with an orange light that had nothing to do with sunlight. 'Why on earth are they bombing Kensington again?' I said in dismay. Then I remembered the cat. 'Ash!' I cried.

Leo wound his way through the devastation. More than once

we had to turn back on ourselves to drive through. There were ambulances and fire engines rushing around, and people everywhere. We seemed to be on the edge of the worst. Most of the people we saw were heading into the city or fleeing it. We had yet to pass a bomb site. This changed when we got to my street.

I was sitting up by now, gripping the side of the seat. I had completely forgotten about my headache.

Then we saw it. My building still stood but the one four doors down was going up in flames. Leo pulled the car up, and before he could prevent us, both Bernie and I were out and in the street, running towards the blaze.

Four fire teams were training hoses on the building, and they seemed to be winning the battle against the flames. I felt dreadful about it, but I was so relived my flat wasn't damaged.

'Did they get everyone out?' I asked an old man, who was standing watching.

'I don't know, love. I'm waiting to get through to the next street. See if my house is still standing. They lathered us pretty good tonight, those Jerry bastards.'

Bernie went off to speak to the firemen about whether it was safe for us to go inside. I thought it unlikely, but I knew she wanted to be off the streets by the time daylight came. It wasn't that likely anyone would recognise her, but it was an upmarket enough area that it wasn't impossible.

I was standing there, holding my head, and wondering where Leo had got to when I heard the roar of a motorbike. It pulled up close to me. A large man in a leather coat, goggles and leather cap came towards me and stripped off his gloves.

'Are you all right, Hope?' asked Fitzroy.

I threw myself into his arms. He smelt of petrol, oil and smoke, but he held me tight. 'Don't worry about the flat,' he said. 'It's not a problem to find you somewhere else. As long as you're safe.' He pushed me a little away from him, taking in my dress. 'You weren't here?'

'No, I went to one of Leo's parties with Ingrid.'

'I shall have to talk to that young man,' said Fitzroy.

Leo came over. 'They think they have the fire under control, sir. We can go back in as long as we're prepared to vacate if the wind changes.'

Fitzroy was the taller of the two, but he managed to seem even bigger in the shadows and firelight. 'What on earth do you think you've been doing, Major?'

Before I could warn him, Leo said, 'I know, sir. But I really had no idea she would be in any danger.'

'Hope?' said Fitzroy, taking me by the shoulders. 'Have you hurt yourself again?'

'Someone pushed me down the stairs,' I said indignantly. I pulled myself away from him, and was violently sick.

'Where's your car, you damned fool!' said Fitzroy, scooping me up in his arms like I was a rag doll.

I didn't hear what Leo answered. I sank back into a comfortable soft darkness. Fitzroy was here and everything would be all right now.

Chapter Thirty-five

I woke up in a bed too large and too comfortable to be my own. The curtains were ajar, letting a soft afternoon light into the room. 'Where am I?' I asked.

A shadow by the window came towards me. Fitzroy had a file in his hand. 'Don't you recognise it?' he asked. 'You used to come and stay here when you were little.'

'Your old flat! But that's a long way from Kensington.'

'Yes, and a long way from the bombing targets so far. I'm debating whether or not to take you back into the country with me.'

'I'm fine,' I said, struggling to sit up against what appeared to be a sinful amount of pillows. My stepfather came over and, with a practised hand, rearranged them for me.

'Yes, you are. He said you might not remember, but I got one of my people to come out and look you over. I believe his verdict was much like the one you got from the doctor at that terrible party. Leo should have known not to trust anyone there.'

'He had to go along with it because of Dashwood,' I said. 'He's not in on whatever is going on.'

'I take it neither are you?'

'Only to know that it must be about Nazi sympathisers, and I didn't even catch on to that before tonight.'

'I must check with Leo if he was specifically told not to tell you, before I bawl him out again.'

'It wasn't his fault.'

'Of course it was,' said Fitzroy impatiently. 'You've more

experience at these things than him. He should have made you aware of the potential dangers.' He paced across to the window and back again. 'Normally I would take you straight home, but I am concerned it will upset your mother to see you injured yet again and in so short a time.'

I took a deep breath. 'It isn't my home,' I said. 'And I am not a child.'

Fitzroy stopped mid-pace and turned on his heel. 'Of course it's your home. You're not a child, but you are my wife's daughter, and my god-daughter, I feel a duty of responsibility to you quite apart from whatever affection I may hold you in.'

'I love you too, stepfather,' I said.

'Yes, well,' said Fitzroy, looking away and making an awkward coughing sound. 'You see my predicament. I neither want to upset your mother nor treat you like a child, but for whatever reasons, things do seem to keep going wrong for you.'

'I had noticed.'

'Any more hallucinations?'

'I thought we had decided they weren't hallucinations?'

'Stress corrupted impressions then?'

'No.'

'It can't be good for you forever landing on your head, Hope.'

I looked at him in astonishment. 'Are you teasing me about this?'

Fitzroy shrugged. 'I don't think we should share this with your mother. I'm heading back to her this evening, so I will have to trust you to sort out whatever you have got yourself into.' He came and sat on the edge of the bed and took my hand. 'I can't always be around to pull you out of the fire. I might want to be, but it's neither possible nor good for you.' He squeezed my hand.

'I know. I'm grateful . . . Is this why you rarely tell me what the actual mission is?'

'What makes you think I know,' said my stepfather with a boyish grin. Then more seriously he said, 'Sometimes you have a hunch something is off, and you can't put your finger on it. That's when you use the most observant of your operatives, and send them with as little bias as possible, so they can assess the situation. Sometimes, though I would never admit it to anyone else, I am as much in the dark as you are.'

'I have one of those hunches – about what you term my hallucinations,' I said.

'Then you must be very careful. You are not without bias in this situation. If you are right, then your recent accidents may indeed not be accidents, and you have no idea where the danger is coming from.'

'Yes,' I said, feeling a cold hand clutch at my heart.

Fitzroy stood up. 'Use this place until yours is proved to be structurally sound. But try not to let Ingrid keep bringing men back here. She has a terribly dirty fireman in my shower right now.' He gave me a wink. Then he bent over and kissed me on the top of the head and left. As usual he didn't say goodbye. He never did.

I waited a short while until I thought he would have gone. I knew it would upset both of us to see him go. Back at home in White Orchards I had a large, scruffy old teddy bear. I'd had him since I was very young. I'd named it Fitz, and though I had never told Fitzroy to his face, as I grew up he felt to me like that bear come to life, who would always protect me. (I believe if he was to compare himself to any animal Fitzroy would consider himself a lion and not a scruffy old bear.) I might moan about him, but I did still consider him to be my protector and that wasn't fair. I needed to outgrow my childhood guardian, and I needed to learn to take care of myself. It didn't help, of course, that despite recognising my need to become independent Fitzroy could still unexpectedly sweep in, as he had last night, and take control. It was like he couldn't help himself.

I got up, used Fitzroy's en suite to shower and got dressed. Someone had fetched some of my things from the flat while I had been asleep. Then I went through to meet the dirty fireman. I already half-suspected who it must be. I opened the door quietly and saw Bernie and Harvey sitting with their backs to me on the settee gazing into the fire and talking in low voices. They had their arms around each other. There was no sign of Leo.

'Good afternoon,' I said brightly, and the pair of them sprang apart like guilty teenagers. I went round to sit in the wing-backed chair by the fire, but was interrupted by both of them getting up to hug me.

'This is terribly un-British,' I said. 'Do you think the war is changing us as a nation?'

They both laughed and let go. I am generally not comfortable with physical signs of affection unless it is family or, I now knew, a lover.

'Did you really not know Bernie was alive?' said Harvey.

'I told you that,' protested Bernie.

'Sit down,' I said. 'All that jumping around is making me dizzy, and no I didn't know.'

'When I saw her by the fire I thought I must have died and gone to heaven,' said Harvey, 'until I realised Bernie was the last person I'd expect to be an angel!'

She swatted him playfully. Harvey didn't seem to mind. Then he frowned. 'What's this about Fitzroy saying there might be people seeking to harm you, Hope? Do you know who?'

'I think it must be to do with those bodies I saw when I first came to town,' I said. 'They were murdered, but placed in a bombed-out area and set on fire,' I explained to Bernie.

'How exciting!'

'Harvey thought he had seen something similar, but he changed his mind,' I said.

'I admit I was frightened, trapped in a building on fire. Thinking about it now, I realise I was wrong,' said Harvey. 'I think it's likely that's what happened to Hope too. Stress. Fear.'

'Hope!' said Bernie. 'Never! She's made of stronger stuff.'

'You don't know what it's like, Bernie,' protested Harvey.

A mulish expression crept across Bernie's face. Before the argument started, I asked, 'Where's Leo?'

'Oh, Fitzroy said he could have the motorbike if he came back with him to get his car. Can you imagine Leo riding pillion with him?' said Bernie.

'Not with his eyes open,' I said. 'Does Leo even know how to ride a motorbike?'

'It can't be that hard,' said Bernie airily. 'He'll be fine. Leo is a poppet.'

'Poppet?' said Harvey.

'Hmm,' said Bernie. 'I asked him to get hold of your fire superintendent, captain or whatever he's called, and bring him over so we could chat about any strange happenings during the raids.'

'You didn't,' said Harvey in a strangled voice. 'Tell me you're joking, Bernie.'

'Lovely man. I met him at the fire before we ran into each other. Eddie Peele.'

Harvey dropped his head into his hands. 'Oh God!' he said.

Chapter Thirty-six

Struck by a sudden fit of hostess responsibility, Bernie decided to make toast and sausages for us all in Fitzroy's well-equipped kitchen. 'It's the least we can do if the man has been putting out fires all over London for the whole night, and is on again tonight. You'll get some too. It's for all of us,' said Bernie.

'Even the poppet?' I asked.

'Especially the poppet,' said Bernie.

I could almost swear I heard Harvey grinding his teeth. While Bernie was still in the kitchen he came over to me. 'Look, can't you put a stop to all this? Peele is my boss, and you can guess the kind of experiences we have to endure.'

'Then why did you tell Bernie about my hallucinations?'

'I didn't. That was Fitzroy. While you were sleeping he briefed us all about a lot of things.'

'That was nice of him,' I said. 'What did he say?'

'Not much more than you told me. Except he told us to be careful. He also said it might all be a mare's nest, whatever that is. Is it a code?'

'No. It's an old-fashioned expression that means the whole thing is nonsense.'

'Right,' said Harvey, still looking worried. 'Maybe I should leave.'

'Do you not get on with this Mr Peele, or is it the thought of hearing Bernie calling Leo a "poppet" again?'

'No, he's a grand chap. I don't want him to think I'm trying to get him into trouble. You lot can be a bit like an inquisition when you gang up.'

'Hence the sausages,' I said. 'Bernie is a clever girl.'

'Oh, I know that. I'm glad she's back with us. I'll tell you, I want to take a swing at that husband of hers. If I was called out to a fire where he was I wouldn't even—'

Bernie came back with a large, loaded plate. 'I thought we could all have little plates and napkins in here rather than use the dining room.'

'I suppose I could light the fire in there,' said Harvey gloomily.

'Oh no, it's not that,' said Bernie. 'I want the man to be slightly uncomfortable, juggling plates and food. It'll be harder for him to lie to us.'

'Why do you think he would lie?' asked Harvey.

'Because you are behaving so oddly, Harvey. I know you too well,' said Bernie. 'There's something going on here, and I intend to get to the bottom of it.'

At this moment the doorbell rang. I went to answer it and found Leo in the company of an older middle-aged man, with twinkly eyes and bright ginger hair. 'Good afternoon,' he said offering me a hand, 'do I smell sausages?' It was said with a touch of humour. I immediately liked him, and from Leo's relaxed body language, I thought he must do too. Either that or he was glad to see the back of Fitzroy.

'Come in,' I said. 'My friend Ingrid thought you might need feeding up before you go on duty tonight, Mr Peele.'

'I've actually got tonight off,' said Peele. 'Do I still get some? And please call me Eddie.'

I took him through to the main room to join the others, but Harvey and Bernie were both in the kitchen. 'Seems like a decent chap,' I said to Leo when Peele went off to wash his hands.

'I like him,' said Leo. 'I've thanked him for saving the flat, but you might like to as well. He waved it aside, but he seemed pleased. I don't think these chaps get a lot of appreciation at the time. When they're on duty it's all danger, trauma and . . . well, you know.'

I nodded. 'I will. But I take it you have the impression that he's not the kind of man to be mixed up in any kind of shady stuff?'

'Too soon to be sure,' said Leo. 'My first impression is very positive, but you know as well as I do that that can be deceptive. By the way, your stepfather utterly chewed me out. I feel like I've been mauled by a bear.'

'Well, if it soothes your ego I can tell you that Bernie thinks you're a poppet!'

'Poppet,' said Leo grimacing. 'That's not what I was hoping for.'

I didn't get to ask him what he was hoping for as everyone and the food arrived at this point. We passed a convivial evening. Leo dug out some beer for the men, and Bernie drank lemonade with me in deference to my head injury, although I saw her take some swigs from Harvey's beer when she thought no one was looking. We talked about everything and anything. Leo and I took turns to interpose questions that might lead Eddie into saying something indiscreet, and even Bernie added one or two rather direct questions. She got away with this because of her long eyelashes and the extra button she had undone on her sweater.

'Seen anything unusual on these night watches?' she asked. 'I bet lots of people are up to things they shouldn't be in the dark.' Leo flinched a little at the obviousness, but Bernie had said it with strong enough sexual overtones that it sounded like she was talking about hanky-panky.

'It's a war,' said Eddie. 'People get up to all sorts when life goes to pot. That's why it's important that we keep London running as normally as possible. That's what the guv'nor says and I agree with him. It's easy to lose sight of all kinds of things when you don't know if you're going to be alive tomorrow. But I always think it's important to be able to look yourself in the eye in the mirror the next day. That's how I deal with it at least. Still, there are others who are partying the night away in nightclubs, would you believe? Just because something is one storey down doesn't make it as safe as a shelter. We've had to pull people out of all sorts,' said Eddie. 'Fancy dinners, cocktail parties, the works. And I tell you, they're just like everyone else, frightened and bloody. Sorry, ladies.'

I used this opening to thank him for saving our flat. He positively glowed under the praise, but insisted he was only doing his job. 'You could have knocked me down with a feather when this young man,' he indicated Leo, 'turned up and invited me over to say thank you. It's very kind of you.'

I muttered about the least we can do, and how lucky we were to have somewhere else to stay. 'A relative's flat,' I said.

'Yeah, that is lucky,' said Eddie. 'You know poor old Harvey's family were bombed out? His father and the kids are in one of the hostels, aren't they, Harvey? Kings Cross, wasn't it?'

'You didn't say,' I said to Harvey. 'I would have helped.'

Harvey got up abruptly and left the room. Eddie took that moment to rise. 'He's still a bit tender about it all. This has been grand, but I should make a move. I'm not on tonight, but I'll sleep down at the firehouse in case they need any extra help. Those Jerries are giving us a right old hiding.'

After we'd bid him a fond farewell, Bernie, Leo and I threw ourselves down into chairs by the fire.

'I thought we handled that rather well,' said Bernie. 'You two with your subtle questions were very good. You clearly work well as a team.'

'Thank you, ma'am,' I said with a mock salute.

'I almost died when you asked him about things going on under the cover of darkness. I thought you were being far too direct,' said Leo.

'Not when I'm wearing this sweater,' said Bernie. 'But did you see his response? Not a flicker.'

'No, I'm inclined to agree he is not our man,' said Leo.

'Harvey, however,' said Bernie, 'has clearly been lying through his teeth.'

Chapter Thirty-seven

'I have not!'

Harvey's face turned bright red. I couldn't tell if he was embarrassed, angry or guilty. Leo and I exchanged glances.

'Oh, come on,' said Bernie. 'I can always tell when you're lying.'

'So I didn't tell Hope my family were bombed out. Big deal. It's none of her business. I'd hardly have told Leo – I don't even know him.'

'I mean you're lying now,' said Bernie in a remarkably calm voice. 'You're doing your thing.'

'I am not!' said Harvey, clasping his hands.

'Too late,' said Bernie. 'You were scratching your left little finger almost all the time your boss was here. So what's up?'

'Maybe we could all do with some tea,' suggested Leo. 'It's been a difficult day.' He turned to me. 'Is it okay with Fitzroy for us all to stay here?'

'Yeah, he's fine with it. He's got several properties in London. He brought us here because he thinks this area is least likely to be bombed. I used to come and stay here when I was little. I think he thought somewhere familiar would make me feel safer.'

Leo raised an eyebrow. 'I can't say I've seen his softer side,' he said, 'but if you say so. He did say there was a shelter in the basement if we needed it.'

'Let's hope not,' I said with a shudder.

'I think I'll be going,' said Harvey, standing. 'I can't imagine the duke wants me to stay around.'

'I don't think he'd mind in the slightest,' I said. 'He's bailed you out more than once. He wouldn't have done that if he didn't like you.'

'Oh, how lovely!' said Harvey in mocking accents. 'Let's all be nice to poor Harvey. Poor, poor Harvey who doesn't have forty-seven flats and wasn't born with a silver spoon up his backside.'

'Hey,' said Leo, 'don't lump me in with them. I don't even have one flat.'

'And I'm dead,' said Bernie.

'I thought we were friends,' I said quietly. 'It wouldn't have been charity if you had come to me for help. It would have been because of that. Because we're friends.'

Harvey's eyes were bright and hard. 'I'd love to believe that, Hope. But you're the girl who's always been given everything. Bernie here gets to start a whole new life because she got into a messed-up marriage – and she let us think she was dead. Dead!' He stormed across to the window. I could see his shoulders shaking.

'It is no one's fault who they are born as,' said Bernie, two high spots of colour on her cheeks, 'it's what you do with your life that counts. And I couldn't tell anyone. Fitzroy said it wasn't possible for lots of reasons. Not least that my husband is an extremely vengeful and powerful man.'

'But you found someone more powerful to help you, didn't you?' said Harvey over his shoulder. 'Your sort always do.'

I tugged at Leo's sleeve and pulled him down slightly, so I could whisper in his ear. 'We should go into my bedroom,' I said.

Leo's eyes opened very wide. 'I don't think now is the time . . .'

'I didn't mean that, idiot,' I said. 'I don't care if we play snap. We should leave these two alone. Now, back out slowly, like you would from a pair of dangerous wild animals.'

Very carefully, we inched our way back to my bedroom. Harvey and Bernie continued to yell at each other. I heaved a big sigh as I closed the door.

'What the hell is all that about?' asked Leo. 'And do you realise we've left the beer next door?'

'And the tea in the kitchen,' I said with a sudden grin. 'I'm sorry, Leo. I think we need to let those two work it out alone.'

'This isn't really the time for a lovers' quarrel,' said Leo. 'We have to work out if we're really in a mess and, if we are, how to get out of it. I, in particular, have been tasked with ensuring that you sustain no further harm or Fitzroy said he would take actions that would mean I would never have any children of my own.'

'He said that?'

'In more vernacular language, but yes.'

'That's ridiculous,' I said. 'But I bet he has a drinks cabinet in here somewhere. Let's find it while we wait and I'll explain – about those two.' I jerked my head towards the door just as we heard a small crash. 'Don't worry,' I said. 'Harvey would never hurt her.'

'But would she hurt him?' said Leo, but he was already checking the panelling for secret stashes.

When we had found Fitzroy's gin supply, and had filled our two glasses, we sat down on opposite sides of the bed. I took a deep gulp.

'Right, I have no idea if Harvey and Bernie were ever lovers, and to be honest I would never ask. They've always been close, but I thought it was a brother and sister type thing. They've always loved winding each other up. It might have started out in '39, when we all first met, as a bit of a joke for Bernie, befriending someone poor . . . a bit of rough . . .'

'And for you?' interrupted Leo.

I shook my head. 'Harvey is smart and he has street smarts. When he failed to pull a con on me, I made him do a favour for me instead of telling the police. I made him my asset afterwards. You've seen yourself, when we were in Scotland, that he has a talent for our sort of thing.'

'I thought he was a tea leaf?'

'Not a thief, more of a con man,' I said. 'And one with his own sense of scruples. He never tried to "gull" – is that the term? – anyone poor or anyone worse off than himself, and it was always about supporting his family. His mother died, and his father was badly injured in the last war. He has several siblings younger than himself, and he sort of took on the role of supporting the family.'

Leo nodded. 'I can see how that might happen, but a criminal?'

'He's right in saying he didn't have a lot of options. Trouble is, despite being brought onside, and paid for being an asset, he's fallen back into his old ways more than once. There's always been a reason – like not wanting to take money from friends – but . . .'

'They are poor reasons,' said Leo, filling in the blanks. 'It wasn't you personally paying him, it was the department.'

'He's very proud.'

'But not too proud to break the law.'

'Thing is,' I said, 'I think he's always felt things were stacked against him and his family. If you asked, he might tell you more, but he did really love those aircraft up north, and he got a brilliant reference from the squadron leader saying he was a gifted mechanic and knew more about aeroplanes after two weeks than some people know in a lifetime.'

'So he got into the RAF?'

'Yes, and was thrown back out again almost at once by some snotty-nosed colonel who didn't think he was the right sort to become an officer.'

'Ah . . . and working as a mechanic?'

'I don't know, but I think Harvey had had enough. He can't fight because of his leg.'

'Fitzroy put him in the MO?'

'I think so. Or maybe engineered it? I suspect he didn't fix the RAF thing, not because he couldn't, but because he has strong doubts about Harvey's ability to stay on the straight and narrow.'

'It's all been a bit rum for him, hasn't it?' said Leo.

I nodded. 'I don't think any of the three of us, Harvey, Bernie or I had it easy. Harvey was poor. Bernie had parents who didn't particularly care about her.'

'And you?'

‘Oh, I got the best of it. I had an odd and isolated life that has left me very much an outsider. I find it hard to form friendships or to trust people. But I had people who loved me dearly, and I think that’s the most important part.’

‘You have your own estate and you’re the stepdaughter of a duke, who is one of the most senior intelligence officers in the service.’

‘Yes,’ I said. ‘That doesn’t do any harm, I suppose. As long as I’m allowed to act as an adult and choose my own life. It’s terribly complicated growing up in a family of spies. They all play mind games all the time. They can’t help it. But listen, it’s gone quiet. Let’s go back through and find out what’s happened.’

‘If Harvey is still standing,’ said Leo ominously.

‘Better bring the gin then.’

Chapter Thirty-eight

'Hello, poppet!'

We found Bernie seated alone in the main room.

'Harvey's washing his face and making himself presentable.' She took a sip from a whisky glass. 'I have to say it's all rather shocking – and if I'm shocked . . .' She twisted her mouth in a wry smile, but her eyes remained worried.

'Is it bad?' I asked, taking the seat by the fire again. Leo hovered in the background, presumably still trying to work out which one of us she had meant by 'poppet' and fearing the worst.

'Pretty bloody,' said Bernie.

'What's he done? Killed someone?' asked Leo from the comparative safety of the window.

'Well, that's the norm now, isn't it? I mean, I killed myself, but you and Hope must have . . .'

My blood pounded in my ears. My mouth went dry, I was on edge waiting to be found out. It was over in a flash. 'It's not a joking matter,' I managed to say.

Bernie must have seen something in my face because she said, 'Yes, of course.' Then in a smaller voice she asked, 'Leo, do you have a gun in that holster?'

Leo's eyebrows shot into his hairline.

'No, I mean really. Do you have a gun on you?'

'Both Hope and I do,' said Leo. 'We're army officers.'

'But you wouldn't just shoot someone, would you?' said Bernie.

'If it was necessary,' said Leo frowning.

'Do you have someone in mind?' I asked.

'Oh dear,' said Bernie. 'Please don't do anything rash.'

Harvey came back into the room. He looked wretched. His eyes were red rimmed and his face was grey. The skin across his cheekbones was taut like parchment. He moved in a jagged sort of way. Bernie leapt up to take him by the hand and led him to sit beside her on the sofa. She kept hold of his hand. 'I haven't told them,' she said. 'It's better coming from you.' Harvey gave a barely imperceptible nod.

'Working for the MO doesn't earn me a lot,' said Harvey. 'That's fair enough. It's not a hard job. The fire service stuff is entirely voluntary. When I was learning to fly it was different. If I was careful I could stretch money out to cover Dad and my two younger siblings. Two of the others have already joined up – we got news a few weeks ago that John is MIA. Then this officer at the flying centre took a dislike to me. Now, I know I can be a cheeky sod, but I really wanted to fly. I was keeping my nose clean. Never a word out of place. I was all "Yes, sir, no sir". You'd hardly have recognised me, Hope.' He looked up at us for the first time and gave me a weak smile. 'But the first time he heard me speak, he said "Where the hell are you from? Who's your family?" It went downhill from there. Somehow he found out I had a record. I couldn't deny that, but when he described me and my lot as not better than we ought to be – in less polite language – I ended up telling him my dad was a decorated war hero from the last war and more than twice the man he'd ever be. My dad is.' He looked straight at Leo this time. 'He's a bona fide hero. Gassed though. No one thought he'd make this long. We nearly did lose him when Mum died. It was like all the life went out of him.'

No one said anything, we listened.

'I'm not trying to get your sympathy,' said Harvey. This time he looked round and met each of our gazes. 'I know there is no excuse for what I've done.'

It was then I started putting two and two together. Leo twigged too because he said, 'I'm not sure I want to hear this. Some things can't be unsaid.'

'I know,' said Harvey. 'But it's because of what is going on now I need to tell you.'

'That gives him some kind of immunity, doesn't it?' said Bernie earnestly.

'If he's about to say what I think he is, then no,' said Leo. 'You're in the army, aren't you, Harvey?'

'Hope's stepfather took me on. He'd heard I'd been booted off the flying course. When they wouldn't even let me transfer to being a mechanic, he raised merry hell. He's a decent bloke, Fitzroy. He might be a duke, but you'd never know it. But he's army and he couldn't get them to reinstate me, so he got me the post at Mass Observation. I couldn't march, after being shot in the leg.'

'But it doesn't pay well enough to support your family,' said Leo flatly.

Harvey shook his head.

'So you have been taking advantage of the opportunity that going through newly bombed-out buildings gave you,' said Leo, his voice flat and cold. 'You've been looting.'

Harvey hung his head. 'I know I could be court-martialled and shot.'

'You will be if you are found guilty,' said Leo. 'It's unconscionable. Even Fitzroy can't get you out of this.'

'But he's stopped,' said Bernie. 'We don't have to tell anyone.'

'He's told a major in the army,' I said. I added 'Leo' when she looked blank. 'He can't overlook it.'

'Neither can you, Hope,' said Leo. 'You're also a serving officer. Why the hell did you tell us, man? You could have stopped and we would have been none the wiser.'

'But he had to tell you,' said Bernie. 'It's not only him. There's a whole gang of firemen at it. Harvey thinks it might even be wider than that.'

'What?' said Leo. 'You're saying Eddie Peele was in on it?'

'Didn't you hear him pointedly comment on Harvey's family

being bombed-out?' I said. 'He was warning you, wasn't he? He's in on it.'

'He brought me in,' said Harvey.

'I think you should tell us what happened,' I said. 'All of it.' My mind was racing. There was no way on earth I was going to let Harvey be shot, but I knew that such a fundamental betrayal of the services was not something even Fitzroy could or would overlook. His only hope was to convince everyone in this room not to repeat what he had said. Bernie and I cared for him. Leo didn't, and while he might bend rules occasionally, letting this go would be as much against his nature as Fitzroy's. Discipline and order are more vital during war than at any other time. It is too easy for everything to fall into chaos. Maybe Bernie was right. He could turn King's evidence. But how would the word of a convicted criminal stand against an upstanding man like Fire Captain Eddie Peele?

What Harvey told us was as unsurprising as it was believable and as it was also unbelievable. 'Basically,' said Leo at the end of his story, 'you steal from houses and warehouses damaged by bombs. You say some of the others are not above lifting jewellery off corpses, and that some will even take things when the ambulances are ferrying people away. You, on the other hand, have only stolen from empty homes. I am unaware that the law makes any difference in the types of theft you mention. The penalty for looting is fixed.'

'But isn't that for people who are caught doing it?' said Bernie. 'Harvey won't do it again.'

'It's not that simple,' said Leo. 'Every time someone pulls Harvey's arse out of the fire he leaps back into the flames again. And it seems to me each time is worse. Besides, if we don't turn him in and he gets caught again we're accessories after the fact.'

'But . . .' said Bernie.

'He will still need money for the family and he won't take it from you or Hope.'

Bernie's eyes were filling with tears. Harvey started shouting at Leo that he shouldn't take it out on Bernie. It was all getting rather uncomfortable, so I picked up one of Fitzroy's crystal glasses and smashed it on the hearth.

Once I had everyone's attention, I said, 'Now, let me tell you what we are going to do.'

Chapter Thirty-nine

'Harvey, you will send your family to my estate at White Orchards, where those that are able will help on the land. Your father can be seen at my aunt Merry's hospital there. She and her husband have a lot of experience from treating men in the last war, and while they will clearly not be able to cure your father, they may be able to make things a little easier for him.'

Harvey opened his mouth to speak.

'Shut it!' I said. 'You will do this because this is what is best for them. And because I want you to do this. And because you owe me and my family a dozen times over. Leo is right in what he says. Every chance we have given you has ended up with you going back to committing crimes. Life has treated you unfairly, but I refuse to believe that every time your only option was crime. I think you fall back on what you know best. You are an habitual criminal and I am done with it.'

Harvey stood up. 'So you'll be handing me over then? I take it you'll look after my family?' He said the last as if he thought I wouldn't.

'Oh, I will do that,' I said. I took a breath. I knew my voice was getting louder. 'Did you ever think how your father might feel if you were executed for looting – and him a war hero? I don't imagine you could have done anything worse.'

'That's a low blow, Hope,' said Leo softly.

'It's true,' I said. 'But no, I won't be handing you over and neither will anyone else here be doing so.' Mentally I crossed my fingers, and hoped my plan would work. I continued in a confident manner that I knew I was copying from Fitzroy, 'I am an intelligence officer and I have been investigating strange occurrences during the London bombings. Harvey was, and is still, my asset, as well as working for the MO.'

'Oh, Hope, how clever!' said Bernie. 'You are going to claim he was undercover all along. He was on a covert mission and had to fit in.'

'I am not going to claim anything. That is what I will say if I am forced to explain. This will not be going in any report. All I will say is that Harvey observed irregularities during his time with the fire service. We cannot accuse these people without them accusing Harvey. We don't want to get into a who-says-what war.'

Leo was watching me carefully. 'It might work,' he said. 'As your commanding officer—'

'You're not,' I said. 'Not for this. This is all on me. I've run operations before. I am bringing you in on what I intend to do, but it is after the fact.'

'You don't need to do this, Hope,' said Harvey in a calmer voice. 'I can't let you.'

I did raise my voice at this. I barked, as I had heard certain officers do, 'You do not have a choice.'

'What's your plan?' said Bernie. 'Is it to do with the bodies you saw? The stuff Fitzroy told you to sort out?'

I nodded. 'I'm hoping it's more than that. Here, pass me some paper from that drawer, Bernie. I need to show you something.'

On the paper I wrote:

SUSPECTS

Bombings
Perkins
Prentice

Party
Anselm
Ottiline
Dashwood

Fire service
Peele

Ministry of Information Insider
Dashwood
Unknown?

I pulled over a small table and put the paper on it between us. I knew I was pulling a lot of threads together, and I wasn't entirely sure it was going to work. I left Cole's name off the list because it would have complicated things too much, and I really didn't have time to explain the history. But if I left him out entirely it made even less sense. I asked Bernie to get me a cup of tea, pleading a headache, while I marshalled my thoughts. In the meantime, the men looked at the paper with puzzled expressions. In Fitzroy's extremely comfortable flat they resembled, more than anything, two gentlemen trying to solve the Sunday crossword. If the stakes hadn't been so high it would have been funny.

After I had drunk some of my tea, I took stock of my companions. There was a desperate air about Harvey. He wanted to take me up on my offer for his family and I could see the glimmerings of hope in his eyes, but he sat there wound tighter than a whip cord. Bernie sat on the edge of her seat torn between excitement and – well, being Bernie, excitement. What surprised me most was that she was placing her trust in me so completely. She looked at me with her eyes bright and her hands clasped. Confident I was going to save the day. The person I had to convince was Leo.

'Right, to begin with I'm going to have to tell you something that you will never be able to mention to anyone outside this room. If you do, I won't be able to help you. You are also going to have to take it on trust that I am telling the truth. Can you all do that?'

Harvey and Bernie nodded. 'If you give us your word you are being truthful,' said Leo. Bernie gasped at his response and Harvey frowned. But it was no more than I would have expected from a fellow intelligence officer – at least one who was as nice as Leo. Others would simply have chosen not to believe me.

'I am,' I said. 'I give you my word.'

Leo nodded.

'Thank you,' I said to him. 'Now, there was an operation, code-named Matchbook.'

'Match*book*?' said Leo, stressing the second syllable.

'Yes, Matchbook. As you may or may not know there are myriad different departments both in the army intelligence services and in the general army itself, who are all working like mad to give Britain a chance. Some of the ideas they come up with are crazy, some are brilliant, and some like Matchbook are taken down almost as soon as they have started. The thing is, and this is another thing not to say outside these walls, that Britain is in a bad situation. We might be winning the battle for air superiority – and frankly that's going totally against the odds – but we aren't going to win unless someone comes up with a miracle or three. Which is what these departments are desperate to do.'

'Or the Americans join the battle,' said Leo.

'I don't see that happening any time soon. Why send your people into war when they aren't the ones in danger,' I said. 'Everything Britain and America stand for might be in danger, but it's a hard task for a leader to convince his people to sacrifice their children when it's not their war – yet.

'Anyway, that's beside the point. Operation Matchbook was a small operation in the scheme of things, but it was definitely one of those out on a limb. The idea behind it was that people who were potentially dangerous to the realm might be, well, taken out, rather than stored somewhere at His Majesty's pleasure. Resources are becoming critical and the idea was that individuals who were strongly suspected of working against Britain could be dealt with rather than taking up said resources.'

'Anyone who is found to be a spy is shot,' said Leo.

'I think they had in mind this was a faster, less obvious way of dealing with certain situations.'

'Was Fitzroy involved in this? He couldn't have been . . .' said Bernie.

'No, he wasn't. You're right in thinking it would go against his code of ethics.' Leo snorted. I ignored him. 'But he knew about it. After the fact. Now, I don't know if certain people heard about the idea of Matchbook and got the idea from it, or if people across London, gangsters, Fascists, etc. were already doing this. What I do know – well, suspect – is that after Operation Matchbook ended, some parties carried on using the idea in a well-organised manner.'

'The bodies you saw!' said Bernie.

'Petey, a messenger boy I spoke to, talked about a gravedigger out in the raids. It was something that spooked him. I think he thought he was seeing some kind of figure of death, but I finally realised he meant he had seen someone burying bodies – burying victims. He talked about it in front of the air-raid wardens. Prentice and Perkins must have heard. Perkins works on the lights at the studio. Like the one that nearly killed me.'

'You have to admit that disposing of murder victims in a bombing raid is a clever, if evil, idea,' said Leo. 'Why did we stop doing it?'

'Politicians,' I said.

'Ah,' said Leo.

'Thing is, for it to work properly, the bodies have to burn.'

'I never saw anything like that,' said Harvey.

'Come on, Hope. That's a stretch,' said Leo.

'Harvey, I bet you were told not to mention falling on that body to anyone else? And I bet you were introduced to the extra benefits of being a fireman after that happened.'

'Bloody hell,' said Harvey. 'You're right.'

'It's still a leap,' said Leo.

'But it makes sense,' says Harvey. 'I mean, Eddie knew I was hard up and struggling with the family – that was the lure. But why bring me in? It's only less for the rest.'

'But what you're suggesting, Hope,' said Leo, 'is that there is some kind of symbiotic relationship between whoever is placing these bodies and the looters?'

'The fire service – or some of them,' said Bernie 'ensure the bodies get burnt. Who else would you ask to set a fire other than the men who really know how fire works?'

'That's the important thing,' I said, taking a sip of tea. It was now cold, and my head had started to hurt for real. 'I'm not for a moment suggesting the whole fire service is involved – any more than I would suggest the whole intelligence service is.'

'Our lot?' said Leo startled.

'Someone had to tell them about Matchbook,' I said. 'I have one name, but no proof.'

'That's alarming,' said Leo. 'You mean Warren, don't you?'

'As I said I have no proof – yet.'

'But who is *they*?' asked Bernie.

'I don't know, but I have some options for people who might be involved.'

'Your list!' said Bernie.

'They are all people who were around when someone attempted to take your life?' asked Leo.

'Yes. Some of them could have heard me talk about what I saw. Some of them are suspicious in their own right – your party people, Leo. Some of them we already know are up to no good. Eddie Peele and his lot.'

'Dashwood? Really?' asked Leo.

'He keeps turning up,' I said. 'It could have been him who pushed me on the stairs.'

'I can't see that,' said Leo.

'The bad apples in the fire service are working with someone else. It could be the Fascists.'

'Anselm and Ottiline,' said Leo.

'It could be the crime world. Any of the others could have links to it.'

'But it's all circumstantial,' said Leo. 'How the devil do we prove any of it?'

I gave him a slow smile. 'We set a trap.'

Chapter Forty

By the time we had thrashed out the elements of the trap it was close on four a.m., and my head had gone from throbbing to being on the verge of explosion. However, there was no longer any talk of turning Harvey in and everyone, even Leo, was keen as mustard to catch whoever was behind this. I could only hope I was right, and it all came to something.

As a group we decided that it was better to act quickly. Leo told me that Fitzroy had left a message to say I was taken off my night duty until this matter was sorted. Bernie had wanted to run the plan past Fitzroy, but I insisted that she had left it in my and Leo's hands. By linking Leo in, I could count on him backing me up about being able to work without direct oversight. I knew he wanted to prove himself to my stepfather, or at least get into his good books, so his reproductive rights were no longer in jeopardy.

'So it's agreed,' I said. 'We'll make a start tomorrow. Harvey and I can sit up a few hours and work something out. It's probably best if we get Bernie to write up the final version. No one knows her handwriting.'

'You look all in, Hope,' said Leo. 'Let me work on it with Harvey and you get to bed. Before you protest, remember I'm the one who wrote all those legends. I know what I'm doing.' He gave me a hard look. I knew he was talking about work at the SOE. My head lanced with pain and I winced.

'I've no doubt you can do a good job,' I said to Leo. 'Just try not to fight with Harvey.' Leo looked offended. 'You've both said nasty things about each other tonight, and I know it must rankle. On both sides. We don't have time for that now. You can sort things out after this is all over.'

Both men frowned at me. Bernie broke in, 'She's right, you know. Hope's been brought up on this stuff since she was a baby. Taught her first cypher code practically before she learned to read. I know you outrank her, Leo, but I think you should give Hope her head.'

I blinked at this. Bernie rarely championed anyone. Not because she didn't like or admire people, but more because it took a lot to turn her attention away from her own affairs. She was not normally a team player. However, since her disastrous marriage, it seemed she had begun to change. I wondered how she would cope in France. Then it struck me. I was the only one who knew she was going. She was likely to be taking on one of the legends, the backstories, that Leo had created and he had no idea. I had to hope she would keep the secret, as she was meant to. Fitzroy had frequently described her as having a mouth as wide as the Channel.

'Actually, Bernie, could I have a quiet word with you in private? We can leave the others to the story.'

If Bernie had been a dog I would have seen her ears prick up. She followed me into my bedroom and sat down on the bed. 'Do I smell gin?'

'You're uncanny,' I said. 'Leo's got the bottle next door. He thought we might need to bathe Harvey's wounds.'

'As if I would hurt Harvs! You were the one doing the glass-smashing. Your stepfather is going to be annoyed. That was one of his favourites.'

'Never mind that now,' I said, wondering how Bernie knew which glasses Fitzroy preferred. 'I think you should know Leo was the main recruiting officer for the SOE. He was meant to be going up north to train the first batch. I thought we'd been sidelined . . .'

'You were working with him?'

I nodded. 'I was assigned to him.'

'That's one way of putting it,' said Bernie, giving me a cheeky pout.

'I realise now that Fitzroy sent us here so I didn't meet you. You must have been up there?'

'Yes,' said Bernie. 'I had to learn how to operate a radio. I'm rather good at it as it turns out. I have a very nice "fist".'

'The thing is, Leo was getting a bit overwrought about having to send what he sees as amateurs into a hostile environment with only a very basic training. I know you were all made aware of the risks when you signed on—'

'But he's feeling responsible,' said Bernie. 'And a bit guilty. It's really not very nice of you to lead him around with a ring through his nose when he's going through all that.'

'I am not!' I said.

'All those little secret conversations, and the looks you two exchange?'

'What? No! It's all been work – or almost all of it. I wouldn't hurt Leo.'

'Yes, well, I don't suppose you would mean to do so, but I can imagine how rotten he feels. He's sending us off and he didn't get to even do the final training. It must be weighing on him. But no, don't worry. I won't mention where I'm off to.'

'Did Fitzroy make you join the SOE?'

'Oh goodness no. He was dead set against the idea. He thinks they are all very brave and all that, but that—'

'Their odds are short?'

She nodded. 'Exactly. It was me that pushed for it. All his other ideas for me disappearing were very, very dull, and besides, I wanted to do my bit.'

I struggled a little with Fitzroy advocating anything dull, but said, 'Yes, that makes sense. I always thought that under the irritation he was quite fond of you.'

'Niece-like,' she said. 'Go to sleep, Hope. I'll make sure the boys don't fight.'

*

I awoke in the morning with a cracking headache and a strong suspicion that we had found a decoy bottle of gin, and that it was deliberately bad. I got up and threw back the curtains. It was a glorious sunny day that made a mockery of the tape on the windows. How could war exist in a world as wonderful as this? But it did. Any deep philosophical thoughts that might have followed vanished as I smelled bacon and sausages. Bernie must be cooking breakfast. I hurried into Fitzroy's private bathroom and showered as quickly as I could. My priority now was to get to the kitchen before Leo and Harvey ate all the food.

When I emerged from my room, hair still damp, I found it was Leo who was cooking. He had even found an apron to wear. Fortunately, it was not pink and frilly or I would have laughed at him and hurt his feelings. Griffin must obviously have acquired some manly ones.

'Hello,' I said, looking into the well-filled frying pan. 'All for me?'

'No,' said Leo. 'All for me!'

I grabbed some plates from the cupboard and put them in the warming drawer.

'It's almost as though he knew we were coming,' said Leo as he broke eggs into a fresh pan. 'You wouldn't believe the amount of food here.'

'I would,' I said, filling Fitzroy's new-fangled coffee machine and getting it on the hob.

'I couldn't figure out how to use that thing,' said Leo. 'Does that make me dense? I was up half the night making up the legend with Harvey. Then it occurred to us it was as important what we all said about it, as what was in it. I mean, if everything goes according to plan it's not as though it will be read by anyone.'

'I get that,' I said. 'But you're right. What's in it will determine what rumours we spread.'

'And how,' said Leo. 'It would be rather fishy if they were known to come from us.'

'I agree . . .' The doorbell rang. 'That'll be the bread and milk delivery,' I said.

'You're joshing me,' said Leo. 'He doesn't?'

'Oh, he does,' I said and went to greet Fitzroy's delivery man.

Breakfast was quite jolly. We'd all slept in decent beds and were being well fed. There hadn't been an air raid, so we'd slept through, and even Harvey was looking the better for his rest. We shared the papers Leo and Harvey had written and read them.

'This is rather good,' said Bernie. 'I like her. She sounds like a right nosy parker. Just the sort who would sniff out any havey-cavey business. Although I'm still not sure I understand why she's writing this.'

'Nah, you've hit the nail right on the head, Bernie,' said Harvey. 'The Mass Observation project advertised in the newspapers to get people who would write a diary to submit to the MOI. Most of 'em think it's all about recording these historical moments, and that their words will end up in museums and stuff. But it's really about taking the temperature of the morale of the country. We've got all these people, from all walks of life, writing about their daily impressions and sending them to us. Some of these diarists seem to take this as permission to spy on their neighbours – and be right nosy parkers like you say. Not all of them. There's this gent in Tunbridge Wells – even I can see he writes like a dream – should have been a novelist. It's fascinating.'

'Exactly the sort of thing Eddie Peele and his lot should be worried about,' I said. 'So if I have this correct you've created a diary entry for a Mrs Wilson, a widow, no children, whose main hobby is getting into other people's business and disapproving of them?'

'Yes,' said Leo.

'We also realised we had to have more than one entry,' said Harvey. 'That's what took the time.'

'I think I might become a novelist after the war,' said Leo. 'It was a lot of fun. Bernie helped.'

I pushed down a pang that my sore head had caused me to miss joining in. I picked up one page. 'So she starts off about Mrs Henderson's jewellery going missing when she's taken into hospital. Then she starts hearing about other stuff going missing.'

'But the *pièce de résistance*,' said Bernie, 'is her getting caught out coming home from the bingo one night during a raid, and having to take shelter in a bomb site, only to witness a man offloading a body into the basement opposite, which shortly after goes on fire.'

'Is it too much?' asked Leo.

'No,' I said. 'You've spread it over a lot of time. I didn't realise you would do so much. It's brilliant. From these words I can imagine her beautifully.'

'The kind of old biddy whose nose you'd want to tweak,' said Harvey, 'but obviously never would.'

'So we all know what we're doing? I think you've got the hardest part, Bernie.'

'It will be good practice,' said Bernie.

'For what?' asked Leo.

'Contributing to the war effort,' said Bernie brightly. 'Now who's going to help me clean these dishes?'

As one we all remembered that we needed to do something important and vanished from the kitchen.

'People!' cried Bernie in disgust.

Chapter Forty-one

Nine p.m. and I was eating an apple under my desk at the studio. Leo, of course, had known I was there. He'd locked me in and left a note on the door that said, *Important Papers Do Not Disturb*. I had the second key, and in a short while I was going to let myself out for a quick recce. Harvey had assured me that the MO office kept regular office hours. They read the diary entries, collated them, wrote up their overall impressions of what was happening, handed these over and then catalogued the original papers. For someone who was not highly literate, like Harvey, it must have seemed an onerous task, but most of his co-workers were out the door sharp at six p.m. unless there was some kind of flap going on. Even in the short time he'd been there I could see that Harvey's language skills were improving. Fitzroy was crafty enough to set him on a job that would also see him gaining useful skills. I couldn't yet see Harvey as an intelligence officer. I don't think any of us could. But whatever he learned would stand him in good stead after the war – whenever that was. Anyway, this morning he filed Mrs Wilson's papers. He hadn't written them up in his report because we had every intention of pulling them after we had our culprit. If we got our culprit. If our culprit existed.

I took one final bite and put my apple core silently and neatly at the bottom of my wastepaper basket. Last time I'd been in the MOI after dark I had been headed down not up. I knew there were very few personnel in the lowest basement at night. How many others stayed in the building, I didn't know. Again, I had to hope that a 'flap' wouldn't happen. A flap constituted any emergency that we had to deal with at once and required staff to be called back in. But then if it happened, I would claim exactly that – that I too was answering a summons. I noticed the floor down here was awfully dusty. Did anyone ever clean in here? I got up and brushed myself down. Thank goodness khaki didn't show much. Or was that the idea? Just as red coats were given the colour of their blood, were we now given the colour of English mud? I crept over to the door to listen. Leo had reckoned I could leave a desk lamp on and not be disturbed, but I hadn't risked it. Inside I'd sat in the dark for several hours. I was pretty sure that at one point I had dropped off. My head still ached, and I was glad I had opted to do the least onerous task and the others had agreed.

I could hear nothing beyond the door, so carefully I inserted the key and turned it. There was a scraping thunk noise that sounded thunderous in the dark. I held my breath, but there was no sound of running footsteps. Carefully, I opened the door and stepped out, closing it behind me. I then fumbled a bit, inserting the key while keeping my back to the door. I didn't think anyone was likely to be here, other than possibly a watchman, but the fewer people who knew I was here the better. After all, I would be doing this every night until someone took the bait.

My office opened out directly into the studio. Unlike Leo's, which was down the corridor. We'd decided his was more likely to be checked. My office was technically a junk room I happened to have the use of. In front of me loomed the big electric lights, dark and coiled in cables. To the left I could make out a giant wind-making machine that Leo was terribly proud about having. Although I couldn't for the life of me think how I was going to work it into a script.

Beyond that stood the sets. There's something creepy about seeing film sets from the outside. Especially in the dark when they are all shadows and angles. Looking into a segment of life, like a living room of a small suburban house, but with the walls cut away, reminded me of the bomb sites I'd seen. Sometimes the whole side of a building would be gone, but there would still be pictures and mirrors untouched on the remaining walls. A film set reminded me too much of that – like a giant hand had broken open someone's life and left it out, like a doll's house, for the director to play with.

I leaned against the door and waited. I could hear nothing. I was nearly certain I was alone, but I felt spooked. Goodness knows how I would manage this tomorrow. Tonight there had been no chance anyone would respond to the rumours the others were out creating. But tomorrow was a different story. Harvey was going to be on guard during the day in case someone was bold enough to try and take the papers during daylight. I would need to sneak in as close to six p.m. as I could. I was counting on the crowds going to and from the canteen to help me hide, but it was going to be difficult. That was why I was here tonight, when no one else should be in, to have a proper look around the MO office and corridors.

I couldn't stand here all night. I stepped away from the door and very carefully picked my way through the studio. For once the cables were coiled away neatly, and all the props had been stored. I tiptoed through easily.

I decided to opt for the stairs. There were several flights, but there were also landings. If I heard anyone I could attempt to hide in the shadows. When a lift door opens there isn't anywhere to go. I turned left out of the studio and started up the stairs. They were marble with metal handrails. Any sound here echoed, and without any form of insulation, such as carpet, it was freezing cold. I walked on the tips of my toes. I had had to wear regulation uniform. Next time I would bring soft shoes that I could use. Although if I was caught wearing them it would suggest a premeditated clandestine entry and I'd be for it unless Fitzroy could bail me out.

I got up the stairs with only one scare. The building was quiet tonight. I passed a few offices where I heard low murmurings, and the clerical floor where I had worked was still busy, but I brazened that out by simply walking past. No one either recognised me or challenged me. It was when I came up to the top floor that I caught sight of a watchman's torch, and had to slip behind a pillar. It was easy enough to spot him, and easy enough to hide, but my heart beat so hard in my chest I thought I was going to burst.

Finally I got to the double doors that led into the MO offices. Gently, I pushed them open. It was near pitch dark. The windows were blacked out, of course, and two desk lamps had been left on. This gave me the sense of an enormously long room, possibly the entire length of the rest of the building, stretching out into darkness. There were three rows of desks spaced equally apart. The ones on the far right had typewriters on them. The others the usual trays for files and pots of stationery materials.

Along all the walls, and stretching as far as I could see, which wasn't right to the end, were filing cabinets. I slid along the wall, allowing the door to close softly behind me, and tried to get my bearings. Harvey had told me which cabinet he had put the file in, but I hadn't realised how very big the space would be.

The smell of stale smoke hung in the air. I fancied there was also an undertone of male sweat. I could imagine it during the day. Harvey said the only girls worked on the typewriters. I pictured an almost newspaper-like office, with people smoking, drinking coffee and writing up reports. Presumably somewhere at the back was the desk or desks where those reports ended up. Or perhaps messengers took them elsewhere in the building. It didn't really matter from my perspective. What I needed to do was step away from the wall, find the right cabinet and find a decent place to hide once I got here. Could I find a desk so in shadow no one would see if I was underneath?

I couldn't hear anything but my own breathing. It sounded horribly loud. The hairs on the back of my neck were up. I could feel myself half-curling involuntarily, ready to sprint, but there was nothing here. I felt spooked, but blow me if I could think of a reason.

I stepped away from the wall and took a few steps into the room. Nothing happened. No one rushed to turn on the lights or shout at me. The carpet had a sticky quality to it that spoke of spilled drinks and cigarettes. Men were disgusting. But the effect was to deaden the sound of my footsteps. I decided that, rather like an unconfident swimmer being thrown into the centre of a pool, I would walk out to the middle desk and then, only when I was very sure, I would turn on another lamp and check the cabinets nearby. Harvey had said they were done by section of the country and then alphabetically.

I walked out into the middle of the room and then the air-raid sirens all over London went off.

I dropped to my knees and crawled under a desk. I knew this was not a sensible thing to do. The best thing would be to get down into the basement, but I could hear running footsteps in the corridor outside. Even in the ordered rush I would be seen coming out of a dark section of the building. There would be questions I couldn't afford to answer. I sat down and hugged my knees to my chest. Was there anywhere in here that could provide some safety? It didn't look like it. I would have to hope that the building escaped being bombed.

Eventually the sirens stopped. I could probably sneak out now, but it must have been a late warning because almost immediately there was the sound of aeroplanes overhead and the building was rocked by explosions.

This was crazy. There was no one left up here. I needed to get out. I got to my hands and knees, crawled out from under the desk. The carpet felt disgusting on my hands, tacky and slimy. Then I stood up and bolted for the door. I had only taken a few hurried steps when an arm caught me around the waist, and I felt the cold muzzle of a gun prod the small of my back.

'Going somewhere?' said a familiar male voice. 'But neither of us have got what we came for yet.'

'There's a raid on,' I said. 'We need to get to shelter.'

'Don't worry. I have it on the best authority that they won't be bombing this side of the river tonight. We're – or rather I – am perfectly safe. It is so very helpful of you to turn up. I was in quite a pickle trying to understand this filing system, but I expect you, my dear Hope – or should I say Sunflower? – have a much better idea of where Mrs Wilson's diaries are being kept. Let's have a little light, shall we?'

He pulled me over to the side of the room, switched off the lamp nearby, and pulled up the blackout shade. A fiery orange light illuminated the room. From the window up on the ninth floor I could see the East End. Almost all of it was ablaze. In the reflection I also saw the man behind me, and the gun he levelled at my back.

I was caught as off guard as any poor person living down by the docks. The Nazis had taken their raids to a new level. As the flames licked up against the night sky, the ghastly mixture of orange and black created a hellscape on earth. I wondered if Harvey had got his father out in time. If he had got out in time. Who would the fire take this time, and who would be blamed?

'You're very calm,' said the figure behind me. 'In fact, you don't seem surprised at all.'

I took a deep breath. 'You were one of several suspects.'

The man gave a low laugh. 'Yes, that sounds like you. Hedging your bets until the last minute. But this time you've left it too late.'

'I didn't want it to be you. But you can't have been doing this alone? Who are you working for?' It was too far to jump out of the window, even if I could have smashed the pane. My only chance was to keep him talking until an opportunity presented itself. If an opportunity . . .

'Oh, I was to tell you, from Prometheus himself, that this isn't personal.'

'That's your head cheese's code name? I am honoured.' This time I couldn't keep the sarcasm out of my voice.

'But it is. Personal. I'm taking all this very personally.'

'I'm sorry about that,' I said. 'I liked you.'

There was a sudden intake of breath at that. I struggled not to tense my shoulder blades. Would he pull the trigger now?

'So tell me, little Sunflower. How would you like to die?'

'That is not an option I prefer to take,' I said. I licked my lips. My mouth was dry. 'Isn't there an agreement we can come to, Dashwood?'

'I wish there were,' he said. 'When I was asked to keep an eye on you I'd hoped we were going to bring you in, but Prometheus said you were too much your mother's daughter, and with Fitzroy having such influence over you, there was no possibility of luring you to our side.'

I remembered now how he had mentioned Fitzroy's connection to me, where there should have been no way he could have known. How had I missed that? My only chance was to keep him talking. 'Who is Prometheus?'

'Now, you know I can't tell you that.'

'Why not? I thought you were going to kill me?'

'I too have seen a lot of movies and read a lot of books, Sunflower – or do you prefer Hope? There is no chance of you being rescued, so extending our conversation is cruel.'

'I take it you overheard Leo at a party,' I said. 'For all you know he is next door waiting for my signal.'

'He isn't,' said Dashwood. 'I disabled his car before I left. You see, I really couldn't take the chance that there might be a Mrs Wilson, and she might have seen something.'

'You couldn't, or Prometheus couldn't?'

'My poor girl, you are too smart for your own good, aren't you?'

'What will your son and daughter think of what you're doing?'

'They will never know I killed you.'

'I meant being in bed with Fascists.' He didn't respond. 'Criminals,' I tried.

'My son was killed by friendly fire, and my daughter will be best served by my enriching myself. I have seen first hand that only money can protect one.'

About now would be a great time for Cole to appear or even

Fitzroy to ride in over the hill, but no one stepped out of the shadows and the door remained resolutely closed.

Dashwood released his grip around me, but kept the gun firmly in the small of my back. 'I have killed before,' he said. 'It was true what I told you about being in the first show. They said that would be the end of it. Seeing my brothers, my father, my friends blown to nothing over a worthless piece of earth. I doubt you can imagine it. But at least it was over.' He pushed the gun harder into my back. 'Look out there, Hope. You can see London burning. This time the casualties aren't only soldiers. They are the old, the frail, women and children. It will never be over. There will always be war and death and destruction.'

'Not if we stop it,' I said.

'You're naive. It will never stop, but I will be able to protect my daughter with the money I make.'

'But at what cost?' I said.

'You mean my soul? That is already too mired in blackness. Now, my dear, it really is time to die. If you offer no resistance and go where I tell you to, I can do this more quickly and painlessly. If you don't do as I ask I will be forced to shoot you.'

'Someone would hear.'

'Over the bombing?' said Dashwood.

Then right on cue a bomb landed nearby and the room shook. I took my only opportunity and spun fast in an attempt to knock the gun away from my back before he could fire. I didn't get it right.

I turned fast, sweeping at the hand behind me. The building shook again, and I failed to grasp his wrist. I felt a suddenly trail of burning heat across my back. The pain was all consuming, and for a moment I saw nothing but white light. But it was only a moment. I realised I had been shot, and now fully turned I went for the gun. His grip was already loose and I managed to knock it out of his hands. It landed somewhere in the darkness. I held on to his arm, swung myself back and down, sweeping my leg across his. We both went down. He hit the desk sending it off towards the cabinet. I heard myself scream as I landed on the ground. Pain shot through me and I passed out for a split second. It was barely a heartbeat or two, but Dashwood now had me on the ground. I could feel one of the desk legs pressing into my side. He'd pinned me with his weight by kneeling on my legs. He was a big man and the pressure was agonising. He loomed over me and the flickering of orange light from the fires outside made his sharp, handsome features demonic. His hands were round my neck, and I could barely breathe.

'Give up. Let me finish this!'

I tried to twist my body to the right, to the left, but he was too heavy. I could feel my consciousness slipping away. I reached up towards his head, trying to catch his lips, his ears. Anything I could catch that would cause him pain. My arms were too short. I pushed an elbow between his arms and tried to twist them and ease the hold. It distracted him slightly and I threw my weight as hard as I could to my left. I screamed again in pain. By some miracle I managed to get him off balance. I flipped on to my stomach. Bile rose in my throat, and I could feel myself on the verge of passing out again. I reached out a hand to the desk above, grabbing for support. My fingers closed on something. A pencil.

Then I was being dragged backwards and down again. He flipped me over. This time he lay flat on top of me. He was panting hard. His face was less than two inches away from me. His breath smelt of whisky and smoke. 'Will you just die!' he said.

He pushed his forearm into my neck and leaned into it. My throat was being crushed. I could not move my body. His weight was too much.

But his head was nearer than before.

I used my elbow to clip his throat. It was a weak hit. I had no room. He barely coughed. But he did raise his head a little more from mine. I punched up with my right hand and drove the pencil straight into his eye.

This time he screamed.

He launched himself to one side, and staggered to his feet. His hands went to his face. 'What have you done?' he screamed. 'My eye! Dear God!' He took hold of the end of the pencil, but either it was in too deep or he could not bring himself to remove it.

I leaned against the desk. I could barely stand. Everything hurt, and breathing was hard. My throat was beginning to swell. My leg knocked against a chair. Dashwood was screaming and clawing at his ruined eye, but unlike me he was still mobile. 'What have you done, you bitch? I'll kill you! I'll kill you!' He came towards me. My arms felt limp and useless. My body sagged, and my mind was dull. I was almost spent.

With one final effort, I grabbed hold of the chair and swung it as hard as I could at the nightmarish figure in front of me.

The chair caught him solidly in his midriff, and catapulted him backwards. He rolled over the desk, over the cabinet and crashed through into the window. For a moment I thought the blackout tape would hold the pane and him, but then it gave way in a shower of falling glass and he was gone. I heard him scream until he hit the ground nine floors below. Then I sank on to my knees, still holding the edge of the chair. It tipped away from me. I fell forward and into blackness.

Chapter Forty-two

'I dread to think of what your mother is going to say,' said Fitzroy, sitting on the edge of my bed and sipping his whisky. 'Griffin calls it a flesh wound, but it's going to leave a scar. I have this awful feeling she will blame me. She's been quite snappy lately.' He looked at me dolefully and I laughed, even though it hurt.

It was a week since Dashwood had died, and I was finally back at the castle after a spell in a London hospital. I should still be there, but my mother had protested and had Fitzroy fetch me home. Now I lay against a mountain of feather pillows, and this was the first day I had managed to eat a solid meal.

'You are still rather purple about the face,' said Fitzroy, inspecting me a little too closely for my liking. 'But that will all fade. Griffin says he'll let you have a mirror in a day or so, and maybe by the end of the week he will let Euphemia see you. He told her you looked much worse than you are, and she needed to wait, so as not to be shocked, and shock the baby. Or something like that.'

'You've been hiding,' I said. It hurt to talk, and my voice sounded ragged.

He grinned. 'I have. I'd heard pregnant women could be a bit fractious, but it seems when you bring home their only daughter shot, and half-strangled, they get more than a little cross.'

'Not your fault,' I managed to say.

'I agree with you,' said Fitzroy. 'Your mother doesn't.' He put his cup down on the side. 'Besides, I wanted to be with you. I had no idea you would put yourself in such danger.' I tried to speak. 'Yes, I know. No one thought it was liable to be Dashwood, so Leo was keeping his eye on the wrong people at the party. By the time he realised Dashwood had done a bunk, his car had been disabled. Apparently, he stole another and drove like a demon to get to you. He found you and called for help.'

'Pity not earlier,' I said.

'I have to pull you from that case now. You got us the code name of the senior man, and some other minor names. Other operatives will take it from there. You've made yourself too conspicuous to carry on. But never mind, I have some interesting matters lined up for you.'

'Bernie?' I asked.

Fitzroy shook his head. 'I'm sorry, my dear. She was called up. Off to the SOE safe house for deployment. She wrote you a letter. You can read it later.'

'Do you think she will come back?'

'Can't keep a bad girl down,' said Fitzroy with a grin. When I didn't smile back, he said, 'I didn't want her to do this. I thought it too dangerous, but she's more than able to make her own decisions. She's changed a lot from when you first knew her. I think she stands a chance, yes. If I didn't, I'd have locked her in the cellar.' That did make me smile.

There was a knock on the door. Leo poked his head round. 'Could you hurry and get better, please, Hope?' he said.

'Aren't you enjoying your time with the duchess and me?' asked Fitzroy.

Leo wisely didn't say anything.

'Come in,' said Fitzroy. 'Don't hover. You're not a mayfly. Now the reason Hope got into trouble was she was working alone again. She'd sent the rest of you off to spread rumours and walked into the lion's den by herself.'

I tried to protest and failed.

'Anyway,' said Fitzroy, 'I've decided to officially partner you two up but, as Hope and you have both pointed out on more than one occasion, there is a disparity in rank. So I've decided to leave it up to you, Leo. Hope is the more experienced Intelligence Officer and has been longer in training. You, on the other hand, have earned your rank fair and square. I looked you up. So what is it to be? Do I promote Hope? Or do I demote you?'

Historical Note

I do include historical characters and events in all my wartime novels, so I thought it might be about time for me to add some historical notes for those who might be interested.

Fitzroy and Euphemia's disagreement over methods in Cairo is about the formation of the SAS by David Stirling. Churchill had asked for a group who would 'butcher and bolt'. From this the basis of the SAS formed. Fitzroy, who is romantic and possibly old-fashioned, holds to the importance of honour and fair play during war. Euphemia, while against killing in principle, acknowledges that desperate times require desperate measures when the security of the country is on the line.

Today the SAS are regarded as the most elite fighting force in the world (along with the SBS) and could never be described by Churchill's original idea.

Hope was given the code name 'Sunflower' by Colin Gubbins, the brigadier who ended up running the SOE.

In the early days of the Blitz the Luftwaffe dropped incendiary bombs on their first raid. These were explosives designed to cause fires. One landed in front of my father as he was running to the garden shelter. It didn't ignite. Instead there was a note inside, written in French, that said, *From your French friends.* Without some brave stranger's defiance of the Nazi regime, I wouldn't be here today.

Once the Luftwaffe had lit up London with fire the second wave of bombers with heavy explosives hit the capital. The rescue services would by this time be on the street and often caught in the subsequent destruction. My grandfather was in charge of two fire engines in the East End. (He was one of the ones who kicked incendiaries off the buildings. Unlike Harvey, he didn't fall through any roofs, but he and some of his men did once have to be rescued when, at dawn, they saw how very high they had climbed.)

Operation Matchbook did not exist. However, there are reports of bodies being hidden during raids and a significant amount of looting taking place. While the Blitz spirit certainly existed in some forms, there were still unscrupulous individuals who were prepared to capitalise on one of the worst events in living history. Operation Matchbox was real. It was created to provide housing and facilities for selected German scientists and technicians for operational use. The US equivalent was Operation Paperclip. Fitzroy mentions it during the war, and it is hardly a surprise that he was already involved in the planning for what would happen after the allies had won.

Fitzroy's department is a fictitious one. In reality what became MI5 was reformed in the twenties after a number of agents in Ireland went native. Fitzroy was never involved in this operation, and so kept his position longer than anyone else in the service. This has allowed him to build his own department in counter-terrorism. The reality is that during World War Two there were a great many separate departments competing for funding, and coming up with all kinds of ideas to bring the war to the end.

We hope you have enjoyed reading *Hope Under Fire*.

For further information about Caroline Dunford's Hope Stapleford adventures, and to find out all about Caroline's Euphemia Martins mysteries,
visit: caroline-dunford.squarespace.com.

And if you'd like to read Caroline Dunford's short stories featuring Fitzroy
please email carolinedunfordauthor@gmail.com
with your request.

If you enjoyed *Hope Under Fire*, don't miss
Hope's previous adventures . . .

With war approaching, innocence is the first casualty. Hope soon finds herself thrust into a web of political intrigue that threatens the very heart of the nation . . .

Available now

Fearing for her life, Hope must confront Nazi sympathisers among the country's elite secret service before she can learn who to trust . . .

Available now

ACCENT

Glowing orbs, grieving mothers and the legacy of dead German pilots are only some of the challenges Hope must face to complete her latest mission . . .

Available now

ACCENT

And don't miss Caroline Dunford's thrilling First World War mysteries, featuring Hope Stapleford's indomitable mother Euphemia Martins and spymaster Fitzroy.

Troubling secrets from the past cast a deadly shadow on the present as Euphemia journeys from London to the University of Edinburgh's medical school to uncover the shocking truth behind a murder . . .

Available now

ACCENT

The First World War is underway, and Euphemia Martins is sent undercover to a theatre where the actors are playing roles both on and off stage, and her toughest challenge is knowing who to trust . . .

Available now

ACCENT